THE COIN

Book 2 of *The Vessels* trilogy

ANNA M. ELIAS

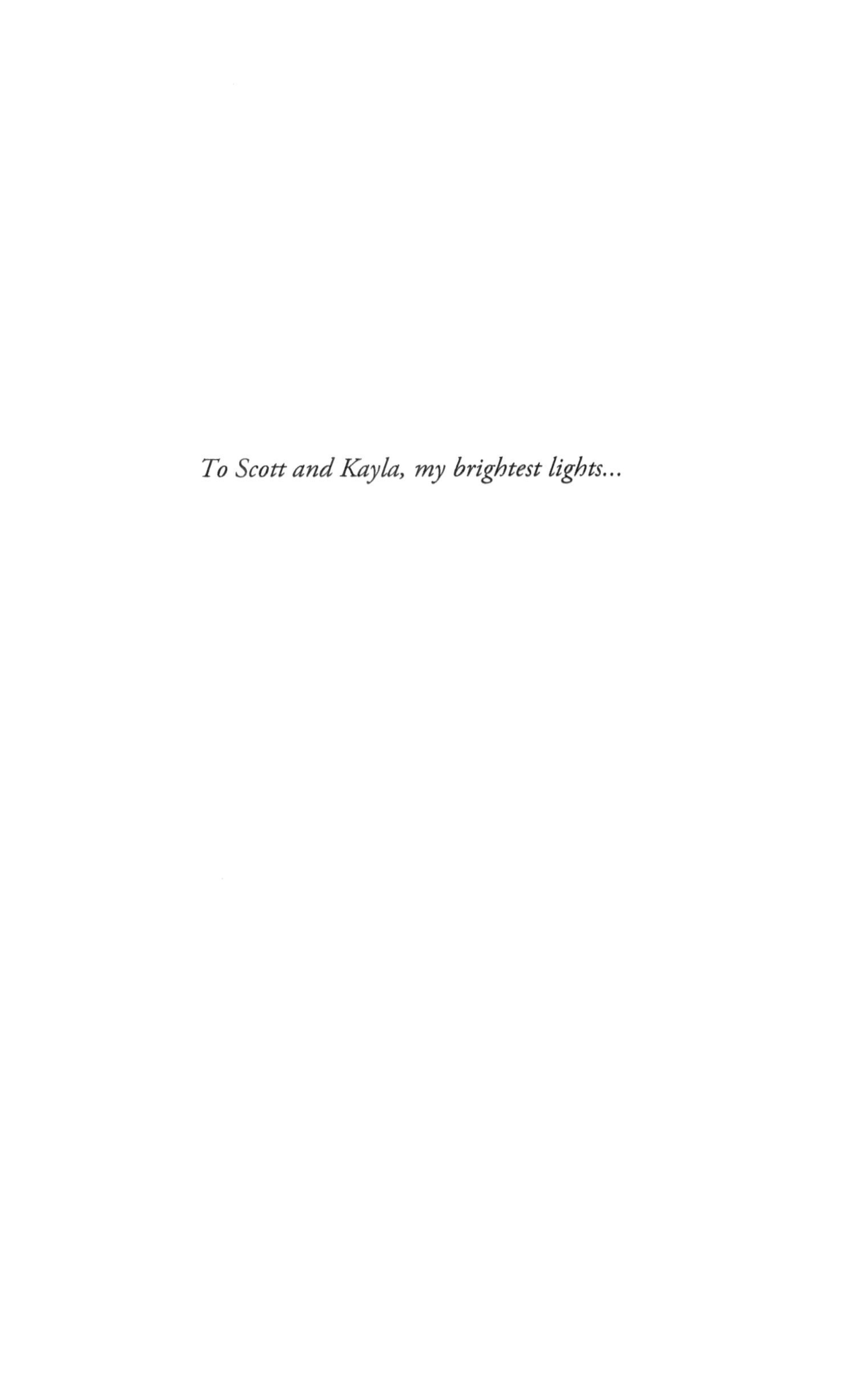

To Scott and Kayla, my brightest lights…

PROLOGUE

The soldiers' sharp voices speared the night as the woman fled from her mountain village in Uganda. She cut through the jungle and dove behind a boulder in a bed of lichen. Chimpanzees chattered angrily from the branches overhead.

She pressed her back against the stone, bathed in shadow by the forest canopy. She wiped the blood from her face and prayed the noisy animals would not give her away.

Boots crunched along the path she had just taken. Rifles clicked against bands of bullets draping the soldiers' chests.

Her village was not the first to be raided by this greedy faction of rebels from the neighboring Congo, and it would not be the last, but she had gotten away thanks to this small, ghostly ball of light that slipped into her soon after the attack. The thing had snaked around her organs and muscles and made her strong enough to sprint off like a gazelle. She'd barely felt the knife wound in her leg, the bullet in her chest, or the bloody hole where one ear had been severed—and that scared her more than the soldiers did.

More footsteps, more angry voices, more men hunting her: the one who got away. If only those chimps would be quiet.

The thing moved inside her again. She had never experienced

anything like it—not any of the times she'd been pregnant or sick, not even when she'd been beaten and raped by another band of soldiers. This feeling was deeper, darker, and growing stronger.

Inside, the rogue spirit tapped the woman's adrenaline like high-octane fuel. He remembered well that same fight or flight gush in his own human body before he died, especially on those occasions when he'd had to kill.

He sharpened the woman's remaining ear to discern three pairs of boots stomping on the grass overhead, about ten meters away. One boot kicked a small rock onto her face. The woman bit back a yelp before the rogue could stifle it. She was strong, a good host, considering how far he needed to go.

She waited until the stomping boots had passed, then stood up before the rogue could stop her. A rifle touched her head.

"We meet again," an older man said, his voice hard as stone. He reeked of sweat, anger, and lust.

The rogue chastised himself for not hearing the man sneak up, but the senses in non-vessel humans were more difficult to use, especially when focused on other things. And the monkey chatter had been so loud.

The rogue braced the woman's machete-sliced thigh and pivoted her toward the man. He appeared to be a general of some sort, with bars and medals across his olive-colored uniform. A pink scar snaked across one black cheek. Short gray hair peeked out below his angled cap.

Blood whooshed loudly through the woman's veins as the man pressed close, his chest touching hers. The general's lips twisted in a lewd smile before he yanked her hair to turn her head and see the bloody hole where her ear had been. His breath and skin stunk of cigarettes.

The woman started to scream, but the rogue held her tongue and shot her hands out to grab the general's throat, clamping her fingers around his windpipe like a tiger's jaw. His eyes bugged as she squeezed.

The general dropped his rifle. He scratched and clawed at the hands crushing his trachea, but the rogue bent her uninjured leg and slammed her knee upward between his thighs. The man let go of a cry that died between her hands.

Her eyes widened, and she struggled to loosen her grip, but the rogue held her tight until the general's muscled arms went limp and his body dropped to the ground, still and unmoving.

Was he dead? Had she killed him? What would they do to her if they found out?

The rogue snipped her fears and made her sprint across the heather-filled meadow to a stand of trees on the opposite side. A few soldiers yelled, and gunfire ripped the air overhead, but the rogue honed the woman's eyesight to see through the pitch-black woods as she ran. He numbed her pain so she could jump over rocks and dodge fallen logs until the soldiers fell behind. Once alone, the rogue ducked her behind a cluster of trees and spun her body apart in a gust of wind and emerald green light.

High in the snow-capped mountains of Peru, Diego shivered inside his wool sweater. He popped the last bite of freshly caught fish into his mouth while Chief Inti drained his bowl of potato stew. The

Aymara tribesmen had left over an hour ago, their bonfire now a glow of flickering embers. The four vessels in this South American program were safely off on their next spirit journeys, and Diego and Chief Inti had remained to share dinner and conversation on the shore of this ancient lake, 4,500 meters above sea level in the Andes Mountains.

A twig cracked, and Diego sat up. Movement stirred in the patchy forest of gnarled Queñua and Yagual trees. "What is that?" he asked. "A wolf? Puma?"

The chief cocked his head to listen. A few more dry twigs filled the silence. "Sounds small. Perhaps a chinchilla foraging. It's gone now."

Diego checked his watch. "Dios mío. I better go. Early day tomorrow." He zipped his down coat while Chief Inti kicked dirt over the embers. Smoke hissed in protest.

The chief tugged on his brightly colored woven hat. Small coins stitched around the edges encircled his face. His blunt, black, and gray hair stuck out under the chin-length flaps covering each ear.

"To a safe journey and return," Chief Inti said in his native Aymara. The two men clasped arms, and the chief disappeared like a colorful bird into the trees.

Diego walked off in the opposite direction to his Jeep, dodging the trees where twigs had just cracked. Late as it was, tired as he felt, his mind whirred with the things he had to take care of at the center tomorrow. In Reno, he had started the fifth and newest North American Vessels Program four months ago inside a casino-turned homeless shelter downtown. He'd had to cede this program to Sam, his best friend and former Army pal, sooner than expected to come here and take over this second global program established decades ago in the mountains of Peru. It was based inside a refugee center for abused, enslaved, and trafficked children, most of them girls, all of them orphaned or abandoned, who came from across South America and parts of Asia. Finding strong vessels from among such humble brokenness was seldom difficult.

Diego had never told Sam why he'd had to leave Reno so quickly, that a rogue spirit had killed the director here by breaking her bones and blasting apart her strong, healthy heart. He also did not share with Sam the concern among the program directors and Spirit Guard about the growing number of spirits that seemed to be going rogue.

Diego slipped behind the wheel and strapped on his seatbelt for the bumpy ride down the mountain. Once he reached the main highway, he was still more than an hour from the refugee center located on the outskirts of Tacna, a small, commercial city about eighty-five kilometers away. He started the engine, backed out, and headed down the narrow road. The tires bumped and bounced as he wound along the trail toward Tacna's arid, almost desert-like climate. Diego loved many things about his home country of Peru, its geography most of all: from the Andes Mountains to the Amazon Rainforest to an entire western coastline of the Pacific Ocean. There was something for everyone.

A light glinted in the rearview mirror. What other car might be out here this time of night? Hikers or hunters, perhaps, heading home from the distant part of this vast national park that was public, accessible, and far removed from Chief Inti's private land.

The Jeep hit a rut, and the light in his mirror disappeared. The other car must have turned off onto one of the dirt trails that veined through the park.

Then it reappeared, brighter, closer, and bigger—from *inside the Jeep.*

Diego jerked the wheel, and one tire caught on the ledge of the deep ravine before he fought to get it back on the road.

The ball of light grew brighter, reflecting something dark and shadowy in the back seat. The figure shifted and sat up. A black woman's face filled the mirror.

Diego screamed as their eyes met. *Oh God*, he thought. *This must be the rogue Captain Hugh just told us about, who got out through the program in Africa.*

Diego gripped the wheel, his knuckles bone white. *Stall*, he told himself. The highway to Tacna was just ahead. The program's Spirit Guard would know what to do. If only he'd accepted the spare coin Captain Hugh had offered.

"W-Wh-Who are you?" he asked.

The woman struggled to speak, wheezing in a language he did not understand. Something wet glinted on her black skin. *Blood?* It coated her neck, shoulder, and the front of her dress. *What has it done to her?*

"W-Why are you here?" Diego asked, unable to hide the quiver in his voice.

The woman said nothing, but the marble-sized light drifted toward him.

"No." Diego's eyes widened even more. "Stay back."

It hovered behind his seat, then lowered out of sight. "No. Please. I'm not ready. I have no … Ahhhhhhh!"

Diego screamed as an icy-hot poker seared through the seat, burned through his thick jacket and sweater, and slipped inside the skin of his back. The pain expanded as this thing squeezed around his stomach, liver and lungs, gripped his heart, and coated his muscles like invisible armor.

Diego caught a glimpse of the woman. Her eyes turned to saucers, and she mumbled strange words.

Diego's fingers gripped the wheel again, this time of their own accord.

The woman reached for the door, but the rogue pressed Diego's foot on the gas and lurched the Jeep around the bend. The move knocked her back into her seat and scattered scree off the cliff as they raced toward the highway ahead.

CHAPTER ONE

TAL

Emerald light glowed from deep within the churning black waters of Prism Lake high in the mountains north of Reno. The full September moon silvered the water's surface, and light from the large bonfire licked at stacks of oddly shaped white tufa rocks that lined the shore like toppled pillows or clumps of cauliflower. A group of Anaho men and women danced around the flames. The beads and feathers stitched to their deerskin garments twisted in time to the beating drums, and their singsong chant sent sparks soaring under the canopy of stars.

An owl's cry split the frosty air, and the ground shuddered underfoot as the ancient ship broke the roiling surface. Tal stood by Sam and Chief Black as the forged metal vessel settled into place.

The tattoo around Tal's left ankle began to warm, and its iridescent tangle of specially inked vines lit up like colorful jewels beneath the leg of her pants. Avani and Link, fellow vessels with matching tattoos, felt the same prickle. The three of them had helped Sam found this newest vessels program four months ago, when he, Doc, and Liam had saved them from their own lives and brought them into this crazy new realm that continued to change with every visit from this ship.

Aaron had been the fourth vessel, joining late, last, and pretty much by accident. He had also been the first to die, sacrificing himself to stop the rogue spirit from killing others. It had churned Aaron's insides apart even before he crashed the plane into the Pacific.

A loud growl echoed around the mountains above as a bobcat emerged from a nearby stand of trees. The animal stood unusually large, almost the size of a tiger, with thick muscles rippling against a blanket of spotted fur. Pointed ears tipped with white furry tufts framed its eyes. They beamed like golden-green torches in the moon's glow. The beast loped toward them, leaping into the air as a cat but landing as a handsome, lightly bearded man with a broad chest, shoulder-length brown hair, and the same eyes "All clear," he said, striding toward the group on shore.

"Thank you, Liam," Chief Black replied, never taking his eyes off the lake.

Liam was the program's shape-shifting Spirit Guard. Disguised as the shelter's handyman he was, in reality, assigned by Elysium for vessel and program protection.

"Have you heard anything more from Ron?" Doctor Eva Lawson asked, her British accent soft on the light, steady breeze.

Sam ran fingers through his salt-and-pepper hair. "Not yet."

"You will, Samuel," the chief said. Wind tugged at his headdress, rippling the long fall of hawk feathers. "Your son is too angry to remain silent for long."

Tal looked down. Bile soured her throat. She had been the one to make the call four months ago, to alert the state licensing office that had then alerted the governor's office about Sam's name not being on the paperwork for the homeless shelter where they lived. She had no way of knowing that oversight was intentional, that Diego Ruiz, Sam's best friend who had started the shelter, deliberately kept Sam's name secret to prevent Sam's son, Nevada's Governor Ron Galt, from finding out about him or the secret vessels program based inside. Tal's call had shot that effort to hell and had put Sam and his shelter squarely in the governor's crosshairs for closure.

Metal clanked as a walkway extended toward shore. Small white lights illuminated its length. A thin rim of phosphorescence outlined Captain Hugh Benham's ship and wrapped the churning water and the white tufa rocks in an eerie emerald cloud. The foam-topped waves licked the walkway as it settled into place over their heads.

The tribal dancers stopped, the bonfire soared, and a wolf howled from high in the mountains above. Tal took a deep breath, allowing the smell of fresh lake water to settle her nerves. Spirits had already taken her to cities in Australia, Europe, and five different states in the U.S. Excitement tingled, along with trepidation, as she wondered where this next seven-day journey might lead.

Link and Avani shifted slightly. Sam waited with Liam as Chief Black stepped onto the walkway and started across the rough water as if going to meet a friend.

Tal had once asked Liam why the spirits used this ship to reach the five vessels programs around the world. Why was it needed to enter through the specific inland, isolated mountain lakes in each via their respective indigenous tribes and private, native lands? Why not just *beam in* from some pre-Elysium waiting room, or vaporize across the veil between planes?

She had not expected his simple answer: they needed the passage to prepare. Captain Hugh's instruction, the ship's womblike state, and the ancient waters of each program's lake that baptized their arrivals and returns all helped the spirits reduce their former human ills like pain, anger, and hate in favor of Elysium's triad of love, compassion, and forgiveness.

Evidently, even spirits needed help becoming better spirits.

A hatch spun open, and Captain Hugh Benham emerged, his wide shoulders cutting the white light from inside the ship. He was tall and barrel-chested, and he wore the same Royal British Navy uniform and sported the same youthful build he'd had in 1805 when he died battling Napoleon. His sapphire eyes glistened in the night, framed by a mane of black hair pulled back in a ponytail. This brave, distinguished, yet humble commander had become Elysium's choice for Spirit Ship Captain, and he'd ferried souls back and forth across the divide ever since. He also initiated each new vessel with a ritualistic blessing that opened their tattoo portal.

The captain stepped onto the plank and walked across the churning water to meet Chief Black. They clasped arms in greeting, the captain's wool uniform pressed against the chief's beaded deerskin tunic, then walked to shore. Captain Hugh greeted Sam, Liam, and each of the vessels: Tal first, followed by Avani and Link.

A current shot through Tal as their hands connected. It took her back to the first time they'd met and the initial soul-searing blessing he and Chief Black had bestowed.

Captain Hugh faced the group. His expression darkened. "There's another rogue."

"Eric Bonner?" Sam choked on the name.

"No. Eric remains in The Lot," the captain said. "This one hid on board among the other spirits, then broke free during my first stop in Africa."

Eric was the vengeful rogue that had killed Aaron. Spirits were allowed three chances to return and right past wrongs. Being inside a vessel host gave them access to the emotions of their former human selves. Those feelings could grow deeper the longer they stayed, and could potentially prevent a successful journey. It's why their journeys only lasted seven days. Eric had barely returned his third and final time when he killed his first vessel, butchered one non-vessel human and nearly killed another, then outran Spirit Guard twice before Aaron sacrificed himself to end his spree.

"What does this rogue want?" Eva asked.

Captain Hugh shook his head. "We don't know yet, but he's cunning and impatient. Whatever he's after will become obvious soon enough."

"Where is he now?" Liam asked, the picture of calm. It would take Armageddon to ruffle him.

"He left Africa," the captain replied. "Spirit Guard are searching. Here." He gave Sam one of the program's unusual coins that were usually reserved for the vessels. "Take this spare. In the event he turns up while they're gone." He turned to Tal, Link, and Avani. "You have yours?"

All three nodded.

Tal fingered the thin, round, titanium-like coin in her pocket, rubbing the raised vines and the *SObY—Serve Others before Yourself*—letters twisting around its edge. Clutching it for ten seconds was like calling Spirit Guard 9-1-1.

Tal's other hand reached around to touch the small spot on top of her shoulder blade where Doc had implanted the wafer-thin, custom-made chip Blaze had designed. It lay under the surface, snuggled between layers of muscle as an invisible beacon to his

GPS.

She looked at Blaze, grateful, and the skinny teen nodded as if sharing her thought. Aaron had received his tattoo, but he was too new of a vessel to have the coin, and the rogue had refused to let him use the cell phone Sam had assigned. But Aaron had the chip, and that allowed Blaze to track him as Eric beamed them from Atlanta to Memphis to San Francisco and out over the Pacific. Even so, no one knew Aaron had stolen a small plane or that he planned to crash it into the ocean to kill himself and stop the rogue until he defied Eric's barbaric torture enough to call in and say goodbye.

"Perhaps this rogue is good," Doc piped up, her accent similar to Captain Hugh's though they hailed from different parts of London, and had lived centuries apart.

"Perhaps," he answered. "But we won't know until we find him. Or learn the condition of the humans he leaves behind."

The wind caught in Doc's bramble of auburn curls. She tucked one behind her ear, a nervous habit Tal had come to recognize.

"It's time," Captain Hugh told them.

Link exhaled. Avani nodded.

Tal swallowed again. Fall leaves shivered, and another owl screeched.

The captain turned toward the lake and extended his arms palms up as three tiny, glowing balls of mist rose from the ship. Smoky pearls set loose from their giant shell.

Tal, Avani, and Link grabbed their left ankles. The tattoos on each burned as the orbs floated close.

"You'd think we'd get used to this," Avani said through gritted teeth.

"Good thing it fades," Link added.

"Not fast enough," Tal mumbled.

The pain eventually eased as the spirits drew near, but the tattoos continued to shimmer like iridescent gems. The tattoo's same *SObY* acronym was well hidden inside the tightly-woven lattice of inked tendrils, and a dove nested at the center, hidden inside a Celtic-looking symbol knotted over their ankles. Tal had seen the bird only once when her tattoo was still fresh and filling that part in on its own.

"Who wishes to go first?" Captain Hugh asked.

The three vessels rotated with each journey, and it was Avani's turn to step up. But before she could move, one of the misty orbs pulsed brightly, lifting and lowering as if on invisible strings near Captain Hugh's chest. His brow lifted slightly.

"This one asks to go first," he said. "With Tal."

Tal stiffened. Spirits chose their vessels and dictated the journeys, but seldom did they care who went first. Sam put a reassuring hand on her shoulder.

Tal rubbed her hands. A spirit's intention had to be good, or it was not allowed to return. And it couldn't be the rogue because Captain Hugh would know. Even so, why was it anxious to get started, and what could it possibly want?

Tal moved into position with Chief Black on her left side, Liam on her right, and the captain in front. The spirit floated behind her to complete the circle.

The three men spread their arms to touch hands, and Chief Black began to chant. Echoing his words, the Anaho once again danced to drums around the fire. Air billowed and twisted around the spirit as it expanded and grew into human-like form. Two eyes took shape on its face, and when its head lined up with Tal's, their eyes merged into bright green beams until the spirit disappeared through Tal's jacket and into her back.

Icy heat spread and shifted as it grew to fill the spaces between her organs and to wrap itself around her muscles and bones. The spirit bent her arms and legs and turned her head, test-driving control. It also acquiesced when she brought her limbs back into place. Her brown eyes sparkled with a dusting of green.

"Everything okay?" Sam asked, watching her for anything unusual.

Tal smiled and held up one thumb. Sam and the others relaxed.

Captain Hugh clapped a hand on her shoulder. "Godspeed."

Wind stirred the dirt and leaves at her feet. A familiar bolt of light cut the air, and the lake disappeared.

When Tal swirled back into herself again, she was standing outside the rusted skeleton of the same Pittsburgh steel mill where her life had careened off the cliff five months earlier. A bust gone wrong had claimed her police partner and best friend, Jake, and she had been falsely accused of causing it. Chief Demmings had taken her gun and badge and forced her on leave until further investigation.

Detective Tucker Manning had made those allegations. Jake's former partner and best friend had hated Tal from the moment she had arrived, and he used her insubordination, her push to rush in after seeing the unexpected gunmen, as a way to remove her from the force. But Tal had subsequently seen Tucker accepting money from the drug dealer who got away, the one who had arranged the gunmen to begin with. Tal didn't know why or what Tucker was up to, but she was confident he would kill anyone who found out.

The brisk fall air cut through Tal's jacket as she looked out over this ghostly mill perched on the banks of the Monongahela River. Jake had died in her arms that night, taking a bullet meant for her, professing his love to her with his final breath. She had not returned his feelings, not in time, and he had gone to his grave without knowing she felt the same.

Maybe her punishment fit the crime. Tucker had found a way to get her fired from the career she loved, and she had almost succeeded in killing herself on the streets of Reno before Liam had found her, Eva had saved her, and Sam had turned her into one of his "ghost hosts."

The spirit vibrated a gentle reprimand.

Sorry, she said, using the traditional method of thought-speak to communicate. Sam didn't like "ghost host," either.

Wind howled through the old buildings as it had that night, shaking the metal panels and rattling locks and chains. Tal wiped the sweat from her palms..

The spirit gently urged her down the same grassy embankment she'd taken that night. Trees cast shadows to her left, while the building moaned to her right.

Voices came alive in her mind.

"*We got company*," she had told Jake over the headset.

"*Who?*"

"*Don't know, but they got facemasks and AR-15s. I'm checking it out.*"

"*Wait.*" Jake had been right to worry. If only she had listened.

Tal once more stepped from the grassy slope onto the weed-choked sidewalk toward the same rusty, half-open metal door on broken hinges.

THE COIN

Crickets chirped loudly, followed by a chorus of frogs. Tal paused to look across the river, then turned her gaze south to the Pittsburgh skyline and the nearest of countless bridges that spanned all three rivers in this city.

Metal chains clanged against a fence, jerking Tal from her reverie. Her eyes adjusted to the mill's shadows and silhouettes, and once again she saw the drug dealer's car parked in the pothole-riddled lot beyond the door. Ghostly footsteps echoed as Jake, Tucker, and Tucker's partner, Dave, rushed in to back her up. Jake had scolded her impetuousness out of care and concern. Tucker had blamed it for causing Jake's death.

Metal slammed.

Tal ducked and reached for her Glock, but her fingers dug against empty denim. No gun. No holster.

No need, the spirit added.

Tal knew it was right, but her police training ran deep. She tugged at the heavy door, its bottom scraping in complaint against the concrete. Leaves fluttered in a stand of dogwood trees. Tal zipped her jacket closed and stepped inside.

The warehouse had not changed since she'd last seen it—wide-open and empty, with moonlight slicing through rows of broken windows and glinting off glass shards on the floor. A grid of floor-to-ceiling beams punctured the space and cast shadows across the paint-chipped walls and the rickety metal table where the dealers had stacked their dope. Tal paused by the wooden pallets where Jake had died, her breath catching at the dark spot of dried blood still staining the floor. The musty smells of mildew and animal droppings stung her nose.

"Police! Hands in the air!" Jake had commanded.

The three dealers had obeyed, but both gunmen had stepped

out from behind nearby beams and opened fire. One of them grinned at Tal from under his mask—as if he recognized his target.

Tal had been too stunned at his police-issued body armor to react. He prepared to fire when someone shoved her out of the way. *"Jake!"*

Tal watched the ghost of herself cradle his body behind the rotted pile of pallets, his blood draining from multiple holes where the gunman's armor-piercing bullets had punctured his Kevlar vest. Jake's ghost reached up again, as he had that night, to brush the tears from her cheek.

"I love you, Tallon."

His blue eyes closed. His arm drooped.

"Jake? No!"

Her words echoed to silence as the orb of his soul rose through his lips a second time and disappeared.

The clang of wind on metal slammed Tal back and she dried her eyes. She may have been impetuous that night, guilty of urging Jake and the others into position sooner than they had planned, but his death was not her fault. Those gunmen were a surprise.

The spirit turned Tal to face the rickety table. *Remember.*

Remember what?

Silence.

Tal detected a young male quality to this spirit's voice. She wondered if he might have been one of the two dealers who died that night, perhaps coming back to forgive the one dealer who got him involved, then got away.

Moonlight painted a ghostly image of the three drug dealers stacking measured bags of white powder on the table when the cops burst in.

"Police! Hands in the air!" Jake's voice split the silence again.

Tal closed her eyes.

The spirit opened them. *Watch.*

The mirage became more solid—a spectral movie where all three dealers obeyed Jake's command until the gunmen emerged. One of them turned toward Tal. She now saw the look on Jake's face when the man took aim, how Jake dove to push her out of the way before shots were fired. She tried to close her eyes again.

The spirit kept them open. *Look.*

She saw a hologram-like image of the two dead drug dealers on the floor by the table. The third dealer, the supplier they'd been targeting, got away.

The spirit turned her toward the door, where two more forms took shape on the concrete floor just inside. They were dressed in black, arms and legs akimbo, pools of red blooming underneath.

The gunmen.

See. The spirit filled her mind with moments she had not seen before, focused as she was on Jake, the paramedics, and the black bag that had carried him out. She saw Tucker berating her and Chief Demmings claiming her badge and gun, the two men nailing the coffin closed on her career, and her reason to live since the death of her young son, Darden.

Her mind's eye returned to the gunmen sprawled by the door as police officers removed their masks, took pictures for evidence, and prepared the body bags. One gunman was white with short red hair, the other black with a deep scar marring his face. Both were young—teenagers, by the looks of it.

Darryl Kazinski and Eli Johnson, the spirit told her. *High school dropouts with no homes, no hope. Joined the same gang at fifteen. Ran guns and drugs by eighteen. Dead at nineteen.*

What a waste, Tal thought. She and Jake had busted gangs like this all around Pittsburgh. Most members were juveniles, and their sentences were light. But, once they got out, with nowhere else to go, they usually ended up back in the gang. Some made it out. Most didn't. What if something like that had happened to Darden?

Why are we here? Tal snarled. She hadn't meant to sound harsh, but misguided or not, these gunmen had taken everything from her that night. *Why are you showing me this?*

The spirit played back her memory to the moment both gunmen stepped out. She could just make out bits of Darryl's white face under his mask farther away. The second gunman stood closer, grinning at her as he leveled his weapon all over again.

I am Eli, the spirit told her.

CHAPTER TWO

LINK

Link walked anxiously along the busy boardwalk, nervous that each tourist he passed might recognize him and turn him in for the reward. He'd been a fugitive for almost six months, and the price on his head had continually gone up. Last he'd checked, it was seventy thousand. This would go on forever until he proved he had not killed Trevor. He'd been trying to save him. Until then, Link prayed his disguise would be enough to keep him free and clear.

The spirit pulsed with encouragement, and billowed his lungs with soothing ocean air.

Two seagulls fought over a french fry. A couple laughed while eating ice cream. Link relaxed. He'd be okay. For now.

To his right, under the nearby ambient light and the distant blanket of stars, lay a hedge of sand dunes that led to the Atlantic Ocean and the famous Jersey Shore. To his left rose the wall of casinos, shops, and restaurants that made up Atlantic City. Well, the famous boardwalk, anyway. Two college-aged girls passed by trailing a clean, soapy scent of coconut, almond, and strawberry. An empty plastic bag took flight in their wake, twisting and dancing on the scented air.

Even this late at night, tourists wandered the four-mile stretch of boardwalk. They bought taffy and funnel cakes, ate pizza, and charged their phones at stations attached to light poles along the path. Strips of neon outlined most buildings, casino signs flashed their ads, and loudspeakers pumped pop and rock music throughout. An open-air tram stopped nearby to pick up the two girls and some other passengers.

The steel pier extended about a thousand feet from the boardwalk to the ocean, the far end disappearing into the moonlit waves. A large Ferris wheel blinked with dancing lights and kept a bright eye over the rides running below it in both directions.

Visions of a hurricane blew through Link's mind and the devastation it brought to this place.

Eight years ago, the spirit said.

He sounded young, male, and sad, or maybe nostalgic, which was odd since spirits did not typically feel emotions.

The rogue that killed Aaron had reconnected to all of its former pain and suffering through the various humans and vessels it had used. Link touched the coin in his pocket, grateful for its immediate access to help if needed.

Not sadness, the voice said, urging Link back to the moment. Arcade bells chimed in the background. *That storm was part of my journey. The final reason I left.*

Link's fellow gang member and despised prison cellmate, Alejo, had talked about having family up here when Sandy hit. Though just a category one, Sandy had affected something like twenty-five states between Florida and Maine, caused millions of dollars in damage, and had flooded Atlantic City.

It looked like this before Sandy hit. The spirit turned Link's head toward the wedge of ocean just visible beyond the dunes, and an overwhelming love flooded in. *Except the beach was wider.*

They passed the Hard Rock Café and continued to the newly constructed Empire Palace just beyond, a ten-story hotel and casino designed to look like an Aztec ruin. The tiered stone entry, draped in a veil of real vines, tapered up three stories to a flat peak. Spotlights aimed up from below to give it an ancient, mystic flair. Faux stone speakers played instrumental music—old-world rhythms made from hand drums, beaded shakers, and wooden flutes mixed with chirping insects and birdsong.

He started working here after I died.

"Who?" The word blurted out. Link caught himself. *Sorry. Who?*

My dad.

He made Link open the door to a wide, windowless room designed to look like the inside of the Aztec temple. Thick, leafy plants and vines covered more faux-stone walls. LED flames licked from torch-like sconces along the wall. One stone ladder climbed to a tall, pointed pinnacle on the ceiling that opened up to a painted blue sky with puffy clouds. It offered the illusion of perpetual day to keep gamblers from knowing night had fallen.

Bells and whistles chirped from banks of Aztec- and Mayan-themed slot machines. A handful of bleary-eyed patrons drank and gambled at the myriad tables and roulette wheels customized for this ancient Mesoamerican civilization. They battled a small army of costumed dealers and croupiers to beat the uneven odds.

It dawned on Link how casinos were a kind of temple. They were built to lure patrons like human sacrifices, tether them to gambling altars, and bleed them of money in sacrifice to the corporate gods.

The spirit shot reprimanding tingles up Link's spine.

Sorry. Link looked around at the various employees. *What does your dad do?*

He's a security guard.

Link froze. *You brought me here to find a* cop?

Security guard, the spirit corrected.

Every spirit knew their vessel's story before merging into their body, and none could willingly cause harm—unless it went rogue. But it could, and usually did, choose a particular vessel in order to affect that vessel's life in some way, too, during the journey, like forcing Link to find and face a cop.

Security guard.

Either way, Link groused, forcing his feet to walk deeper inside.

A handful of security guards crossed the brightly patterned carpet wearing khaki-brown uniforms and colorful, feathered caps. Their clothes, while appropriately themed, also allowed for easy movement and speed when handling conflict.

Or detaining a felon.

The spirit ignored Link and scanned each guard. *He's not here.* He guided Link to a booth at the far end of the room, where two ladies sat inside a gilded cage designed to hang at floor level from one of the stone pillars. Both women wore skimpy, sleeveless Aztec empress costumes with plunging necklines and lots of bright feathers. Both women also sat ready to change any form of money into chips for gambling or turn those rare winning chips into money if such luck prevailed.

Link approached one of them. Her nametag read Marie. She was about Doc's age, pretty but with too much makeup that caught in the fine wrinkles near her eyes. Her hot pink lipstick matched her feathers, and she smelled of cheap, sweet perfume.

She tucked back a piece of bleached blonde hair and surveyed Link with stern gray eyes. "Need to see some ID, sweetheart."

Link had no idea what to say, but the spirit stepped up.

"Is Kevin Dawson working tonight?" His voice sounded kind and gentle inside Link's.

Marie's eyes sparkled at the name before she stifled it. "What's he do, sweetie?"

This must be protocol.

"Security guard," he replied.

Link shuddered again.

Marie studied Link's bleached-tipped brown hair, his silver capped tooth, and the contacts that turned his hazel brown eyes a dull jade. She recognized artifice.

"You a friend of his, honey?"

"Family. We used to live in Asbury Park."

He was from the Jersey Shore. That explained his accent. Link had met someone from Long Branch when he was in jail before he'd busted out. Well, before Blaze had created the whole laundry-room, exploding gas torch thing that had busted him out.

"I'm only here a few days," the spirit continued. "Was hoping to catch him before I left."

"Lemme check, honey," she said, flipping through a binder on her desk.

Her accent reminded Link of Sam's. Maybe she was from Chicago, too. She scanned the pages quickly, no doubt knowing the answer already.

"He's on 'til six," she replied. "But he's at lunch right now."

Lunch? At two in the morning? "Do you know where?" Link asked.

She pointed a hot pink fingernail toward the lobby. "Go out those doors, turn right and walk just past the diner. He likes the potato and corn chowder at the Grand Incan." Her eyes twinkled again before she turned to the next customer.

Link walked through the lush, maze-like lobby to the sliding exit doors. They opened to a wide corridor designed to look like an extension of the temple, with walls and ceilings painted to look out over distant mountains and other pyramid-shaped parts of the temple. A daytime setting, of course, to repress any connection to night or their gamblers' need to sleep.

LED torches flickered along the corridor between shops, boutiques, and eateries that included famous chains and familiar franchises. A few of the restaurants were original, though, like The Grand Incan.

Link did not remember much from high school history, but he was pretty sure the Aztecs, Incans, and Mayans were not quite this interchangeable. Then again, none of the patrons seemed to care.

Mural-painted walls inside the restaurant made it appear perched on a mountain, with grassy terraced fields cascading down rocky sides. A life-sized llama statue greeted customers at the door.

The place was mostly empty, but one large man sat alone at a plastic, granite looking bistro table near the front. He wore the same security uniform with his colorful feathered cap perched on the table next to him, and he ate thick soup that smelled of root vegetables, corn, and spicy chicken. A bit of potato caught in his red and gray beard. No gray had touched his cropped chestnut hair, however, and it shone in the flickering lights like a worn penny. He wiped off the piece of food with a paper napkin and continued eating.

Link nervously plucked a menu from a stand by the llama statue. He inched closer to Kevin's table, pretending to need the light that hung above it for reading.

"Kevin Dawson?" the spirit asked.

Link's hands trembled on the menu.

The man looked up. "Who's asking?"

His voice was gruff and humorless. The spirit studied his dad's face and eyes.

"Well?" Kevin asked with less patience.

"I, um, I have someone here who wants to see you," Link stammered.

The man looked around the room, thick ropy muscles turning his neck. "Who?"

Silence. Link squirmed.

Kevin lowered his feet from the stool rung and prepared to stand. "Well?"

"It's me," the spirit said at last. "It's your son. Teddy."

Kevin's eyebrows shot up. He crushed the plastic cup inside his fist, squeezing soda and ice onto the table. "What did you say?"

Link stepped back, spying possible exits, but Teddy rooted him near the table.

Soda dripped off the edges, and remnants of avocado littered Kevin's bowl. Link's stomach growled. He had not eaten since breakfast.

"It's me, Dad. I came back to see you. To tell you it's okay."

The veins popped in Kevin's neck, and his face turned as red as his beard. "I don't know who you think you are, asshole," he hissed. "But my son is dead, and I will not tolerate you or anyone—"

"Your name is Kevin James Dawson," Teddy spoke quickly.

"You were born in Brooklyn and moved to the Jersey Shore after marrying Mom. You worked as a police officer there for almost twenty years."

You brought me to a COP? Link dropped the menu. His heart threatened to stop.

Security guard.

Kevin's blue eyes seared Link. "Who are you?"

"Mom died shortly after I did," Teddy continued, keeping Link's voice steady, unthreatening. "You quit the force and moved here."

Kevin tossed tip money on the table and stood towering over Link. He leaned down, his breath a curtain of cayenne, red pepper, and the surprising smell of cinnamon.

"Anyone can know that," he said, jaw clenched under his beard. "Being a cop and a security guard is public record. Now get the hell out of here before I—"

"It's me, Dad. Honest. I came back to say it's okay about my death, about leaving me there. You didn't understand."

Hurt flickered, quickly swallowed by rage. Kevin squeezed Link's arm hard enough to cut off circulation.

"My son was a faggot," he whispered. "He brought it on himself. Whoever you are, whatever you *were* with him, doesn't mean shit to me. This is your last warning. Get the hell out before I throw you out."

Link had already noticed the small security camera mounted on the ceiling. Others like it had watched him since entering the casino. He could be recognized by any one of them. The last thing he needed was a scene.

The spirit must have agreed because he stepped Link back.

Kevin grabbed his hat. "Now go crawl back into whatever hole you slimed out of and leave me the hell alone." He stormed away.

Link picked up his dropped menu and stuck it back in the stand by the chipped plastic llama.

Are you insane? he asked, hurrying out the door and into the expanse of the hall. *If he calls the cops, I'm done.* WE *are done.*

Teddy flooded Link with calm to flush his fear away.

Link's hands stopped trembling as he exited into the cool night air. He inhaled until his lungs caught fire, then exhaled slowly, counting to ten, before repeating the cycle again. *In, out. In, out.* Tal had taught him this trick to handle even the scariest moments. *Okay, what now?* he asked.

Teddy answered by turning toward the dunes. Though Link had never been to a beach of any kind, he suddenly could not wait to stick his feet in the sand, and feel the moist, salty air on his lips.

CHAPTER THREE

AVANI

Avani dodged the black olives that littered the ground beneath the lone olive tree outside this windowless building. Purple neon cast an amethyst blush across the handful of cars in the lot while lights from the famous Las Vegas Strip two blocks away fired up the night sky.

The building's sign read *Desert Haven Gentlemen's Club.* A smaller sign near the door flashed *Girls, Girls, Girls!*

I have to be a stripper? Avani balked. She could almost smell the booze and sweat from patrons stuffing cash in her garter.

The spirit fired off a gentle blast of heat.

Sorry. Avani rolled her neck and shoulders. Spirits chose their vessels and their journeys. That was the deal.

She's still here. The spirit tingled happily and stepped them inside.

She? Avani had assumed they were here for a man.

The room was dimly lit. Pop music blared. A male bouncer, wearing a tight black T-shirt over his muscled chest, sat perched on a stool by the door. His bored look disappeared when Avani entered. He scanned her lithe body, her long, raven-black hair, and her wise black eyes.

"Twenty bucks," he told her. "Includes two drinks."

"I'm looking for Elaine Fox," the spirit replied, her voice making Avani's more coarse and sultry.

The spirit was female, no big shock there. But her familiarity and confidence in a place like this worried Avani.

"Yeah, she's here," the bouncer said with a leer as if picturing Avani undressed and on stage. "But I can help, if you're looking for work."

How quickly this man had reduced her intelligence, education, and life experiences to the size of her breasts and the fit of her jeans. Anger sparked.

The spirit snuffed it out.

Sorry.

"Elaine's an old friend," she told him. "I'm just passing through and want to say hi."

The bouncer cocked his head. "*Old* friend?"

At least he's looking above my neck, Avani thought.

The spirit ignored her and smiled. "Age is in the eye of the beholder, I guess."

The spirits could not lie, but neither did they have to share every detail.

"Does she know you're coming?" he asked.

"It's a—surprise," she replied with a shift of Avani's hips.

The big man gestured her in. "Straight down the hall. Last door on the left, past the water fountain." He ogled Avani's bottom as she passed.

She fired back a look.

See them with your heart. Listen with your soul.

I know, Avani grumbled. But knowing it did not make this

core vessels' statement any easier to achieve.

Lights throbbed on stage, where a woman danced topless. She wrapped her slender torso around a pole in time to the heavy bass. She slid off and dropped to her hands and knees, crawling toward the edge like a lioness, teasing patrons with her bare buttocks and the narrow triangle of sequined cloth between her thighs.

Avani frowned as men stuffed ten-, twenty-, even fifty-dollar bills into the floss-like band at her waist. *It's like chumming for sharks.*

See them with your heart. Listen with your soul, the spirit said again, firmer this time.

I know.

No, you don't. Not her story, not theirs. And yet you judge both.

Avani crossed the room and walked quickly toward the hall. She noted the number of male eyes following her, many with the same lascivious looks they gave the dancer. She flashed to Sonny's attack, his hands groping, his hips slamming hers against the brick.

Compassion is in the why, the spirit said, dissolving those memories into smoke. *Why someone would move from admiring to wanting, from looking to taking, from friend to foe. Understanding the why doesn't justify their actions or let them off the hook, but it does offer the compassion that allows the forgiveness that creates the healing. You did this with Sonny.*

The short back hall was painted the same peacock teal as the rest of the building, with purple neon signs over both bathroom doors on the left. The kitchen door opened just beyond, a gateway of fried and greasy smells.

I didn't forgive him. I still can't.

You showed compassion to him and his family in spite of your hurt. Forgiveness will come. Healing will follow.

There it was, the nudge toward next steps with Sonny. Another reason this spirit had chosen her.

They passed the water fountain, rust ringing the spigot, and continued toward the last office on the left, farthest from the noise. A soft light spilled from inside the cracked door and across the hall carpet.

Avani peeked in to see a middle-aged woman seated behind a desk. She was dressed in black pants and a blue, long-sleeve tunic, with a large, colorful costume necklace and just enough makeup to enhance her eyes and lips. The heavily ringed fingers on her right hand expertly punched numbers on a calculator while her eyes remained locked on a computer screen. Her left hand brought a large, iced beverage to her lips.

Avani winced. It was vodka and cranberry juice. A strong one, by the smell of it.

The spirit knocked gently and opened the door.

The woman jumped, then her blue eyes narrowed. "If you're looking for work, honey, you gotta come back tomorrow and talk to—"

"Elaine?" the spirit said.

The woman looked. "Do I know you?"

The spirit stepped Avani closer. "You did. Years ago."

Elaine leaned back in her chair, eyes flat and disbelieving. She sipped the drink with her left hand while her right hand slid to the edge of the desk. Her thumb hovered over something underneath.

The spirit sensed a hidden alarm.

"Who are you?" Elaine asked, firmer this time. "How do I know you?"

The spirit trained Avani's finger toward a picture on Elaine's desk, a framed photo of two young, beautiful girls with long hair and bare, toned midriffs. They stood arm-in-arm, wearing high heels and skimpy dance costumes, and grinned at the camera. One girl was obviously Elaine, thinner and with naturally dark hair. The other girl stood taller, with long blonde hair and hazel eyes.

"It's me, Elaine. It's Amber."

Elaine's laughter sounded like gravel scraping. Avani imagined it was from years of smoking, given the cigarette butts piled in the ashtray on her desk and the thick, rancid smell of nicotine painting the office walls and carpet.

"Yeah, right." Elaine scoffed. "And I'm Liza Minnelli."

Amber smiled. "I died two years after that picture was taken."

Elaine stopped laughing. "That was thirty years ago."

"You found my body."

The drink slipped from Elaine's hand and hit the desk. It tipped over, and Elaine jumped up and yanked a ledger and some papers out of the way before the liquid reached them.

Amber grabbed tissues from a box and used them to sop up some runaway liquid.

"You called the police," she said, squeezing the tissues into Elaine's glass to reuse them. "You came to my funeral. One of the few who did."

Elaine watched Avani wring the tissues again. "Amber did that. Reuse things to save money." Her eyes hardened. "Who are you? What kind of joke is this?"

Amber's green flecks sparkled brightly inside Avani's black eyes, "You threw two red roses on my grave, one from you and one from Jeffrey."

Elaine stumbled back and fell into her chair. "What do you want?" she stammered. "Why are you here?" Her right hand grabbed the desk, thumb over the hidden button.

"I came back to find him. To fix what's broken."

Elaine shook her head.

"I never should have let him go. But now, I can give him what he needs."

Elaine's hand dropped from the desk. She slowly rose to her feet and braved small, uncertain steps toward Avani. "Amber?"

Amber held out Avani's arms, and Elaine stepped in. The women embraced, their renewed connection kindling Avani's tattoo.

They held one another a long time before Elaine let go and stepped back. She fetched another tissue to dry her tears. "But how come … why did … who let you do this?"

"The other side is infinite," Amber said. "Full of mercy and second chances. I came back to see you, to find Jeffrey, and to ask forgiveness from you both. I should never have given up on him, on me, on life."

"We were kids," Elaine said, seeking Amber inside this stranger. "Working, sharing an apartment, doing the best we could to make ends meet and survive our shitty lives. What you did for Jeffrey … *that is* what he needed."

"He was four."

Amber's words held no regret. Avani was continually amazed at how the spirits could address the worst and darkest chapters of their past human lives without judgment or self-loathing. Why was that so impossible to do while human?

"Is he here, in Vegas?" she asked.

Elaine toyed with one of the rings on her finger. "It's not your fault."

"What about *The Oasis*?"

Elaine stared at her hands. "He tore it down and rebuilt it as a high-end club called *The Palace*." She looked up. "He did it to spite you, Amber. To erase you from his past." She paused. "I'm sorry."

Amber waited for Elaine to continue.

"Jeffrey said he wanted a fresh start. No mother other than the one who raised him, and she died a few years back." Her fingers found her necklace. A tiny smile crossed her lips. "I can still see us dancing on that stage. You and me, Candy and Angel. We were the best."

"Please tell me he kept Hal."

Elaine brightened. "Jeffrey has two clubs in Vegas and three others in the south. Hal runs the newest one in Miami, near South Beach."

"Jeffrey always liked Hal, even as a boy."

Elaine lowered her hands and peered at Avani. "Jeffrey's not that boy anymore, Amber. He … the girls …" She took a breath and paused to blow it out. "He pimps them out to his high-end customers and takes half their pay. If they try to leave, he threatens them or their family."

Avani saw red, but Amber did not respond. She must have already known this. Spirits knew most everything about the humans they returned to find. So why did she need to see Elaine?

"He deals drugs, too, through his private dinners and parties," Elaine continued. "I know it's wrong, but … he pays me well to stay quiet and keep his books clean." She looked down. "I have kids, too, you know? And grandkids. We need the money."

Avani tightened with disgust.

Amber tossed out Avani's feelings and lifted Elaine's chin. "You're good for him, too, Elaine."

A tear leaked out. Elaine's chin quivered.

"I'm sorry for what I put you through," Amber continued. "The booze, the men, the drugs. Finding my body the way you did. Please forgive me."

There it was. The other reason they had come.

A sob tore loose, and Elaine threw her arms around Avani.

Avani's tattoo heated more this time and amplified her senses. The office lamp became a bright sun. The music suddenly pounded from the far room, and the second hand on her watch thundered around its face. Minutes passed like hours before Amber let go and Elaine pulled back. All sights and sounds returned to normal.

"It's not your fault," Elaine whispered. "Life was hard. You did the best you could." Her mood darkened. "And you don't need his forgiveness, Amber. Not anymore. Not after what he's become."

Amber took Elaine's hands. "*What he's become* is why I'm here."

CHAPTER FOUR

SAM

"You're all done, Tom," Eva told the wisp of a gray-haired homeless man seated at her clinic table in the downtown Reno shelter. "But your blood pressure is *critical.*"

Sam waited for her to remove the cuff from Tom's bone-thin arm before knocking. "Sorry to interrupt. Thought you were done."

"Almost," Doc said. "Tom's the last."

"Here." Tom dug something from his pocket. "Happy Birthday."

Sam opened his palm, and Tom dropped in a limp, withered daisy.

"Thanks."

"I can't afford no medicine," Tom told Doc, his voice thick from the same nicotine that clung to his dirty clothes.

"It's why I'm here." She unlocked her medicine cabinet, removed a small prescription bottle of pills, and handed them over. "A thirty-day supply. Come back when they're out, and we'll see about a refill."

"If someone don't steal 'em first."

"Wait." Sam dug out a container of mints from his pocket and gave it to Tom. "Put them in here."

Tom ate the last two mints and smiled. He still had most of his teeth. He held out the container, and Doc filled it with some pills.

"Thanks, boss," Tom said, smiling through his stubbly beard. "Don't know what we'd do without this place." He pocketed the mint container and shuffled slightly. "I can't sleep so good, either." He pointed to the metal cabinet. "Jerry said you gave him somethin' to help when his leg broke."

"Those are for emergencies, Tom." Doc closed the cabinet door and locked it. "Pain killers are not sleeping pills."

"Every day's an emergency out there, Doc. Just a matter of what kind."

"Go eat dinner."

"All right, all right." Tom grabbed his dirty, sweat-stained ball cap, limped to the doorway, and tossed Sam a rusty salute before walking out.

Doc adjusted one of the bent flower petals in Sam's hand. "I'm afraid I don't have anything. You were quite clear on *no gifts*."

"At least one of you listens."

"Happy Birthday." Blaze burst into the room with a goofy grin, holding a small laptop wrapped in a blue ribbon. A small dent became visible in one corner as he handed it to Sam.

"Blaze," Sam started.

"It's not a gift, I swear. I refurbished it. Three gigs of RAM, thirty-two gig storage, twelve-hour battery, and a twelve-inch screen, so even *you* can see it."

"Do I need one of these?"

"Dude. Seriously?"

Doc chuckled.

Sam put Tom's flower onto the clinic table and opened the device.

Blaze leaned against the table, proud. "Loaded all your favorite software, plus some games you need to, like, at least know about."

"Thank you, Blaze. I'll, um, give 'em a look." He closed the lid.

"Uh-oh," Blaze said. "I know that look. Are the vessels okay? I haven't seen anything going gizmo on the GPS."

"They're fine," Sam replied.

"Then spill it." Doc leaned next to Blaze and crossed her arms.

Sam sighed and put down the tablet. "Stephanie called."

"Another one?" Doc asked, incredulous. "What are they inspecting *this* time?"

Sam removed his glasses and rubbed his brow. "Not sure. She thinks it's the upper floors. Where that wiring has been exposed."

"Think the new contractor's on the take?" Doc asked. "I'm sure our dear governor is not above paying for such … insight."

Sam's pulse thrummed in his ears. "Ron's insisting Diego sign off."

"Diego always signs off," Doc replied.

Sam hesitated. "In person."

"What?" Blaze jerked upright from the table.

"How?" Doc's auburn curls caught fire in the LED exam light.

"Liam and I will talk to him," Sam replied. "Meantime, I doubt they'll limit their search to the upstairs." He sighed. "We have two days to secure anything and everything to do with the vessels."

"Two days?" Blaze snapped. "Can't you, like, put it off for a week?"

"I wish," Sam replied. "But, if we're lucky and everything else appears in order, they'll just fine us for exposed wiring and give us some seemingly impossible deadline to get it fixed. We've dealt with that before."

Doc toyed with the tablet's bow. "What happens if Diego cannot come?"

Sam looked down.

Blaze looked between them. "He will, right? He gets, like, just how wacked this gov-nut is. No offense, Sam."

Eva nudged Blaze over and set aside Tom's withered flower like it was gold. "*In God We Trust* my arse," she said, stripping Tom's used paper liner from the exam table. "All these bloody inspections, deadlines, fines, and disruptions simply because our *governor*, who seemingly represents *all* the people in his state, only wants to help the rich ones, with no concern for what happens to people like Tom who need this place to survive." She wadded the paper and threw it out.

Sam looked down.

Doc paused to collect herself. "I'm sorry, Sam. I know he's your son. But—"

"Happy Birthday, Sam." Liam startled them from the doorway.

"No, it isn't," Sam told him. "Not really."

"You'll want to celebrate this one."

"Thank you, but—"

"Come with me," Liam stated. His golden eyes sparkled, each iris haloed by a dark green ring. "Now, please."

Sam frowned. It wasn't like Liam to be so forthright unless something was wrong.

They all followed Liam to the lobby, where the last rays of

evening sun cut through the front window blinds and across two female figures.

Liam moved aside, and the older woman took a hesitant step closer. "Happy Birthday, Sam."

Sam stumbled back. His breath turned to glue. "G-Gale?" Sam hadn't seen his only daughter since she'd attended her mother's funeral four years ago. They had not spoken since she graduated high school.

Gale placed a hand on the stiff, unsmiling teenage girl next to her. "This is your granddaughter. Malina."

It was late by the time Sam toured Gale and Malina around the shelter, by the time they'd finished dinner in the cafeteria. The homeless guests had gone, and laughter echoed from the kitchen staff as they cleaned up.

"The place is amazing, Sam," Gale said, leaning back to sip her coffee.

Sam could not believe he was looking at his daughter again after all these years. Her face, her hair, her smile—his little girl grown up. He soaked it in for fear she'd leave again. "It's all Diego," he told her. "Who else buys a condemned casino and hotel and sees *this* in it?"

"How is he these days?"

"Enjoying life in Peru." Sam glanced at Liam. It was true enough.

Malina huffed in her seat and turned away, fingers flying across her phone. Texting, most likely, Sam imagined. She had barely touched her dinner.

THE COIN

Gale took another sip of coffee. She looked so much like her mother, Fergie, but her mannerisms, the way she held her cup and inhaled the coffee's aroma, were all Sam. He smiled to himself.

"I'm sorry for the bad timing," she said. "It's just that I, well, *we* ..." she looked at Malina, "wanted to surprise you for your birthday."

Malina glared at her mom before returning to her phone.

"Put that down and eat, please," Gale reprimanded again.

That was the third or fourth time she'd called out Malina since dinner began. Her voice was firmer this time, and Malina tossed the phone on the table and poked at her peas and potatoes.

"It's been so long," Gale told Sam. "I didn't know if I should call first, if you'd take my call. I just ... took a chance. I'm sorry for interrupting."

Sam squeezed her hand. They hadn't exchanged a word in over twenty years, much less a meal, some coffee, or a hug. She had grown into a beautiful woman, but the scared little girl still hunkered inside.

"You're here now, and that's what matters. I'll have more time after this inspection to show you two around. Take you to my favorite fishing hole."

Gale laughed, and Sam's stomach did backflips. She sounded like Fergie, too.

"I can't think of you without picturing a rod and reel in one hand and a string of wiggling fish in the other."

"And your mother glaring at them both."

Gale chuckled.

Malina rolled her eyes and slunk deeper into her seat.

Liam feigned interest in his coffee but looked up at Malina every now and again. Sam couldn't tell if he was curious about the girl or intrigued by her overt efforts to be rude. But he did not look upset, disgusted, or put off, which would have been easy to do. Sam let go of his apprehension about her, too.

"I could never understand Fergie's love for ballet and opera," Sam told Gale. "But somehow, it all worked out."

Gale sighed. "I miss her."

"Me, too," Sam said. "Every day."

Malina exhaled loudly and stabbed some peas with her fork.

"How long are you two in town?" Liam asked, locking his gaze on Malina.

If anyone could find a way to crack her, it would be him.

She squirmed and looked down. Gale spoke up. "We, um … I'm not sure. I wanted to see you, and you've never met your granddaughter, and—"

"She made my dad hate us, and he left," Malina snapped at Sam. "So now he's with some other woman, and we have to move here. It sucks. Just like this food."

"Malina!" Gale snapped.

"It's true," the girl retorted.

"Sorry," Gale said, silencing her daughter with a look. "She's usually nicer than this."

Sam somehow doubted that.

"He's coming back for me," Malina hissed at her mom. "He told me so. It's why we have to go home. It's why we can't live here. He'll never find me in this stupid place."

"That's *enough*," Gale said.

Malina jumped to her feet. "Yes. It is." She stormed toward the kitchen and the door that led outside.

"Malina? Where are you going? Malina!"

The door slammed and Gale started after her, but Liam put a

hand on her shoulder. "I'll go. You and Sam talk," he said, cool and unfazed. "She'll be okay." He followed Malina out the same door, closing it gently this time.

"This is a lot for her," Sam told Gale. "She just needs time."

Gale sat back down, tears welling.

Sam wanted to wrap her in his arms around her, but offered his handkerchief instead.

"Vince came home one night and announced he was leaving." She dried her eyes with the neatly folded square of cloth. "Said I couldn't give him what he needed anymore, that our marriage had dried up. Then he packed his bags and drove straight to the home of his secretary." She twisted the linen in her hand. "Turns out they'd been having an affair for two years. I just thought he and I were going through a rough patch, you know? Finances, work, teenager stuff, but—divorce papers came a month later and, well, here we are." She sighed heavily. "Malina's only sixteen."

Sam flashed to the moment he'd told Fergie about his affair. It was his first and only indiscretion in their forty-five years of marriage, but it had consumed him for almost a year. He had never really known how badly it hurt Fergie until now, seeing that level of pain, shock, and anger reflected in Gale. How had Fergie ever forgiven him? How could she have taken him back? Thank God her desire to keep her family together was stronger than the hurt.

"I'm so sorry," he said.

A long moment of silence passed before she worked up the nerve to ask, "What stopped being good enough in Mom that made you want to be with someone else?"

Sam fingered the wedding ring he still wore, turning it around his finger. How ironic that, after all these years, the one thing that brought Gale back to him was a version of what he had done to drive her and her brother away.

He cleared his throat. "When you fall in love with someone, you see only the good. They could spill their whole plate of food in your lap, and you'd laugh." He paused. "But the longer you stay together, the more you see their faults. Eventually, they could drop a pea on the floor, and you'd hate them. The problems grow larger, and the shortcomings grow bigger, including your own." He took off his glasses. "Especially your own."

Laughter from the kitchen jackhammered their conversation.

"You want to feel good again, you know?" Sam said, cleaning his glasses before putting them back on. "That first *in love* high. So you find it with someone else, someone new, usually when you're not looking for it."

She frowned. "But cracks and problems just show up there, too."

"Yes, but at that moment, you don't care. You feel *good* again. Wanted. Desired." He twisted the ring. "I was incredibly fortunate your mother took me back."

"But you also *wanted* to come back." Hurt darkened her eye. "Vince doesn't. And even if he did, I don't think I could let him." She worked the handkerchief into a small triangle before looking up again. "I hate him, Sam. I never want to see him again. And I never want another man in my life because of him." Tears spilled out. She dabbed them again. "And Malina hates me because of it."

Sam took her trembling hands. "Malina doesn't hate you, Gale. She hates herself, thinking *she* failed, too, that *she* is part of the reason her dad left. You and Ron went through the same thing at first." He paused. "You have to help her fill in those cracks to know it's not her fault. The way your mother helped you and Ron. Or, tried to."

Gale collapsed into his arms.

Sam held his daughter while she wept. "Malina will come around. Just give her time."

A few minutes passed before Gale sniffled and mumbled against Sam's shoulder. "Ron really hates you."

"I know."

She sighed. "He's the reason for this inspection, isn't he?"

Sam nodded.

She leaned back in her chair. "I read he was trying to close all the shelters."

"All those that are funded by state dollars. Ours is mostly private, for that reason, but he has been trying to close us since he found out I was involved."

Doc burst in through the back door from the shelter, not far from their seats, her face bone white. "We've got problems."

"What is it?" Sam asked, jumping to his feet. "What's wrong?" With another rogue on the loose, he feared the worst.

"Stephanie called. Two state inspectors showed up tonight from the governor's office. They intend to surprise us first thing in the morning."

The room started to swim. Sam grabbed the table to steady himself. "Blaze?"

Doc glanced sideways at Gale. "We are … tending to that."

"Let me talk to Ron," Gale said, pushing back her chair and standing up.

She was the same size as her mother, with the same thick brown hair streaked with gray and the same laugh lines around her eyes and mouth.

"I'll tell him what you're doing here, the people you're helping. He'll—"

"That ship has sailed, I'm afraid," Sam told her. "Liam will drive you and Malina to the hotel. Settle in. I'll call when this is over." He hugged her one last time and followed Eva back to the lobby.

CHAPTER FIVE

TAL

Why did I have to get this *spirit?* Tal's thoughts ran amok as she nibbled a Chicago-style hot dog three blocks down from her old Pittsburgh precinct. The only thing that could have been worse, or at least as repulsive, was if she had received the spirit of the woman who'd crashed into Owen and Darden because she'd been texting. The woman had survived, of course, but had sent Tal's family flipping end-over-end into a fiery hell that killed them both. Tal prayed never to come across that woman in *any* form.

The spirit tingled to bring her back.

Sorry, she said, then remembered the spirit was Eli, and anger sparked again. A bite of the hot dog stuck in her throat. He pulsed to help it go down.

Tal wanted to hate Eli for choosing her. But every time her revulsion kicked up, he stomped it out with a blast of warmth, a fog of peace, some kind of ethereal benevolence that flipped her loathing to compassion. It was not fair.

Eli pulsed again.

Stop that, she hissed. Damn spirits. They heard every thought.

Tal tossed her empty wrapper into the metal trash and remembered Tucker Manning doing the same thing outside this same favorite street stand four months ago when she had come back to talk with him. That was before she'd seen him taking money from the drug dealer and learned the truth of his involvement in Jake's death.

Now, here they were again, waiting for that same dealer outside that same pawnshop where it happened. Great.

Benz, the spirit told her.

What?

The dealer. His name is Lawrence Cooper, but everyone calls him Benz—his favorite car. He buys a new one every year.

He must make a lot of money.

He sells a lot of drugs.

Bastard.

There's more.

Figures.

The compassion flooded.

Dammit. She tried to stay angry but failed. *Still doesn't justify what he's doing.*

We're here to help with that, Eli told her.

The early fall breeze shook more leaves on a nearby maple. Tal shivered. *Of course, we are.*

The tall buildings cast late afternoon shadows over the busy downtown streets. The workday had just ended, and rush hour was already underway. Tal walked down the crowded sidewalk to get a better view of the pawnshop's long and narrow parking lot across the street. It ran along one side of the building, an alcove with just enough room for a handful of cars, a dumpster, and a waste truck to back in when needed.

She had stood in that same lot about four months ago, chasing after a vision of Darden before he disappeared, and Liam took his place to demand her answer. *In or out? Vessel or not?*

Invite, not demand, Eli corrected.

Or erase my mind if I didn't.

Your memories, Eli countered again. *To keep the program secret.*

Tal frowned. She understood the need to keep things secret, but the threat of losing one's memories, the good and bad, the loved ones and those who'd been lost—*it's a bit extreme*, she told him.

So is the global fallout if knowledge about this program gets into the wrong hands.

Okay, okay. You don't have to get all doomsday about it.

Tal had opted to join the program to keep from losing her mind—*her memories*—and to have a chance to solve this Tucker thing once and for all. Though being a vessel really put a crimp on that because she could not blackmail him, coerce him, or take pictures and turn him in. She'd have to do this the *vessels* way—with forgiveness, compassion, and his shot at redemption. It was *far* more than he deserved.

Eli singed with a wave of heat.

Stop that.

When you do.

She started to grouse, but something moved. She ducked out of sight as the drug dealer emerged from the rear door of his pawnshop and walked to a sporty black Mercedes.

Benz.

He stuffed a brown bag into his jacket, and Tal spied the handle of a .45 sticking up from the back of his pants. He pulled his baseball cap low over his face and beeped the car doors open with his key fob.

Follow him, Eli instructed.

Tal tossed her soda into the trash and slipped behind the wheel of her nondescript blue rental car parked along the street. She ducked down and waited for Benz to pull out and drive past.

He turned right and stopped at the light before Tal merged into traffic behind him. Experience kept her several car lengths back.

She tailed Benz across two bridges and up a hill to an inner city neighborhood marked by broken streetlights, gang-tagged buildings, and a handful of cars blaring rap music. Tal's windows shook with the heavy bass.

Dusk bent the last rays of sunlight into darkness as Benz entered an apartment complex of four-story brick buildings with rusted balconies and some western-facing windows lined with foil to keep out the afternoon sun. An old, worn sign reading Brighton Apartments marked the entry. The grassy areas were mostly dirt, and the parking lot was filled with older, economy-style cars missing hubcaps or riding on spare tires. Children chased feral cats through a common area near overflowing dumpsters.

Tal pulled over as Benz drove in. *All his money, and he lives here?*

He works *here*, Eli corrected. *Kids want out. He gives them the chance.*

Tal waited for Benz to drive halfway into the complex before following. Young women outside their stoops waved as Benz rolled past. Some of the boys gaped at his car. *How could he prey on people like this?* Tal thought. Hopeless and hungry, with families to feed and limited income. Most would have jumped at better jobs and education if they'd had the chance. But they didn't, and they wouldn't as long as systemic racism, political gerrymandering, and unrealistic minimum wage with no health care ruled their world. She and Jake had arrested far too many like them over the years. They wanted a hand up, not a hand out.

Why can't spirits fix that? she snipped.

Eli let her vent before making her pull over to let Benz park.

The same people who had brightened at Benz now frowned at Tal, aloof, mistrustful.

I lived there. Eli pointed to a top-floor unit on the corner above Benz's car. The balcony sagged at one corner and foil lined two cracked windows. *My mother OD'd on the couch. On my fifteenth birthday.*

No judgment marred his voice.

I'm sorry, she said.

Tal's son, Darden, had been killed at age four, his life snuffed out before he could live it. Eli had lived his, but at what cost? And to what end?

Dogs barked across the courtyard.

Benz was my ticket out, Eli said. *Or so it seemed.* He warmed. *We're going to change that.*

He made Tal drive past Benz's car and park outside a downstairs apartment. Loud music thumped from inside, a soundtrack to the voices and laughter. A party was in full swing, and Benz appeared to be the guest of honor. People called his name, slapped hands, and shared hugs as he entered.

Tal turned off the engine, her palms damp on the wheel. She and Jake had busted many such parties to arrest dealers and save local kids from getting involved or addicted. She felt that same rush now, but without her badge, gun, or police backup.

You won't need that, Eli said, nudging her to breathe.

Vessels could not carry weapons, take lives, or cause harm, unless, of course, their own lives were at stake. And that was thoroughly questioned since vessels could rely on resourcefulness, cunning, and, most importantly, the spirits they carried to help them survive. Even so, a gun at her side would sure bolster confidence.

It's time. Eli stepped her out of the car.

Tal crept toward the apartment, careful to stay to one side as she peeked in the open door. It was packed with young men and women, some dancing, most drinking, and a few making out. Two junkies shot their arms full in a far corner. Benz held court from a cushioned chair in the middle of the room. He smoked a joint and sold a young girl a bag of what appeared to be crack.

Tal rolled her neck, steeled her nerve, and stepped inside.

"Hey!" One shirtless, muscled boy yelled from the couch as he pointed to Tal. "Who the fuck is that?"

The talking stopped. All eyes turned.

Let's do this, Eli said.

Your party, Tal replied.

She took a few more steps, and twenty or more handguns appeared, all aimed in her direction, including Benz's .45.

"What d'ya want?" the muscled boy asked.

He appeared to be this party's host. Sweat moistened Tal's lip, but Eli held her steady.

"Wait, I know this bitch," another boy said. He stood up, tall and skinny, not much past thirteen. His hand trembled on his gun. "You're that cop who busted my brother."

Guns cocked with a staccato of metal clicks. Someone turned off the music.

Tal had never felt so vulnerable, so helpless, so less like a cop.

But Eli opened a portal in her mind, a window into this same apartment through his young eyes four years earlier when he was fifteen: an identical party, Benz in the same big chair dealing drugs and showing off his gold rings and tooth.

My mother had just died. I was alone. No family, no hope.

In the vision, Benz put an arm around him and pulled him in like a little brother. He made the boy feel special, wanted.

Humans need that. And we'll take it from the worst places if that's all we can get.

The portal closed, and the room of faces returned to normal, all eyes on Tal.

"Well, bitch?" Benz prodded.

"I *was* a cop," she told the young boy, squaring her shoulders and looking him in the eye. "And I remember your brother—Jackson. I'm sorry for what happened to him. I'm sorry for the lives he took."

The boy glowered but remained silent.

Tal turned to Benz, still seated in the large stuffed chair, center of attention, god of the room, his .45 aimed at her chest. "But I'm not a cop anymore," she said. "Not since the night I met you."

Benz and Tal stared one another down before he sent over a teenage girl, about seventeen, who was dressed in a short jean skirt and a tight midriff top. Tal could see goosebumps on her skin from the cool air outside. The beads in her braided weave clicked against each other as her hands moved expertly along Tal's sides, around her waist, and down her legs to the inside of her shoes. The girl's skin smelled like cheap floral lotion. Her long nails glittered purple and pink with a tiny rhinestone glued to the tip of both ring fingers.

"She's clean," the girl said and sat back down. The others

relaxed and lowered their weapons slightly.

At that moment, and for the first time in her professional life, Tal was grateful she did not have a gun. She would have drawn it, as the others had, and lives could have—no, *would* have—been lost, including the possibility of hers with Eli inside. No wonder vessels were not allowed to carry weapons. Their humanity could really screw things up.

Eli warmed with confirmation.

Benz rose from his cushioned throne and walked closer. His shirt hung open over gold chains and low-slung pants. He circled Tal, gun at her head, finger hugging the trigger. "All you cops gettin' dirty now, or what? You bust our asses, then you come out here wantin' in on the fun. Well, this ain't your party, sister."

Tal frowned. *What's he talking about?*

"So why you really here, bitch?" Benz snarled, his tooth catching the light. "And don't be lyin', or I'll shoot your face off b'fore you finish."

"We're here for you, Benz," Eli answered, his voice low and rich inside Tal's.

Benz pulled back. Several in the crowd sat up.

Tal was stunned, too. Eli sounded older than his years.

Benz kept his gun at Tal's head while peering outside. "Who the fuck is *we*?"

Eli blasted a brilliant emerald light around the room through Tal's eyes.

People screamed. Some ran. Others ducked under tables and into corners.

Tal seized the moment to knock the gun from Benz's hand. He ran for the door, but she stuck a foot out, tripping him. He slammed to the ground but scrambled back up to run again. She grabbed his arms, and Eli pinned them behind his back.

He fought and kicked, but the spirit's strength was no match.

Benz yelled for help, but every face turned away at the light blazing from Tal's eyes.

Eli summoned a gale that knocked over chairs and bottles, snatched guns from hands, and swirled white powder into vapor trails. Bodies blew onto the floor and against walls. Benz watched in horror as the barrel of his .45 twisted into a pretzel on the floor before another torrent of wind and light ripped the room away.

Dust devils twirled across the floor as a whirlwind of tissue, bone, and spirit spun back together into Tal, Eli, and Benz. They stood between slashes of moonlight in the empty warehouse, Tal still pinning the dealer's arms behind his back.

Tal scanned the room, the rickety table, and her heart sank. *Not again.*

Eli loosened her grip, and Benz yanked free. He stumbled back and knocked the table sideways, its bent metal legs scraping indignantly against the concrete. He teetered, trying to stand, but his tall frame and heavy muscles tipped him onto the floor with a thud.

"W-Who a-are you?" he stammered, crabbing backward to get away.

"Ghost of Christmas past," Tal said, fury blooming.

Eli stepped her closer, his green essence reflecting from her eyes off Benz's face.

"What the hell is this?" Benz whimpered, trying to stand. "Where am I? What happened?"

"Look around," Tal snapped, pushing on his shoulder to keep him down. "This place should ring a bell."

Benz stared at her, then slowly turned his head to scan the room. His frightened eyes lingered on the rusty columns, the partially unhinged metal door, and the cockeyed table.

"Cops busted us here a few months ago. I lost thirty pounds of coke, but—"

"That's *it*?" Tal exploded. "*That's* your takeaway?"

Eli dialed her back.

"A good cop died that night because of you, asshole. I lost my job, my career—*everything*. All because of you and your precious *coke*."

Eli pinned her tongue.

Benz scooted farther away.

Tal inhaled sharply and released it. In. Out. In. Out. *Sorry*, she said at last.

Eli let her go. "What else do you remember?" he asked Benz.

Benz swallowed and pointed at spots around the room. "We used that table for the … merch. Two gunmen hid there, behind those columns. Cops came in there." He stabbed a finger at the metal door.

"What cops?" Tal hissed. "How many?"

"I don't know. Cops are cops. Too many."

Tal snarled. Her fists curled.

Eli swamped her, an ethereal wet blanket. "Look again," he instructed in a deeper voice.

"How many people you got in there?" Benz asked.

"Try," the spirit said with a flourish of green from Tal's eyes.

Benz looked again at the door. His brow furrowed. "One white guy out front and her," he indicated Tal, "plus a couple of others."

"Why were there gunmen?" Tal asked. "Who wanted them? Who gave them police body armor?"

"I don't know."

Her eyes narrowed. She crouched down, breath hot on his cheek. "I think you do."

Eli pulled her back and crossed her arms over her chest. "Who warned you about the bust?"

Benz scrambled to get away from this seemingly possessed woman until his back hit the wall.

Tal leaned in close. "Who?"

"A cop set it up," Benz said, trapped between her and the wall. "This white dude."

"That helps," she scoffed.

"Tucker. His name is Tucker."

"Manning?"

"I guess."

She leaned back. That must be why she saw him taking Benz's money at the pawnshop. He must have provided the body armor, too. Anger surged thinking about the horrors Tucker had inflicted in a matter of minutes, the lives his actions had cost. Just for money.

Eli dialed her back. "Why?" he asked.

"I don't know," Benz stammered. "Dude came to me and offered info if I paid him. Said the 'buyers' were undercover cops that planned to bust me that night. I wanted to pull out, but he said we should let it happen, that he'd make sure I got out. Said one cop knew too much, and he needed us to take 'em out."

Bullets flew in every direction that night, but when Tal had stood up to engage, Eli had grinned at her through his mask, like he *knew* her. Jake died, pushing *her* out of the way. She grabbed the table to steady herself. "But I didn't know anything."

Benz shrugged. "All I know is, the man saved me a fortune. He still tells me what the cops know so I can adjust my location. Then, when he needs me to remove a problem, we set up a bust."

Tal made herself look at Benz without pummeling him. "How many times have you helped him *remove a problem?*"

"Twice. Mostly I just pay him to keep the cops off my tail."

Tal's stomach churned. This dealer pedaled chemically enhanced dope that had killed at least thirty-five people by the time they'd arranged that bust Tucker derailed. God knows how many more had died since. "How much?" she asked.

"Ten g's a month.

"Ten *thousand? A month?*" Tal asked, incredulous. Cops barely made ten thousand per quarter. Tucker was deep into something.

"I was here that night," Eli said.

"Yeah. I know," Benz stared back. "You were one of the cops."

"No," Eli continued. "Me. Your right-hand man."

Benz struggled to his feet and slammed his knee into the wall. He yelped.

Eli stepped close to his face, though his voice remained kind, gentle. "I lived at Brighton. My mother had OD'd. I was fifteen with nowhere to go, no family, no way out. You took me in and taught me to sell drugs, then guns. You taught me to shoot, too, and I was good. And loyal. So you paid me for protection. And for hits."

Benz swiveled his head in disbelief. "No. No, no way. It c-can't be. Eli's d-dead. I saw it."

Eli beamed in Tal's eyes. "I came back, Benz," he said. "For you."

Benz screamed and tripped over the table as he scrambled for the door. He shoved it open and bolted outside. His footsteps pounded off into the night.

Aren't we going after him? Tal asked, bracing for the wind and light.

He's too scared to go far. Eli walked her outside instead. He turned her right across the parking lot where Benz and the other dealers had parked that night.

Tal's tennis shoes got soaked in the dew-covered weeds and grass as Eli led her down a slope toward the river. She cut through a stand of trees and emerged near a cluster of rushes by the water's edge. Tal stepped cautiously. This would be a great place for snakes.

Eli led her toward a clump of brush with the top partially pressed down. He elevated her senses to hear past the crickets, frogs, and lapping river to the sound of anxious breathing and the overwhelming stench of sweat and fear.

"You can't run from this, Benz," Eli told him. "It's bigger than both of us."

Benz held his breath. He did not move.

"Come out," Eli told him. "There's something I have to do."

"Get the hell away from me!" Benz snapped, lunging from the brush.

Thanks to Eli, Tal saw Benz move as if in slow motion—his arms and legs scissoring in flight, his tall, monolithic form gaining purchase on the wet ground. With the spirit's help, Tal easily measured Benz's stride and calculated the distance and speed needed to stop him. She dropped into a squat and thrust one leg out to catch Benz at the ankle. His legs swept out from under him, and he toppled with a thud.

Tal was on him in seconds, straddling his chest and pinning his arms over his head. Eli turned her to lead so Benz couldn't move. His ribs expanded just enough to draw air.

"D-Don't kill me. P-Please. Don't kill me."

"Look at me," Eli told him.

Benz turned his head and squeezed his eyes shut. "No. Leave me alone. *Whatever* you are, please go away."

Eli's voice sharpened. "Look at me!"

Benz turned back. He slowly opened his eyes.

"That's it." Eli's essence poured through Tal's eyes and opened the channel to connect.

Benz stared at her, unable to move. Fear rolled off in waves. "Are you gonna kill me?"

"Look at *me*," Eli told him.

Benz shifted his gaze from looking at Tal's eyes to looking *in* them. His fear shifted as he found Eli. Less terror, more awe.

"That's it," Eli said, leaning closer. "I'm here, Benz, to forgive you."

Benz's jaw unhinged. His eyes bulged.

"I forgive what you did to me, to Darryl, to all of us. For getting us into that life, for selling it as the only option."

Benz gasped. A tear rolled onto his cheek.

"And I forgive you for getting me killed."

Benz started to cry. Tal slipped off to sit next to him, arms around his shoulders, rocking him as he wept.

The Celtic-knot symbol flared inside Tal's tattoo, searing the skin over her ankle. The croaking frogs turned to foghorns, the river roared against its banks, and humidity landed like clear beads on her skin. Benz shook like a rag doll as Eli's forgiveness purged the flotsam of suffering, fear, and rage. Link once described this part of the process as "an emotional exorcism." That pretty much summed it up.

Holding Benz like this deflated Tal's bitterness, too—which was, no doubt, part of Eli's plan.

She needed to forgive this asshole for the part he played in ruining her life, so she could heal and move on. Rocking him like she would a whimpering child, hearing him gasp between sobs, and having this whole thing orchestrated by the spirit of Jake's killer somehow made that forgiveness easier. While it should have incensed her, it ignited more compassion instead.

Eli thrummed with support.

She held Benz a little closer. It was probably the first time he had been allowed to show his emotions openly like this since he was a child. Kids grew up way too fast in his world, and feelings were considered a weakness.

What if she had grown up in similar circumstances? What if Darden had been born at a place like Brighton? What would their family have looked like? What would he have grown up to do or be?

The surge between Eli and Benz lessened, and Eli loosened Tal's arms.

Benz leaned back and wiped his nose and face. He did not seem as scared.

Tal shook her head, amazed yet again at how another human being had transformed right in front of her, emerging from the ash of his past with a new lease on life.

Liam had explained that human time means nothing on the other side. "A day, a month, a millennium, it's the same—infinite and infinitesimal, endless and connected." That truth showed itself again at this moment with Eli and Benz.

The river's roar subsided, the beads of humidity evaporated, and the booming frogs returned to their normal croak.

Eli stood Tal up and extended her hand.

Benz took it, and she helped him up until they stood face-to-face. Well, face-to-shoulder since Benz was about a foot taller.

"I got a second chance to make things right," Eli told him. "And now, so do you."

Uh-oh. Tal stiffened.

"How?" Benz asked.

"You see Tucker soon, yes?"

Oh no. Tal teetered unsteadily. *You have got to be kidding.*

"Saturday night. Got another cop on his tail and he asked me to get rid of him, but—"

"Who?" Tal asked, petrified of where this conversation was leading.

"Some partner or something."

"Dave?"

"Yeah. That's it. White dude. Tall. Brown hair."

Tal buckled. Dave had been Tucker's partner and friend for years since Tal came on board and, in Tucker's mind, stole Jake away.

You knew *about this?* She yelled in silence.

Eli flooded her with peace and focused on Benz. "What time?" he asked.

"Ten o'clock."

We can't. The ship comes that night. We have to—

We'll make it, Eli assured.

"But look, man," Benz said, running a nervous hand across his mouth. "I can't do that shit no more. Not after all this tonight."

"You must," Eli replied. "Keep the plan. Tal and I will be your gunman."

"What?" she yelped.

Shh. Eli stepped her back as air started to gust.

"Wait," Tal said. "This is crazy. What are you talking about?" The idea of repeating that night, even with a spirit inside, even with a dealer who'd grown a heart, was like grating her skin to pieces. She couldn't do it.

You can, Eli told her. Wind eddied around them. "You will walk from this darkness on that night," Eli told Benz. "But more importantly, you will open the door for others to follow."

Light flashed, and Tal disappeared once more.

CHAPTER SIX

CASPIAN

"You okay?" Manuel asked.

Caspian looked befuddled, a pair of clippers in one hand and a cluster of white grapes in the other. He and Manuel were seasonal pickers at this winery near the Vosges Mountains in northeastern France.

"You went 'away' again," the young Frenchman continued in stilted Spanish, pointing to his own head.

Caspian opened his fist to a cluster of white grapes, almost a dozen of them crushed. "Dios mío, the berries!"

"You didn't damage many," Manuel said.

"I'm not to damage *any*," Caspian snapped. He gently removed those he'd crushed and quickly popped them in his mouth. He lightly placed the rest atop a growing mound in his wooden basket and scolded himself for letting the visions take over again.

A young girl with a radiant smile. Bits of dark hair and olive skin. A puddle of blood. *Had he known her? Had he hurt her?*

These snippets came at random, bits and pieces of Caspian's past skittering across his brain like spiders on a web. They had haunted him for years, and he didn't know why.

"You okay?" Manuel asked again, whispering so none of the other pickers would hear.

"Fine. Thank you." Caspian shook off the few spiders and snails from his basket of grapes. He had no memory of his past when he arrived here three seasons ago. No idea of who he was, where he was from, or what his name might be, but they had hired him and taught him to pick.

"Panier," he called out, followed a bit louder by, "Rempli." But the basket carriers were busy helping other pickers on the next two rows, so Caspian hoisted the heavy container brimming with grapes to his shoulder and carried it to the waiting trailer.

Uncertain of his age, but feeling around twenty-five or twenty-six based on Manuel and his youthful vigor, Caspian was not the youngest worker, but he was among the strongest and most desired. His broad shoulders and strong back withstood long hours of work, and he moved quickly and efficiently down the rows. Though this was only their second season together, Manuel was one of the few who could keep up with him. It's why Caspian had requested to work with him. Well, that and their pleasure in sharing languages. Born in Paris, Manuel spoke French and had studied English in school. Caspian spoke fluent Castilian Spanish, though he could not remember why. They enjoyed comparing words and phrases in all three tongues.

A foreman scowled as Caspian offloaded his basket. The grizzled man shoved the empty basket back at him and yelled for Caspian to finish the next row before his break.

Caspian nodded and walked off with a slight smile. He had shared a bed with that man's daughter, Elena, over the last two seasons. At her insatiable insistence, too, though her father did not know that part. She had also been the one to give him his name, saying he looked like "Prince Caspian" from that Narnia movie. He had no idea of his real name, so it stuck.

Thunder rumbled in the distance, marking the onset of a late afternoon summer storm. All twelve pickers quickened their pace. Weather was a god at wineries, and rain meant reduced sweetness. They had to finish this field while the sugar ran high.

Caspian's black hair stuck to his face in the heat, and his linen shirt clung to the muscles of his back as he cut another knot of grapes and placed them carefully in the basket. His strong hands and long fingers cupped them as they had Elena's soft curves.

Later that night, the pickers gathered by the fire after dinner to sing and talk of the day. Some of them, like Manuel, lived near this winery that hugged the border with Germany. Others, like Caspian, were itinerant pickers who hailed from Europe, Australia, and the Americas. All of them spoke their own languages, but a few could translate for the rest, enough to ensure the stories, jokes, and songs could be shared.

Caspian picked up his guitar. Firelight bathed his hands and face as he played and sang songs in Spanish, French, English, and Italian—a little something for everyone. The pickers toasted their wine and sang along.

"Where do you go next?" Manuel asked when it was over, testing his Spanish again.

"Not sure. There's a beautiful olive grove on the Iberian Peninsula. You'd love it there."

Manuel smiled. "Not this time." He blushed. "I met a girl."

The other men teased. Caspian raised his glass.

"Even the strongest men fall at a woman's soft touch." They toasted, and Caspian downed the last of his wine. It warmed his throat as he slid into his sleeping bag, long legs kicking to make room. He shot Manuel a teasing grin. "Sweet dreams."

The other pickers soon followed, the crickets singing them to sleep. Winery work started before sunrise, and the days were twelve to fifteen hours long. Rest was a welcomed reprieve.

Caspian gazed up at the canopy of stars. They were clear and bright, without any ambient light to get in the way. He wanted nothing more than to sleep, but he dreaded the nightmares, the shards of memory that rent his dreams. He focused on constellations like the Big Dipper and Orion and a few orbiting satellites that winked their way across the sky. Long-eared and Barn owls swooped among trees and across the fields to hunt voles and rabbits. Caspian watched them until his eyelids became too heavy.

The young woman again—a diamond on her finger. They make love. The bed catches fire. "Help me," she says. "Please."

"*Please.*" A man's voice. "I need your help."

Caspian's eyes flew open to see an old man's face inches above his—salt-and-pepper hair, clean-shaven, very weak.

Another vision. Another old man. His face bloody and covered in dirt. "Help me."

"Please," the man whispered. He struggled to stand.

Caspian sprung from his sleeping bag, chills cascading down his spine and his left ankle on fire. He feared having stuck his foot in the campfire, but the embers were cold. He rolled up his pant leg and pulled down his sock to find that weird tattoo suddenly *glowing*, the center knot over his ankle burning slightly and shimmering in jewel tones.

He jerked back. "W-Who are you?"

"You are one," the man replied in perfect Spanish. "You can help."

A few men stirred and rolled over, and he thought of waking them. One loud yell would do it.

"No," the man said as if reading his thoughts. His voice was somehow lighter, younger, but equally fluent. "Please. Help us."

Caspian looked around. "*Us?*" The old man was alone.

"You must take this spirit," the old man whispered. "I am too weak."

Caspian's strong legs buckled. Those words were *familiar*. A surprising rage flared from out of nowhere, but the heat from the tattoo shot up his leg and through his body to drive it back. *What the hell is happening to me?*

"You are one of them," the younger voice said through the old man's lips.

"One *what?*"

He grabbed Caspian's arm like a vise. "You are a vessel."

The old man screams from the dirt. His cries mix with pounding hooves and evil mirth.

Caspian tore free and sprinted into the woods. He wanted to put as much distance as possible between himself and that crazy old man.

Caspian ran full speed until he reached the edge of the woods on the far side of the winery. He hurried inside the barn, panting and shaking, and slid down the weathered wall between bales of hay to catch his breath. The barn was built ages ago to store hay for the draft horses before motorized equipment took most of their work. A few horses remained, so the barn was still used.

He trembled, heart pumping and muscles burning. The wood

creaked against his weight, and splinters threatened to pierce his back. He remembered those he got with Elena their first few times out here before they'd become brave enough to meet in her room. Now, red deer and lynx scat covered the floor.

Caspian dug into his sieve-like mind to make sense of the old man, of his talk about spirit, and of the strange tattoo around his ankle that had ignited for the first time in … he couldn't remember. Who had he been? What had he done? And what the hell was a *vessel*?

A burst of strong wind hit the shed from outside, yanking at the rusted tin roof and pulling hay from the bales. A bright light slashed the air, and the old man appeared inside the barn, on his knees.

"Please," he said, his voice even weaker. "You must help."

The man started to collapse, but Caspian instinctively caught him and lowered him to the wooden floor, resting his head on some hay. The man's skin was ashy, his shirt soaked with sweat. He wheezed.

Caspian scanned him for injuries but found nothing bleeding or broken.

"What's wrong? How are you hurt?" There were no Alzheimer's facilities in the area, and people cared for their elderly at home. Maybe he'd wandered off.

The old man's eyes shot open. He grabbed Caspian by the shoulders with that same forceful inner grip. "Please," the other, younger voice said. "Help us."

The old man let go and fell back.

Hurry.

That word came from the old man, but his lips had not moved.

Help me lift him.

Caspian lurched back. That thought was not his. "What is going on?"

Now.

The urgency grounded him, and he stooped to lift the old man. Whatever force was inside helped Caspian stand him upright.

Good. Quickly.

This thing, this force, this *spirit*, used the old man's arms to turn Caspian around. His tattoo shone under his pant leg, and green light burst from Caspian's eyes into the darkness. He turned his head and saw the same thing happening with the old man. Their eyes aligned, and Caspian caught an odd, sweet floral scent before a shiny ball of light the size of an olive pit left the man's mouth and floated toward Caspian's back.

Caspian gripped the barn wall as the orb slipped inside and filled him with a peculiar icy heat. His stomach churned as the thing expanded to fill the crevices around his insides. It was not painful as much as it was unusual and ... *familiar.*

The bearded old man reaches up from the dirt to say something. Fury ignites, and Caspian thrusts out his hands. Was he helping the old man or hurting him?

The spirit moved Caspian's arms and legs as if testing them. He struggled against it at first, then relaxed slightly when it allowed him to share control.

The tattoo cooled to a smolder, but it continued shimmering lightly in jewel tones around his ankle. He covered it with his sock, unable to remember where the tattoo had come from or what it was for. But some deep part of his brain knew it would light up around spirits.

We must go, the same voice replied, this time from inside

Caspian's mind.

"But he needs a hospital. That's—"

Think your words.

Caspian closed his mouth. *He needs a hospital.*

No time. Lift him.

He'll die.

Pick him up.

"But—?" Caspian caught himself. *But why? Who are you?*

NOW. The spirit bent Caspian down to scoop the frail form into his arms.

The poor man was hanging on by a thread. This spirit had nearly cost him his life. Would it do the same to Caspian?

"What's your name?" Caspian asked in Spanish, trying to keep the old man engaged, alive.

"Diego," he whispered. "Diego Ruiz."

Caspian held Diego in his arms like a child. *What now?*

Hold on.

The whirlwind kicked up again. It tossed the hay, rattled the wood, and lashed at their clothes until a bolt of light tore the barn away and landed them on the shore of a vast black lake canopied with stars and surrounded by mountains. Cold bit through his sweater and pants. The old man trembled uncontrollably.

"Where are we?" Caspian's teeth chattered more from fear than cold.

The spirit lowered him to his knees on the rocky shore, tilted his head back, and made him howl, long and mournful, like a trapped or injured wolf.

One moment passed. Another. Two more cries tore from Caspian's throat, each one louder and longer until footsteps pounded in their direction.

People appeared. It was hard to make out details or count how many, but they were not wasting any time. Some lit a bonfire. One wrapped Caspian in a wool blanket while others took Diego and cocooned him in layers of dyed wool. The men and women were all dressed in brightly woven shawls and hand-knitted hats that covered their ears and their short, blunt, black hair. They all spoke some kind of Spanish. Caspian recognized a few of the words, but the language seemed as archaic as these mountains.

The bonfire roared to life. Some men and women danced around it as an older man hovered and chanted over Diego. He was their chief, by the looks of it, wearing a more decorated hat adorned with small coins of some kind and a brightly woven blanket across his shoulder. A white tunic stuck out underneath, over his boots, with bright yellow suns embroidered at the hem. Strands of beads and shells clacked together around his neck, and a large silver medallion swung below his chest. He closed his eyes, lifted his hands, and mumbled more of the same language.

A streak of light ripped open the night, and a woman appeared. She looked like the others, though dressed in civilian clothes and coat, and her golden eyes glowed as if lit from inside. A ring of deep, jade-like green surrounded each iris. The chanting continued as she blessed two cups of steaming liquid. She gave one to Caspian and trickled the other between Diego's lips.

The hot liquid smelled like cocoa, and the chocolate tasted raw, rich, and earthy. The rush of caffeine came quickly, stronger and more invigorating than with any espresso Caspian had ever tried.

Another bonfire on the shore of a different lake. Different snow-capped mountains. A different tribe chanting in a different language Caspian recognizes. They wear coats of thick

white llama hair.

The spirit tuned Caspian's ear like a radio dial until he understood the nearby tribal song and the chief's ancient Mayan words. A feather could have toppled him. *Who are these people?* he asked. *What is happening?*

The chief raised his hands and called out to the heavens. He asked for Diego's life to be spared, for his soul to remain. Caspian's hands shook around the cup of cocoa.

Diego's cup ran dry and he opened his eyes. He blinked and looked around until he spied the chief. Firelight bathed the man's hat and shawl, and it glinted against the medallion over his belly. The chief nodded, and Diego turned his gaze to Caspian.

His coloring had improved, and his eyes shone brighter. The prayers seemed to work. Diego freed one hand from the blanket and beckoned Caspian over.

Caspian obliged and knelt beside him. "You are ... okay?"

"I will be," he whispered. "Thanks to you."

"Will it hurt me, too?"

"This spirit needs you."

"I don't understand."

Diego's eyes closed. He fell asleep.

"Trust your visions," the chief told Caspian. "The spirit will help."

The hair on Caspian's neck shot up. He had not told *anyone* about the visions.

"What do I do?"

"What the spirit needs," the woman answered. She held out a coin and placed it in his hand.

Another coin in Caspian's clenched palm. Same etched vines. Same SObY initials. Same dove flying through. It grows

brighter. He throws it away.

Caspian started to heave this coin, too, but the spirit stopped him and stuck his hand into his pocket and dropped it in there.

"Godspeed," the woman said, and, for the second time that night, Caspian's world spun away.

CHAPTER SEVEN

LINK

Link plucked the colorful bouquet of store-bought flowers from the car seat. Their plastic sheath crinkled as he stepped out of the rental car and into the Atlantic City sun.

He walked across the narrow street and through the large metal gate of Chadwick Memorial Gardens. Link hated cemeteries. He had no family to speak of, so did not understand the concept of visiting loved ones who'd passed, or calling up their dead memories. And the thought of being locked in a box forever, even if you were not alive to know it, was too much like prison. He shook off the thought.

The spirit steered Link off the walkway and onto some grass near a bend in the trail. The late morning sun beat down as he stopped by a stone marker lying flush to the ground, its face weathered with veins of gray and black. Teddy knelt in the grass and ran Link's fingers over the words:

Sally Ann Dawson, Loving Wife & Mother
April 10, 1975 – Dec. 28, 2016

"Your mom?" Link asked aloud, then realized. *I mean, your mom?*

Teddy warmed.

Link noted the date, so close to Christmas. Holidays always made death more tragic.

Teddy made Link remove the plastic wrap from around the flowers and place them in the empty bronze urn affixed to his mother's stone. Most of the flowers held no smell, but the red roses released a hint of sweetness as Teddy turned them for optimum display. He poured water from a plastic bottle into the urn around their stems, then looked at the other name carved on the stone:

Kevin J. Dawson, Loving Husband & Father
November 15, 1972

Link snorted. There was nothing loving about the Kevin he met last night.

He loved her, Teddy said. *And he gave me what he could.*

Like every other spirit Link had served, Teddy held no sense of animosity or bitterness. No matter how badly they'd been hurt in human life, the spirits were like bright, flickering torches that never went out.

He needs to know love, Teddy said. *The kind Mom had.*

Link waited for more, but Teddy made him stand.

Let's go. He's alone.

Link threw the plastic wrap into a metal waste barrel by the cemetery gate and returned to the car. His nerves wound like guitar strings thinking of Kevin's connection to the cops, but Teddy cooled him off. Link took a few breaths, donned his sunglasses, and pulled into traffic.

Atlantic City was more sprawling and residential than Link first thought. Then again, most people who came here did so as tourists to gamble or walk the beach. They did not think of it as someone's home. The same was true in Reno. Tourists almost never left the casinos or the nearby hotels and restaurants to walk the neighborhoods.

Teddy guided Link to a working-class urban neighborhood lined with narrow, two-story homes painted a variety of colors. Most of the small yards featured chained-link fences and few to no trees. More than a few included rusted sheds out back and short driveways in front.

Link pulled over by a plain, two-story white house on the corner with storm windows and paint-chipped wooden siding. This must be Kevin's. The fenced-in yard was slightly bigger and well-kept. One mature maple tree dominated the side yard, its fallen leaves painting the grass yellow and red. The cracked driveway was just wide enough to fit two cars under the open carport. A white Honda was parked to one side. The empty spot next to it glistened with fresh oil.

Teddy's comment, "*He's alone,*" suddenly made more sense.

It's okay. Teddy guided Link to park on the street one house up in case Kevin looked out. Link anxiously eyed the window. Kevin was a security guard and former cop with easy access to more cops. He was bound to find out.

Teddy eased his fears and stepped from the car. Link took a breath and exhaled sharply. In, out. In, out. He followed the sidewalk to Kevin's drive and the short walk up to the front porch. A few flowers grew in pots on either side, and Link suspected a woman's touch. Marie, perhaps? The woman in the gilded cage who knew Kevin's favorite dish at his favorite casino restaurant while feigning the need to check his schedule?

Smells of vegetable soup and fresh bread wafted from the neighbor's house next door. Link's mouth began to water. He hadn't eaten since dinner last night but he pushed that aside and knocked on Kevin's door. He heard footsteps, followed by the *thunk* of a metal lock being turned.

The door swung open, and Kevin snarled. "I told you to stay away—"

"I died in that Chicago nightclub shooting," Teddy said. "You told Mom I burned up in the explosion."

Kevin's jaw dropped momentarily, but he quickly recovered. "You his boyfriend or something? Coming back to cause trouble? I got no money if that's what you're after."

"It's me, Dad. Honest. I came back to see you, to talk to you about that night."

"My son made his choice," Kevin hissed with an angry snarl. "He's gone, and there's nothing I can do about it now." He started to slam the door, but Teddy stuck Link's foot in the way.

"Mom was Sally Ann Bering. You met her in New York when you were still a police officer."

Alarms sounded again with visions of sirens, handcuffs, and prison. Link shoved his hands in his pockets to keep them from shaking.

"Anyone can read that," Kevin said warily. "Same with the news about that nightclub."

"Mom died five months to the day after I did and just two days after you told her what really happened to me, to my remains." He leaned in and spoke softly. "She had cancer, but she died from a broken heart. That is *not* public record."

Anger scorched Kevin's cheeks, and he tried to close the door, but Teddy showered him with a green light from Link's eyes. Kevin staggered back. "And you cannot move on with Marie until you deal with that," Teddy continued.

Kevin's face twisted indignantly, and he grabbed a shotgun from behind the door.

Link turned to run, but Teddy rooted him. He could not move so much as a finger.

"You always did love guns," Teddy told his father.

"It's how good guys keep bad guys away," Kevin retorted.

"Good guys can go bad, too, Dad. You of all people should know that."

Kevin tightened his grip. "Get inside."

Teddy lightened his hold and stepped Link into the house.

Kevin slammed the door and shoved the gun into Link's back, urging him toward the adjacent kitchen. He gestured for Link to sit in a chair at the breakfast table, then picked up his phone and pressed a number. He held it a few seconds, then put it down and walked closer, his gun leveled at Link's chest.

Link's heart threatened to burst, but Teddy looked around at the clean house, the locked gun cabinet, the array of deer heads and large fish mounted on the paneled walls, the floral dishtowels in the kitchen, and lace doilies under the lamps. These few feminine touches brightened the place but were as light and superficial as the potted plants outside—easy to remove if things changed.

A few framed pictures of Kevin dotted the room: as a police officer in New Jersey, at the Empire Casino with Marie, and with a petite blonde woman and a handsome, sandy-haired teenage boy Link assumed was Teddy. Ted had his mother's hazel eyes and sweet smile but his father's square jaw and barrel chest. His mother beamed. Kevin frowned.

Link grimaced at the imbalance, but the spirit warmed equally toward both parents. Link feared being a pretty bad spirit when his time came.

There were a few other pictures of Teddy, as well, including his senior picture and one of him hunting with his dad. He was a boy, unsmiling, holding the rifle like it was a rattlesnake.

"Who are you really?" Kevin snapped. "And what do you want?" His finger curled around the trigger.

Unfazed, Teddy pointed to the hunting picture. "My tenth birthday. My first gun. You made me kill my first buck. That one." He pointed to one of the smaller deer heads hanging up.

A touch of pride crossed Kevin's face.

"And I hated every second."

The pride fizzled.

Teddy pointed to another photo. "My first homecoming." Link stole a glance at the young man in the black tux with the teal bow tie. His lips were smiling, but his eyes were flat.

"You wanted me to take Helen Moore, telling me how much she liked me and how much her family was hoping I'd ask. But I wanted to go with my friends. It grew into this big fight with you, wondering why I spent all of my time with them and not with girls. Why I didn't like Helen and why I didn't have a girlfriend. Mom knew, but …" Teddy paused. "I knew how disappointed you'd be."

Here we go, Link thought, bracing for Kevin's response.

Kevin cleared his throat. "How do you know all this?"

Teddy's emerald light bathed Kevin's cheeks. "I love you, Dad."

"It's impossible," Kevin mumbled.

"Nothing is impossible on the other side."

Kevin shook his head, unable to hear this.

"I love you," Teddy said again. "And I forgive you for turning away and leaving my body there unclaimed."

Remorse crept in. Kevin fought it back.

"Strangers buried me in a donated cemetery lot. A minister contributed her time to perform the services, and a local gay rights organization helped cover the costs of my casket and vault."

Kevin fell into a kitchen chair. "I can't do this again," he mumbled. "I already paid for this with your mother's life."

"It's not about making you pay, Dad," Teddy said, kneeling Link next to Kevin's chair. "I'm here so you can heal."

Tears welled, and Kevin lowered the gun to the linoleum floor. "I told everyone you died saving people in that club," he said. "That you were walking nearby and heard the shots. That you ran in to help, but … the shooter hit that gas line." He wiped his cheeks. Words struggled out from his tight throat. "Your mom learned the truth later on. I didn't want to hurt her, but I couldn't face why you were there. I couldn't face *him*."

Kevin slumped over, and Teddy wrapped him in Link's arms.

The tattoo ignited, and Link's senses deepened to hear, see, and smell even more of the world around him, including a distant siren that suddenly went silent blocks away. Kevin must have called the police. He probably pushed a silent alarm on his phone after forcing Link inside. Link eyed the door. Police would arrive any second to surprise him.

He tensed, ready to bolt. Teddy held him back.

"Kevin?"

Kevin and Link jerked up to see Marie staring at them from across the room. She must have entered through the back door on the other side of the kitchen, off the carport. *How long has she been standing there?* Link asked, worried now that two people could turn him in. *How much did she hear?*

Teddy didn't answer but pulsed with confidence, instead, as if he'd expected this. Or planned it.

"Is that true? What you just said?" Marie asked Kevin.

He looked down.

She pointed to Link. "So he's … *Teddy?*"

"On the inside," Kevin whispered.

Teddy vibrated. His father had acknowledged him.

Link heard the cars roll up. Two of them. The engines turned off, and footsteps hurried across the grass. A loud knock followed at the front door. "Police! Open up." The voice was deep, gruff, demanding.

This is it, Link thought.

You'll be okay, Teddy assured.

Marie and Kevin exchanged a look.

"Police!" the voice shouted, firmer this time. "Open the door."

Link trembled in spite of the spirit's comfort. He looked between Marie and Kevin. The room began to spin.

Finally, Marie straightened her shoulders and passed by them to reach the front door. She screwed on a smile and opened it. "May I help you, Officer?" she asked, standing to block the policeman's view of the kitchen table.

"We received an alarm," he told her. "Is Mr. Dawson here? Is everyone safe?"

Marie glanced fleetingly in Kevin's direction, but he was slumped over in the chair, gun on the floor, sobbing. Link's eyes pleaded for her not to tell.

She turned back to the officer and giggled. "That silly fool," she said. "His family got to town early, so I let them in to surprise him. His nephew came out, and Kevin didn't recognize the poor boy. He thought he was here to rob the place. I'm sorry he called. Everything is fine."

She delivered that lie so honestly. Perhaps she'd been an actress.

Showgirl, Teddy told him. *Before Kevin helped her get work at The Empire.*

"Thank you, ma'am," the officer said, his voice a few degrees softer. "But we need to speak with Mr. Dawson."

"Of course," Marie said, looking toward Kevin again.

Kevin took a deep breath and stood. He plucked a napkin from a container on the table and blew his nose before walking over. Marie stepped back to let him pass, then led Link from the kitchen, past the carport entry, to the back of the house.

They entered the spare bedroom, and Marie quietly shut the door. She ensured the curtains were drawn, then turned on the light and drilled Link with her eyes. "How did you get here?"

"What do you mean?" Teddy asked.

Link was sure he already knew.

"Kevin is a good man," Marie said, trying to keep a protective edge to her voice. "But he has been ripped to shreds since that shooting. I understand a little better now why that is, but—why put him through all that pain again, just when he's gotten over it?"

Teddy took her hands. "Because he cannot heal without it." He squeezed. "And neither can you."

Marie yanked to free her hand, but Teddy held tight. Her heart beat like a rabbit's. "What does that mean?" she asked. "What are you—"

The door opened, and Kevin entered. "Coast is clear," he said, eyes red but brighter.

Link heaved a sigh, and Teddy let go. Marie stumbled back.

Kevin pulled a piece of paper from his pocket and held it up. "You looked familiar the moment I met you."

Marie gasped.

Link buckled, staring at the mug shot of his true self—Javier Gomez, fugitive from Reno—along with some sketches of what he might look like in disguise. Though Link appeared different from any of the sketches, the connection was close enough.

Marie sunk onto the floral bedspread.

Link tried to reach the door, but Teddy anchored him. "Meet me at the cemetery tomorrow," he told Kevin and Marie. "Both of you. Three p.m."

The air split open, and Link disappeared.

CHAPTER EIGHT

AVANI

Avani strolled past art deco hotels strung like painted beads along Miami's South Beach. The humidity was thick as milk, and the air rubbed her skin like fine sandpaper. Various pop songs, some performed by live bands, competed from the hotels as tourists and locals dined al fresco around pots of bright tropical plants and vining flowers.

Between the hotels and the wide beach and turquoise waters of the Atlantic, Ocean Drive hummed with cars, bikes, and young men and women, skin tanned or burned, wearing as little as possible. They walked, jogged, roller bladed, and strutted up and down the sidewalks, making South Beach feel like a tropical Las Vegas with hotels, nightclubs, and beaches instead of casinos.

Avani grew nervous, angry even, at the lustful leers tossed her way.

You are beautiful, the spirit said. *A work of art. It is difficult not to admire you.*

"Admire?" Avani retorted. *They look at me like I'm raw meat.*

At the next street, Amber turned left and led them away from Ocean Drive. *My dad started abusing me when I was eight,* she said, *but my mom refused to believe it. He didn't stop, and she wouldn't listen, so I quit school at sixteen and ran away to Vegas.*

Avani could not fathom this kind of abuse. Her own father had been so kind, smart, and loving. He read books to Avani, shared his love of space and his work at NASA, and taught her how to cook his favorite Indian food. Right up until two white boys stabbed him to death in a post-9/11 hate crime.

I was young, pretty, and built—"raw meat," as you say—but I turned that hunger into "admiration" by becoming a showgirl. It's how I met Elaine. It didn't pay much, and neither one of us had the smarts or money for school, and no way were we going to work the streets or become escorts for johns who could potentially hurt us, so we became strippers.

Amber turned them north onto Washington Avenue, toward 16th Street, past the rows of palm trees, restaurants, gift shops, and low-rise condos and hotels.

We made good money onstage, she continued, *and only gave the lap dances we chose. It was far from perfect, and I'm not saying it's right, but it paid the bills and, believe it or not, watching us dance released the steam valve on some men who might have taken their frustrations out on wives, girlfriends or daughters.*

How old were you? Avani asked. *When you died?*

Twenty-four. Drug overdose.

No hurt. No shame. No sign of self-loathing. She had forgiven herself.

The afternoon heat and humidity frizzed Avani's thick mane of hair. She lifted the hem of her shirt to dry her face, and two young men whistled from a construction site nearby. She quickly lowered the shirt. *See? Raw meat.*

What about Sonny?

Avani clenched her teeth.

Not that Sonny, Amber corrected. *The real one.*

As they walked past a convenience store and Hookah lounge, Avani thought of the nine years of friendship she and Sonny had shared before that horrible night. She remembered the fun times they'd had as kids, the gentle ways he'd expressed his feelings as they grew, and the hurt that had deepened with each refusal.

Even the darkest clouds let in light.

Avani flashed to her father, bleeding to death on the convenience store floor. *Not all of them.*

We're here. The spirit stopped outside another windowless, one-story building like the one in Vegas, painted the same peacock teal with the same purple neon trim around the roof and entry. This one featured an entry bordered on either side by narrow, opaque, glass block windows. A sign over the door read, The Inner Sanctum.

A million butterflies launched in Avani's stomach.

Amber, by contrast, pulsed happily. *Teal and purple were Jeffrey's favorite colors.*

The building covered half a city block and was sandwiched between a tattoo parlor and a Latin grocery. Two young, bikini-clad women with unnaturally large breasts stood by the open front door.

"Free wings, tonight only!" one of them called out.

"All you can eat," the other added salaciously as she handed out coupons to passersby.

Avani hated these places where women were reduced to lumps of titillating flesh, and men wielded a perverse sense of power by paying them.

Things are not always what they seem, the spirit cautioned.

"May I help you?" the brunette woman asked, her voice curt,

sharp.

"I'm looking for Jeffrey Danielson."

"Aren't we all," the blonde one said. Both women laughed.

"It's personal."

"That's the only kind he does, sugar."

More giggles.

"May I see him?"

"You better tell *us* your business, sweetheart," the brunette snapped. "'Cause ain't nobody gets to Mr. Danielson except through us."

Amber stepped up, her voice like course gravel. "Is Hal here?"

The women jerked at the change.

"Hal's always here," the blonde replied. "Why?"

"I need a job," Amber said.

What? Avani reeled. *THIS is why you brought me here?*

She turned to leave, but Amber rooted her.

"I was told to ask for Mr. Danielson or Hal," Amber continued as she blanketed Avani with calm.

"Well, why didn't you say so, honey," the brunette said, stepping aside.

"Good luck," the blonde added.

Avani couldn't believe the change. With that one sentence, those four simple words, she was one of them, allowed into the den to become part of the pack.

Inside, deceptively high ceilings darkened a wide-open room that afforded every table a clear view of the elevated stage. Deco-style lights hung low over each table. Purple neon outlined the bar on one side of the room as well as the wide stage with its three translucent poles on the other.

Music pulsed. A row of wall-mounted screens played televised sports in silence, but most patrons watched the four girls dancing onstage. Each was naked except for a teal-colored thong. A handful of waitresses wearing teal bikini tops and curve-hugging boy shorts delivered food and drinks.

You want me to work *here?* Avani eyed the dancers sliding around the clear poles. *I can't do that. I won't.*

Amber turned her toward the bar. *Remember that these women are someone's daughters, sisters, friends. Or mothers.*

Avani's cheeks reddened. She knew better than to judge on sight. *Sorry.*

Amber guided them to a tall, gray-haired man mixing drinks behind the bar.

"Gotta be twenty-one to order," he said without looking up.

"I'm not here to drink," Amber replied.

"Gotta be twenty-one to stay."

He had a crusty but caring aura that Avani liked immediately.

"Hal?" Amber asked.

He paused to look up. "Who's asking?"

"I need a job."

"Sorry. Gotta be twenty-one for that, too. Afraid it's not your lucky day." He garnished the drink and handed it to a customer on a nearby stool.

"She looks like *that*, and you care about her *birthday?*" the customer retorted. "Come on, Hal. We pay *extra* to buy drinks from girls like her."

Avani shuddered, but Amber pressed on. "Young body, old soul," she said.

"Gee. Never heard that one before." Hal stopped to look her in the eye. His expression was hard, and wrinkles lined his face, but his blue eyes were kind, wise.

"You're a beautiful girl. But go do something else, something better than this." He turned away.

Avani understood why Amber and Elaine liked him so much. "Elaine Fischer sent me."

Hal stopped and turned back. "How do you know Elaine?"

"She's an old friend," Amber replied.

Hal sized up the girl in front of him. "You're young enough to be her granddaughter."

"Friend of the family," Amber corrected.

Avani admired how deftly she navigated these tricky waters of truth.

"She told me where to find you. Call her. She'll vouch for it."

Hal leaned in. He seemed tough, but Avani could tell it was meant to protect more than put off.

"No offense," he said quietly. "But I can smell age on a woman the way some men know perfume. I'd bet my life savings you're not even twenty."

Avani bit her lip. She would turn nineteen next spring.

The girls up front shrieked playfully as Jeffrey Danielson entered. He was young, handsome, and cocksure. But behind the charm lurked an emotional void. Avani could feel it from across the room. It grew stronger as he approached.

Jeffrey scanned her body, undressing her with his eyes as he took her hand. "Please tell me this goddess needs a job."

Hal lowered his gaze to clean a glass. "Not old enough."

Hal's disgust for Jeffrey hit Avani the way horses she had rehabbed on the ranch radiated abuse. Trust was long gone, replaced by hate, fear, or, in Hal's case, a need to defend and protect.

"When did that ever stop us?" Jeffrey chided. "Just put the

right birthdate on her paperwork and get her started."

"That's what I said," the customer added, winking at Avani and sipping his drink.

Jeffrey slapped Avani's butt, his fingers lingering long enough to get a squeeze. "You just passed the interview, sweetheart. Give her a job, Hal. We need this ass working tables in my club."

Avani clenched her fist to punch him. The spirit eased her back.

Jeffrey lightly smacked another waitress's thinly covered backside as she walked by. "Bring my usual, honey," he told her. "In fact, make it two."

"Sure thing, Mr. D," she said with a giggle, then scowled once he left. Jeffrey was anything but loved.

It's why we're here, Amber told her.

Hal put down the glass and grabbed Avani's arm. "Elaine is too nice to send anyone here," he said. "Go. Finish school, find a job, join the Peace Corps, get married. Do whatever it is you want to do in life, but don't do this. Not here. Not with him."

He let go, but Amber took his hand. Her voice thickened in Avani's like smoke. "Jeffrey *is* why I'm here, Hal. I don't expect you to understand, but Elaine did. I only need a few days."

Hal drew back, worried.

"Jeffrey needs what I bring. If he gets it, everyone wins, including them." She nodded to the waitresses and the girls on stage.

Hal twisted the bar rag, but he didn't walk away. "You sure about this?" he asked at last.

She nodded.

He sighed and reached under the counter for a clear, sandwich-sized plastic bag. "Your uniform," he said, then pointed to a backstage door off the rear hall. A small sign at the top read, Employees Only. "Lockers and dressing rooms are through there." He paused. "I sure hope you know what you're doing."

"Thanks, Hal." Amber smiled and turned Avani toward the door.

Avani's second night of work was not much better than the first. She worked just as hard dodging pinches or slaps from some of the more inebriated patrons as she did serving their drinks. Most respected the club's "look, don't touch" policy, but there were some, evidently, who could not resist the temptation of her tight, teal-covered bottom.

Avani threatened to throw a drink at the next man who tried.

Amber navigated her back to the bar. *Only a few more days*, she assured.

Laughter rang from the back as Jeffrey hosted a group of men in his private room, sharing dinner and conducting business. Avani had seen and heard enough already to know that *business* meant drugs, political favors, and gambling. Most of those deals were brokered or sealed through lap dances from chosen girls, along with Samantha's captivating movements on stage. She was the most beautiful, most experienced dancer at the club and Jeffrey's favorite by far. He saved her for only the most important lap dances.

"Vodka tonic with a twist, margarita on the rocks, and a Maker's and Coke," Avani told Hal. He mixed, measured, and poured, a virtuoso juggling orders from three busy waitresses and a slew of customers at the bar.

"How's it going?" he asked, securing a wedge of lime onto one salted rim.

"Made sixty-five in tips, and I'm only two hours in."

"You might want to put some ice on your bottom during your break," he told her. "To stop the sting and keep it from bruising."

"Thanks," she replied. No wonder Hal was beloved.

As he placed the finished drinks on her tray, another waitress hurried up from the back room. Avani recognized her as the blonde woman who had greeted her at the door when she arrived.

"What is it, Hal?" she asked.

"The neighbor called again," he said. "Your mom fell and hit her head."

"Oh no. When?"

"Just happened. She's at home. Go check on her. Avani here can cover 'til you get back."

The woman smiled. "That okay? Really?"

Avani nodded.

"Okay. Thanks. I won't be long." She started to go then turned back. "Watch out," she told Avani. "Jeffrey's in a mood tonight." She hurried toward the backstage door.

"Thanks, Hal," Avani told him. "Sorry you had to lie."

"She needs to check on her mom more often, anyway," he said.

A third waitress came up with a drink order. Hal took it and gave her Avani's tray. "Take this to table one. Avani has to fill in for Cinder."

"Good luck," the third waitress said flatly, taking the tray. "Glad it's not me."

Avani glanced toward the back room.

Hal touched her arm. "Finish what you came for and get out," he warned. "The longer you stay, the harder he makes it for you to leave."

Amber shimmered in Avani's black eyes, a bare green dusting that reflected in Hal's glasses. "Jeffrey needs this," she said. "It will change everything."

Hal looked at her warily, then mixed another drink. "Yeah. Hope so."

Amber made Avani hoist the empty tray, then strode confidently toward the back room.

Every head turned as she entered. The doorway curtains had been pinned back, and the plush teal carpet gave way under her heels. She paused long enough for her eyes to adjust to the low, decorative lighting. It was bright enough to see but dim enough to easily watch the girls on stage forty or fifty yards away.

Jeffrey sat with three men around a table draped in white linen, the only source of white in the room. It was covered with dirty dishes, half-filled glasses, and wadded linen napkins. The men soaked in her every move as Avani bussed their table.

"My wife would get a whole lot more from me if she looked like that," one man said when Avani leaned over to collect his cutlery.

He was overweight, with thinning hair and a thick gold chain buried in a carpet of gray chest hair. Avani shuddered. *What wife would want more of that?*

Amber pulsed a brief reprimand.

Sorry.

"Where's Cinder?" Jeffrey asked gruffly.

Avani prickled at his tight lips and cold eyes, but Amber warmed with a mother's love. "Home," Avani said. "Her mother fell."

Jeffrey snorted angrily. "Happens again, you're replacing her for good."

I'm not out to cost anyone a job.

You won't, Amber said. *In fact, things will be much better for Cinder, and everyone, when we're through.*

According to Hal, Cinder had worked here for five years and had spent most of that time as Jeffrey's private waitress. She was also a favored lap dancer to help broker his biggest deals. She hated it but needed the extra money for her mother's medical care.

Avani feared Jeffrey would expect the same if she were to replace Cinder.

"Works for me," Gold Chain said. "She new?"

"Interviewed yesterday," Jeffrey replied, plucking Avani's ass as he had before.

Avani wanted to smack the leer off his face, but Amber stole control of the room by pouring Avani's body around the men, twisting sensually to collect the plates, tossing her hair as she reached for the glasses. The men hung on her every move, and it reminded her of the Japanese Geisha she had read about in an article. They were taught to enchant their male clientele in much the same way, usually while serving tea. Sometimes their sensual efforts stopped at this simple entertainment. Often, they did not.

"Why would I want a wife," Jeffrey said, draining his glass of champagne, "when I can have all the same privileges for free?"

"And save a helluva lot in cash and headaches doing it," Gold Chain said, reaching for Avani's bare, toned midriff.

Jeffrey grabbed his hand. "Ah, ah, Saul. Gotta pay for that first." He twirled Avani onto his lap and delivered a quick kiss between her bikini-clad breasts. She did not have time to react before he righted her again and turned to his guests. "All of my gems are available, gentlemen, but only one key unlocks that door."

Avani clutched a butter knife.

Amber loosened her fingers and placed the knife with other dirty dishes. *We are here to fix this*, she told Avani. *Not become part of it.*

One journey will not be enough for this guy.

Patience.

Amber measured the last of the champagne equally into the men's glasses and encouraged them to drink.

Jeffrey polished his off and looked past her to the stage where Samantha, draped in the spotlight, wrapped herself around one pole. Her lithe body arched backward, and her legs extended into the air like a *corde lisse* circus performer twirling on hanging silk ropes. She was *mesmerizing.*

"Exciting, isn't it?"

The words startled.

"Welcome back," Jeffrey snapped at her.

Amber made Avani brush some lint from his shoulder. "I'm sorry," she said sweetly. "I was just giving these gentlemen time to finish their champagne."

The men obliged. Jeffrey relaxed slightly.

As Avani reached to clear his glass, he pulled her down to ear level and whispered, "I need my customers to want you girls. And to dream, however mistakenly, that you want them, too." He nodded toward Samantha. "You swing that way, you keep it to yourself. Got it?"

Avani imagined breaking the champagne bottle over his head. She wondered if it might knock some sense into him.

Amber cooled her jets and cooed at Jeffrey like a siren. "Just admiring what you've created for your customers."

He sat back, smug.

Amber leaned down until Avani's breath bathed his cheeks. "May I speak to you in private later?" she whispered. "There's something I'd like to share."

The other men gaped enviously, and Jeffrey puffed up. "You already got the job, sweet cakes," he said loudly for effect. "There's no need to go further unless you just want to sample the goods."

The men laughed.

Avani bit her tongue so hard she tasted blood.

"There's more to me than meets the eye," Amber hinted, a sphinx setting her trap. "And I don't want to share that with anyone else."

Not a lie, Avani thought.

"I'll think about it," Jeffrey said.

But Avani sensed his curiosity. He would be more receptive, more willing to listen, once they were alone.

CHAPTER NINE

CASPIAN

Caspian had no idea what was happening. Night had become day, the mountain lake had been replaced by a strange city full of tall buildings and bridges, and the signs were written in English, which somehow he recognized and understood. They indicated a place called Pittsburgh.

Shrapnel of memories shred his brain. A guard outside a building in Moscow. Caspian speaks fluent Russian. The guard lets him in. He speaks Dutch to a woman diplomat in The Hague. Italian with a gondolier in Venice. *How?*

This way, the spirit said, guiding Caspian across a downtown city street.

Were they speaking in Spanish or English? Caspian's head was still Swiss cheese about it—more holes than understanding.

Caspian stuffed his hands in his pockets as the spirit led him across another busy street. His right hand brushed the lightweight metal coin. He toyed with it nonchalantly, and it began to warm against his skin.

The spirit led them into a large shopping complex built along a river and across from the city skyline. The place teemed with people walking around stores, restaurants, and a large hotel. Two odd vehicles in front looked like boats on wheels. Signs nearby offered "River Tours" of Pittsburgh, the "City of Bridges."

A young woman looked up from a kiosk of watches and jewelry as Caspian passed. Her eyes were the color of blueberries. Her bright pink lips parted in a flirtatious smile, and a sudden desire ripped through, dark and lustful, like nothing he had ever felt before.

Go to her, the spirit said, its voice raspier this time.

Caspian scanned the young woman's lean arms and tanned thighs, her long blonde hair, and her low-cut, bright pink tank top that hugged every curve.

Go, the voice said again.

Caspian started over, curling his fingers a little more around the metal. But as he drew close, his legs slowed as if the spirit were now trying to stop him.

Which is it? Caspian asked in growing frustration.

"Looking for something in particular?" the woman interrupted.

Her smile was luminous. The coin heated.

"Maybe a gift for that special someone?" Her eyes roamed across his face and neck, his broad chest.

"There is no 'special someone.'" He leaned onto the counter.

"Then, maybe you need something special for yourself." Her fingers brushed his arm as she reached toward a display of watches. "I have lots to choose from."

Caspian's yearning intensified. And it seemed to come from the coin.

Give it to her, the raspy voice urged, louder, stronger, drawing Caspian's hand from his pocket with the coin tucked loosely inside.

No, the other spirit voice countered as it pulled his hand back.

The woman's smile waned at this slight tug-of-war.

Caspian was terrified of the battle going on inside his body but too filled with want to care. He extended the coin toward the woman. It began to glow between his fingers.

Not too tight, the raspy voice warned.

Put it back, the other voice commanded.

The woman reached out. "That for me?"

That's it. The raspy voice darkened. *Give it to her.*

Caspian turned her hand over and started to place the coin into her palm when the spirit yanked his hand back, stuffed it into his pocket, and dropped the coin inside. It spun him around and hurried him off.

What the hell are you doing? Caspian roared.

The spirit crossed Caspian's arms over his chest. Without access to the coin, the intense yearning evaporated. He looked back at the woman's stunned, indignant stare before his head snapped forward again.

Never touch the coin, the spirit instructed in its normal, non-raspy voice. *Not unless I tell you.*

But you did *tell me.* Caspian struggled to uncross his arms, but he couldn't even wiggle a finger. *You wanted me to give it to her.*

Not me.

Then who? How many of you are in there?

Just one, the spirit said, walking them deeper into the shopping complex. *But without the ceremony, I may not always be strong enough to stop you.*

What ceremony? Caspian strained to remember, but nothing came.

The one that binds spirits to vessels. Similar to the way you and I joined, but different, stronger.

So why didn't you just pick a real vessel and have the ceremony?
You are a real vessel.

So you keep saying. But why can't I remember it? And what the hell happened back there? If you didn't do that thing with the coin, who did?

I don't know. Just—don't touch it again unless I tell you. The spirit's voice was direct, abrupt.

Caspian let it go and followed the spirit's lead behind a restaurant and ice cream store to an open-air courtyard overlooking the river. A decorative fountain with multi-colored lights surged three stories into the air, waters dancing to loud pop music playing through speakers nearby. The city skyline filled the opposite shore and reflected on the river between them. One of the buildings resembled a glass castle with multiple spires.

The spirit brightened, and Caspian prickled with something slightly familiar, a deep sensation he'd felt working the olive orchard in Spain. *This place is your home?* he asked.

Born and raised. The spirit pointed to the river. *The Monongahela is one of three rivers that make up Pittsburgh. And that,* he pointed to the glass spires, *is PPG Place. Six total buildings over three city blocks made from 20,000 pieces of glass. Their skating rink at Christmas is bigger than the one at Rockefeller Center.*

Who's Rockefeller?

Never mind.

Caspian wanted to ask again about the coin, that other voice, and the maddening lust he'd felt for the woman, but the spirit turned him to face the courtyard of people. He scanned the fountain, the collection of shops and restaurants, and the nearby Monongahela Incline where two boxy, yellow passenger cars moved up and down the hillside on two sets of tracks to a place called Mt. Washington.

This shopping center was once a train station. This city was once filled with steel mills and coal mines. Both have been reinvented and reimagined. Like you.

Reimagined? Caspian's riddled mind struggled to understand. *In what way?*

You were a vessel. Your memories were erased. You started over, reinventing yourself to survive.

The old man in the dirt extends his arm, something clutched in his hand. Caspian reaches out. Horses pound. The man screams. His blood stains the dirt.

Who was he? Caspian asked as the vision withered. *Erased how? What happened?*

Not now. The spirit ducked them around a corner and out of sight as a tall black man entered the courtyard from a bridge connecting to downtown. The man passed the fountain and walked to an ice cream store, his face hidden under the brim of a ball cap.

TAL

Tal followed Benz into the Station Square courtyard and remained a short distance behind and out of sight as he bought ice cream. A memory surged—one of her ordering cake batter ice cream with chocolate chips and sprinkles. It was Darden's favorite, and the last one he ever ate was here, at age four, two months before he died. The crash was seven and a half years ago, but it may as well have been yesterday.

Tal hadn't come here much after that, but she did last April, after Jake's funeral and before her flight to Reno, where she'd planned to end this wretched life. The second to last time was with Jake when their squad had taken down the legendary South Side Gang. They had kissed for the first time in this courtyard, at that slightly indented spot along the wrought iron fence that overlooked the river. Tal tingled at the memory of Jake's touch, the feel of his body pressed against hers. They had both wanted more that night, but she was not ready, and he had not pushed. Six months later, he'd died in her arms.

Benz took his ice cream to a bench near the dancing fountain and sat on one end. He removed his jacket, careful to conceal the .45 tucked into his waistband under his shirt. He puddled the jacket on the bench a short distance away. Tal wondered why until Tucker Manning turned the corner and bought a soda at the same ice cream store.

He sat down to watch the fountain from the other end of that same bench. He sipped nonchalantly as the waters danced, as people strolled past.

Tal snarled at Tucker. *I could take a picture of them and text it to Chief Demmings. Anonymously.*

Eli pumped compassion like a fog. *He would trace your text.*

I could call the tip line and report Benz. Let them send a unit and find—

Something moved. She turned to catch the young, dark-haired man across the courtyard who'd been peeking out since her arrival. He ducked back. Tal did not recognize him, nor did she sense danger, but something about him shot goosebumps up both arms.

Tucker stretched and rested one arm across the top of the

bench, his hand hanging down above Benz's jacket. The two men still had not spoken a word or shared so much as a glance, but Tal waited. Something was coming.

Benz ate the last of his ice cream, crushed the paper cup, and stood to throw it away. He left his jacket.

Tal started to follow, but Eli's spirit held her back.

Tucker lowered his arm after Benz disappeared and rested it on the jacket. He pulled it closer, then waited another moment and put it on. The whole thing happened so slowly, so organically, that no one passing by would be the wiser.

"Well played, asswipe," Tal hissed.

Tucker stuck his hand in one pocket and felt around. His shoulders eased at whatever he found in there, and he stood to leave.

One picture, she said again. *Wearing Benz's jacket. With God knows what in that pocket.*

Eli prickled with a thousand ethereal pins.

Okay, okay. Fine.

Tal waited for Tucker to leave the courtyard before stepping out. Benz was long gone. The dark-haired stranger across the courtyard was, too. Tal didn't understand why, but Eli made her follow Tucker toward the shopping center exit. Tucker passed kiosks on his way out, including one that sold watches. He winked salaciously at the blonde girl wearing the pink top who ran it.

Tal rolled her eyes. Tucker was easily twice that woman's age. And he was married, though he and Katherine had long been separated. Still, they had kids. Three, if Tal remembered correctly. *Disgusting*, she said without censoring her thoughts.

He is broken, Eli corrected.

He needs to pay for what he's done.

He will, just not in the way can imagine.

I know, I know. 'Walk from the darkness on his own. One of Liam's top ten.

Then you should remember.

He said it gently, and without sarcasm, but the words still stung.

Tucker crossed the street ahead of them and disappeared into a parking garage. Tal hurried past the garage opening and entered through a pedestrian door just beyond. She expected to find him at the elevator or climbing the stairs to his car. Instead, he walked slowly up the ramp to the next floor, past a row of parked cars, as if looking for his. But his eyes flitted nervously to the higher level.

Tal had just ducked behind a van to hide when a bald man with thick ropy muscles walked down the ramp. He met Tucker halfway, between two cars, careful to stand clear of any cameras. They spoke quietly but with heat. Tal inched closer, but she could not make out their words.

Tucker pulled a brown bag from Benz's jacket.

The man glanced around, took it, and opened the bag just enough to lift out a wad of cash and spin expertly through the bills. He shoved it back in the bag and stuck the bag in his coat. A pistol appeared in his hand, low and out of sight, aimed at Tucker's gut.

Tucker spoke fast and stepped back as if preparing to run.

Tal's instincts told her to yell, to call for help, but the spirit immobilized her. She couldn't even blink.

The man moved closer, and Tucker's voice changed, pleading. The man shoved him back and put the gun away before strapping on a pair of sunglasses and a hat. He stabbed a final finger at Tucker's chest, then walked down the ramp and past security cameras to exit the garage.

Tucker stumbled briefly, then shoved his hands in Benz's jacket and walked up the ramp out of sight.

Tal plopped down on a curb. *Who was that guy? What's Tucker doing?*

"We'll find out soon enough," a voice replied with a thick Spanish accent.

Tal jumped up and twirled around to see the dark-haired stranger from the courtyard now standing two cars away. His accent surprised her, and his good looks stole her breath, but—*was he reading her thoughts?*

Her tattoo warmed, and her eyes flew to his left ankle.

He lifted his pant leg just enough to reveal the same.

"You're a *vessel?*"

He nodded.

Eli? What's going on? she asked.

The spirit remained silent.

"Who are you?" she asked the stranger, backing up into a van's bumper. "Why are you following me? What does your spirit want with—?"

"Tallon," the stranger said, his voice different and deeper. The accent was gone.

Tal's jaw dropped. Only one person in the world ever called her that.

"Jake?"

The stranger grinned in Jake's face-consuming way, and his brown irises glimmered green.

"Jake!" Tal threw herself at this man and wrapped her arms and legs around him. Jake's spirit hugged her back. Stars shot across her heart.

Half a minute passed before Eli peeled her away. The tattoos returned to normal.

Tal dried her tears.

The stranger cleared his throat and extended a hand. "I, um, I'm Caspian," he said, the Spanish accent back in place.

Tal blushed and shook his hand. "Right. I'm Tal. Tallulah, really, but I go by Tal. Your spirit was my police partner, my best friend." *My heart*, but Tal did not say that part. "Your name is … Caspian?"

"It's what everyone calls me."

She let go of his hand, realizing how odd this would look to anyone watching: a fierce embrace followed by an introductory handshake. Thankfully, there were no people in sight and they were out of camera range. She craned her head. The employee taking payment at the gate could not see them, either.

The Spaniard seemed uncomfortable, or unfamiliar, with the odd and quirky relationship between vessels and spirits. Perhaps he was new. She started to say something when Eli stepped her back toward the stairwell.

Time to go, he said.

"No. Wait. Please." She grabbed onto a sign. *Can't we stay? With Jake? Isn't that why he's here?*

We're here for Benz.

But …

Eli unhooked her fingers and guided her to the stairwell.

Tal held out her hand toward Jake. "No. Please. Just a little longer."

"It's okay," Jake told her.

Eli opened the door to the stairs and leaned Tal in to make sure no one was coming.

"Jake?" She turned back. "Jake, don't leave, okay? It's Tucker.

He's behind all this."

The Spaniard grinned Jake's good-natured smile. "See you soon, Tallon."

The stairwell door closed, and Tal disappeared in a swirl of wind and light.

CHAPTER TEN

GALE

Gale's foot tapped like a drumstick against the hard floor, and the chair squeaked when she shifted to free her polyester skirt from the textured fabric. The secretary's blue eyes, framed by perfect hair and flawless makeup, fired daggers at her from across the room. Gale sheepishly hooked one scuffed pump behind the other to keep it still, and the young lady resumed her work.

The lobby walls were painted white, and plush white furniture covered the dark wooden floors. One large vase of irises, roses, and gardenias dominated the table next to her. Another, slightly smaller one took residence at the corner of the secretary's desk. They provided the room's main color, and their scent reminded Gale of her mother's garden back home. Though Gale had failed to inherit Fergie's green thumb, she could still identify many of her mother's favorite flowers.

Her brother's large, framed portrait anchored the wall adjacent to Gale, with a plaque underneath reading "Governor Ronald Galt, 2016 – Present." It was 2018. Ron was only halfway through his first term. Gale had no doubt there would be more campaigns and elections. His ambitions were too high to stop here.

A phone buzzed. The young woman picked it up, then forced a smile. "The governor will see you now," she said politely, working to hide her contempt for Gale's simple dress, cheap shoes, and plain hair as she rose to go in.

Gale threw back her shoulders and crossed to the short hall leading to Ron's substantial corner office. She may not have his money, power, or notoriety, but she was not short on pride of her own. She inhaled sharply and knocked. Seconds later, Ron's door swung open.

"Gale, what a pleasant surprise," he said flatly, stepping back to let her in.

It was the first time they had spoken in years, the first time she had laid eyes on her brother in more than a decade. His custom-tailored suit reeked of extravagance, as did his expensive furnishings. Even as a kid, Ron had enjoyed the finer things in life, always asking for the more expensive toys and the designer clothes their father's military salary could barely afford.

"The job suits you, big brother." Gale stepped in, and he closed the door. "You look good." They shared a brief hug.

"Thanks. You, as well."

Ron was lying, of course. His cursory, condescending glance gave him away, but Gale didn't care. She had always been more frugal, like their parents, forgoing the expensive cars, clothes, and European trips even when she and Vince were happily married and could afford them. That decision proved wiser now, since the divorce.

Ron led her to the lush, deep brown leather sofa and chairs across from his desk with a stylish coffee table in between. An expensive Persian rug ran underneath the furniture, and the pointed legs of the coffee table, to protect the hardwood floor.

Ron sat in one of the two chairs and crossed his long legs, the subtle crease of his navy suit pants running perfectly straight from his knee to his black leather dress shoe.

"So, to what do I owe the honor of this visit?" he asked, getting to the point with the same forced smile as his receptionist. Ron had no patience for small talk.

Gale sat perched on the end of the couch, feeling incredibly small and inadequate in the overstuffed leather. She guessed that was the point.

"Sorry to bother you, Governor, but—"

"Please. It's Ron," he said, his words slathered in dismissive familiarity.

"Okay. Ron." She cleared her throat. "I came here to see you today for, um, well, because of … Sam. And the shelter."

Ron's eyes hardened, as she knew they would.

"What about them?" he asked.

"I know what you're planning to do there," she said.

"My plans are public. I have nothing to hide."

She heaved a sigh. *Here we go.* "I was just there, Ron."

"What?" He sat up. "Why?"

"Sam's birthday." She hesitated. "Last night. Malina and I stopped by."

"I pay you to stay *away* from him."

"No," Gale replied, her heart pounding. "You pay me to stay quiet about him, about us and our family, and I've done that." She could tolerate a lot, but not an outright lie, not anymore, not after all those her husband had told. "Sam has, too, by the way," she continued, "and without being paid. But—things have changed, Ron. I want to see him, to reconnect. His granddaughter is sixteen, for Christ's sake, and he's never even met her."

Ron stood up. He paced in silence before coming to stand over her.

"You've become just like her, you know," he said, his voice like steel wire. "You look like her, you act like her, and now—you've grown soft and weak like her."

Gale stood, too, shaky and flustered, but she squared her shoulders and rose to her full height, eyes level with Ron's shoulders. She looked up to meet his gaze. "Our *mother* was forgiving and kind. She *loved* us, Ron. What's wrong with *that*?"

"*Everything!*" He spat the word. "I slaved for years to start over on my own, away from Sam and all the bullshit he did to us in Germany. I carved out a new life, a new beginning. I am *not* going to let him, or you, ruin that, just because you suddenly want to 'reconnect.'"

"God, you are bitter." She stepped back. "All these years, and you still hold nothing but hate."

"*Still?* After what Sam did to us? We were *kids*."

"It was an *affair*. One indiscretion. Yes, it was stupid and embarrassing and wrong. And yes, it cost Sam his job and almost his marriage. But Mom forgave him, Ron, and he never did it again. Our family moved on."

"They had a *baby*." He crossed to the window, wrinkles marring the back of his crisply ironed white shirt.

"She had an abortion."

"Even worse! And it cost me *every*thing."

A long silence followed.

Gale could still picture the beautiful blonde, blue-eyed German girl who had stolen Ron's heart. They were only in eighth grade but had been crazy about one another since fourth. Upon learning the news of this abortion, the girl's staunchly Catholic parents forced them apart. After Sam and Fergie moved the family back to the States, Ron wrote his beloved every week, promising to move back after school and begging her to wait for him. He never received so much as a postcard in return.

Six years later, she got married, and the rest of Ron turned to stone. He married, too, and had two children, but it was mostly for appearance and political gain.

"What do you want from me?" he asked, returning to the window.

Gale spoke as gently as she could. "Leave the shelter alone, Ron. Sam and Diego worked hard to build it. Sam raises the money to run it, and it's no skin off your nose. It cares for more homeless people than you can imagine. Especially since you're closing everything else."

Ron stared outside.

Gale shifted nervously and cleared her throat.

Finally, Ron spoke. "Downtown Reno is being gentrified: a win for the city, the community, the businesses, and the tax base. Sam's shelter is in the way. Let him raise the money and move somewhere else."

"But the homeless live where he is."

"The homeless are portable, Gale. They'll find Sam wherever he goes."

"Jesus, Ron. It's not like Sam can just pick up and put a shelter in the suburbs or next to some shopping plaza. Nobody wants a shelter in their backyard. Downtown is the only place that works."

He turned to face her. "There's too much at stake."

"People will die if you close that shelter, Ron. From cold, hunger, sickness. Leave it alone. Gentrify someplace else."

Silence.

"Do you even have a heart anymore?"

Ron smiled, but his eyes sizzled. "You're divorced now, yes?"

Gale shifted. "Almost."

He stepped closer. "And you lost your job at the school?"

How did he know? "Cutbacks," she said. "But I'm a school nurse. I'll find another—"

"And Malina. You have sole care of her now, yes? Or is your ex paying child support?"

Gale looked down. Vince owned a bar. He could never afford child support or alimony. He barely earned enough to feed his girlfriend and the baby they'd made during his marriage.

"We'll be fine," she said.

He must have known she was lying, based on the self-satisfied look strapped to his face. He stepped closer. "And you're relocating to Reno."

"Maybe. I'm not really sure what—"

"You'll need funds to get settled." The smug look broadened. "New apartment, new utilities, new school for Malina, time to look for a new job."

"Yes, but—"

He lowered his voice. "And I more than adequately supply those funds, do I not?"

"You have been, yes."

"I am willing to increase them, Gale, given your current circumstances. You cashed in both bank CDs, and your savings are nearly gone."

Her mouth dropped again. *How did he know so much?* He made a routine deposit, but he did not have access to her balances and activity. He must have bribed a bank teller or official.

"But for me to do so," he continued, standing close enough

for her to smell the starch in his dry cleaned shirt, "you must walk away. Take Malina and move somewhere else, anywhere else, even in Nevada. But not Reno." His breath disturbed a few strands of hair on the top of her head. She brushed them back. "Or I will see to it that you lose every job you try to get until *you* are a homeless, unfit mother, and the state takes Malina away." He paused. "Are we clear?"

Fear clamped her throat. "Yes," she whispered.

"Good." He backed off and let air move between them.

This had not gone at all as Gale had hoped. The brother she had known was gone, replaced with this greedy, self-serving cyborg. Desperate for another way to reach him, her eye landed on a family photo perched on his desk. She swallowed her pride and redirected. "How is Nancy?" she asked. "The kids? I imagine they're almost out of school."

His shoulders relaxed slightly, but his face remained stern.

"Nancy's active in her clubs, Felix is starting his second year at Princeton, and Christoph is a senior in prep school."

German names. Gale wondered if Ron's wife, Nancy, knew of his first love or cared. She was about as disconnected from parenting as Ron was. At least they had hired a caring governess.

Gale glanced around the office. "You must be very proud of your success."

His chest swelled. His eyes brightened. Bingo.

"The constituents seem happy."

Only the ones like you, Gale thought. "Think you'll run again?" She knew the answer, but the ambition pouring off him frightened her.

"I'm considering it."

Greed or lust underscored his words. Probably both.

"In fact," he said with an audacious smile, "I'm considering a run for president."

She knew this was coming, but the words still knocked her sideways.

"Why not?" He shrugged, void of any humility. "I'm a better choice than anyone so far this century. The country could use a good leveling out with fresh blood that would give them an independent executive branch free from party dictums and allegiance, one able to work *all* sides of *any* aisle."

No feeling for his family, no concern for his father, and negligible tolerance for his sister, but unchecked passion for his job. No, for his achievements. No. For the money, control, and power his achievements would bring.

Ron had become power-mad and narcissistic, maybe even sociopathic, given his bent on destroying Sam at all costs. He would never listen—not to her, not to Sam, not to anyone who was not blindly loyal or financially useful. The qualities Ron disdained in other leaders were precisely the ones he was guilty of having, and no one seemed to see it or care. His popularity grew every day.

"I was going to invite you to lunch." Gale could barely utter the words. "If you have—"

"Thanks," he cut her off. "But the day's pretty full. I'll just order a salad and eat here."

Gale hid her relief. "Another time, then."

"Absolutely." He opened his office door.

Gale paused at the threshold. Ron's blue-gray eyes were the color of Sam's but made of ice. He smelled clean, but no amount of soap could scrub the rot from his soul. What would it take to reach him? And would there ever be anyone who could?

Gale started to leave, but he put a hand on her arm. "Are we absolutely clear?" he asked, the question more of a command this time.

Gale's lip curled in disgust. "Oh yes, brother. Your offer was very clear." Her voice sharpened. "But I did not say I would take it."

She strode past him to the hall, counting the seconds until he slammed the door. The secretary was startled at first, then smirked as Gale crossed the lobby and exited the glass door to the elevator beyond. Helping Sam save the shelter would require a lot more effort and resourcefulness than she had anticipated.

CHAPTER ELEVEN

SAM

Sam sat at the desk in his bedroom-turned-office at the Reno shelter. He ran a fingertip along the coin Captain Hugh had given him, touching the embossed dove at its center, the raised vines and hidden letters circling its edge. The coin was too important to carry around, and Sam didn't dare leave it anywhere the inspectors might look. After careful consideration, he folded it into a white handkerchief and tucked it inside a small wooden box that had once held his favorite watch—an anniversary gift from Fergie. He stood on a chair and hid it behind the boring pile of spare sheets, blankets, and towels on the top shelf of his small closet full of clothes and shoes that should hold no interest for anyone.

His cell buzzed with a text from his receptionist, Victoria: *They're early.* He could feel the ire in her words. It was only 7:45 a.m. Leave it to Ron to have his inspectors come an hour before they were due.

Sam locked his vessels files behind the false back wall of his bottom desk drawer, spread his desk with routine papers, opened his computer to a bland budget spreadsheet, and gave himself one final check in the mirror.

In the lobby, two well-dressed men stood confidently by the

front door. One was tall and lean, the other short and stocky. They were accompanied by a young Reno police officer Sam recognized. He worked with at-risk youth, especially those targeted by gangs, and had spent many volunteer hours helping kids at this shelter. He nodded to Sam uneasily.

Sam extended his hand, willing it not to tremble. "Good morning, gentlemen. I'm Sam Fullerton. May I help you?"

Victoria stole glances from her nearby desk while sipping coffee and pretending to organize files as if there were nothing to be concerned about. Meanwhile, she had spent the last three hours waking homeless guests they had allowed in from the cold and urging them out of rooms that were not yet permitted. Sam wished he could pay her double.

"Building inspectors from Carson City," the taller man said, shaking his hand. "I'm Nathan Smith. This is Adam Larson. We've been sent by Governor Galt's office."

Sam pretended to be caught off guard. "Oh, I see. Well, we've passed all local and state inspections. Our bills are paid. Our permits and paperwork are current and on file. Is there something specific the governor needs?" *Other than running his old man out of town?*

The men eyed one another briefly.

"He sent us to, uh, make sure everything really is in order," Nathan said.

"I see." Sam eyed the police officer. "We've not had the pleasure of police escorts during our routine inspections."

The officer shifted uncomfortably.

Adam, the shorter inspector, puffed up defensively. "He's here to make sure you let us do our job."

"Of course. But, don't you need a warrant if police are

involved?"

"You got something to hide that requires a warrant?" Nathan asked.

The officer shifted again, but the two inspectors seemed to relish the conflict. *What had Ron told them?*

"Not at all," Sam replied. "But we all want to honor protocol, and inspections don't normally call for police unless—"

"Unless we have reason to believe you're hiding something," Adam snapped. "Like providing rooms that are not yet approved?"

Victoria bent low over her paperwork.

"Or operating the shelter with exposed wiring that could be a fire hazard?"

Sam's hackles rose. That new contractor was definitely on the take.

Adam grinned, almost gleeful. "This officer will simply ensure you don't close any doors we need opened."

"And," Nathan added, "He can witness Diego Ruiz sign off on our paperwork. As the owner of record." He smiled, malevolent. "At the governor's request."

Sam's head swam. He still had not heard back from Diego.

Doc carefully arranged her medicines in the cabinet. No shelter would normally have prescription antibiotics, blood pressure pills, and cholesterol medicine, and they certainly would not have the Valium, Xanax, and Percocet disguised in bottles of over-the-counter meds. But this was not any normal shelter, even without the vessels program hidden inside.

She had barely relocked the cabinet when a form moved by

the door. She jumped.

"Tom?" She eased, grateful it was not the inspectors.

"Lost my pills," he said.

"But I just gave them to you yesterday."

"Someone stole 'em." His eyes were dull, his face drawn. He smelled of sweat and dirt.

"I'm sorry," Doc replied, gesturing to the paper-draped clinic table. Tom crawled up to take a seat, and she wrapped a pressure cuff around his arm. She plugged her stethoscope in to listen. "198 over 120," she said after a few moments. "You need an emergency room."

"You treat me better. B'sides—" he pointed to her white doctor's coat lying across the desk chair. "You wear one a those, too."

Doc sighed and unlocked the cabinet. She reached in, knocking over some carefully arranged bottles to pluck two different kinds of blood pressure pills from behind. She placed one of each into a single paper cup. He swallowed them down with water she gave him in another cup.

She refilled the water twice more, forcing him to drink while she measured several pills from each bottle into a plastic chewing gum container. She handed it over. "That is a one-week supply. Pop back by in three days so I can check you again."

"You're a lifesaver, Doc." Tom jumped down from the table, his dirt-stained pants clinging to his bony hips. He paused to roll down his sleeve. "Hey, where's that kid who fixes the washing machines? Link, or something like that."

"He's off on an errand. If you'll excuse me, Tom, I have to get ready for—"

"Us?" A tall man said, walking into the room with a police

officer.

Eva froze. He must be one of the inspectors.

A smaller man joined them and nodded to Tom. "Thanks."

"Thanks?" Doc asked, stunned. "For what?"

"See ya later, Doc." Tom slinked out.

Sam shot her a pointed look from the doorway.

Right. Act surprised. Eva turned to the inspectors. "Where are my manners? Good morning, gentlemen. I'm Dr. Eva Lawson," she said, offering a hand.

"Nathan Smith," the taller man said, shaking her hand like a wet fish.

"Inspector Adam Larson," the shorter man piped up, gripping her hand so hard it hurt. "We've been sent by the governor's office to make sure you're in compliance."

"How do you know Tom?" she asked, still composing herself over *that* revelation.

"He's a fixture in this part of town," Adam replied. "Knows the shelters. What they do." He paused, smug. "What they hand out." He nodded to her still-open cabinet. "We need to take a look at your meds."

"What for?"

Adam soured. "To make sure you don't have anything that doesn't belong."

She looked at the police officer. "Don't you need a warrant or something?"

"Not since it's open," Adam said with a smirk.

The officer looked down. Sam sagged against the door.

The room spun. Eva braced herself to make it stop. Tom must have told them. How dare he out her to the very people who could stop her from helping him and others! Then Eva pictured his bony ribs, his rotted teeth, and his high blood pressure. Life on the streets was brutal. Morality, or lack thereof, usually went to the highest bidder. She exhaled and stepped back.

Nathan nodded, and the officer approached her cabinet. He moved aside her white coat and placed the items on her desk: cough syrup, painkillers, fungicides, and ointments.

Eva shifted slightly when he removed a bottle of vitamins from in back and spilled some into the lid.

"Those don't look like any vitamins I've seen," Adam snipped.

"Lotensin," she replied honestly. "The generic, actually. I also have valsartan and some diuretics, as well. Most of the guests who come in here, like Tom, have blood pressure high enough to stroke out. Their pills are frequently stolen, so I keep a supply."

Nathan smirked. "Guests."

Adam chuckled.

"Try walking in their shoes for just one week," Doc snapped. "With little to eat and no healthcare when you're sick. Let's see how well you do."

Nathan angrily gestured for the officer to dig deeper. He extracted a bottle of aspirin.

Doc tensed. Adam noticed.

The cop popped off the lid and shook a few pills into his hand. He sniffed. His brow furrowed. "Oxy?"

"Percocet," she mumbled. She did not return his look or Sam's.

The officer opened another bottle marked acetaminophen. He held up a blue pill with a distinct hole in the middle. "Valium."

"Many of our guests suffer alcohol withdrawal," Eva said defensively. "It helps them cope. I'm a state-certified doctor licensed to distribute. And these medications are locked up at all times, I assure you. Completely controlled."

"Perhaps," Adam quipped. "But I seriously doubt this shelter is licensed to store and/or distribute them." He turned to Sam. "We'll need to see paperwork for this."

"And this," Nathan said from across the room, holding a bag of type O red blood cells from Doc's small freezer.

"That was locked," Doc said angrily.

"Not all the way," Nathan replied, twirling an open padlock on his finger.

"I bet the shelter doesn't have a license for that, either," Adam gloated, no longer attempting to stifle his grin. "Unless, of course, Diego Ruiz can prove otherwise. Is he here?"

Sam struggled to maintain his composure. "He wasn't … expecting you this early."

Eva looked over but Sam avoided her gaze. She had not burdened him with ordering and keeping these prescription meds, and it had never been an issue—until now. This unexpected chink in their armor could bring down the whole place, Diego or not.

Sam unfurled the third set of plans for the inspectors to review while waiting for Diego to arrive. The police officer stood by the door and checked his phone.

Sam's phone vibrated. Gale. Seeing her name made his heart leap, especially after all these years of her silence, but now was not the time, especially if her visit with Ron had gone badly. He pressed the side button to stop the call and hoped she would leave a message.

"Where is he?" Nathan asked, his patience as thin as his lips.

"You've stalled long enough."

"He should be here any minute," Sam said. "Let me show you our permits on the work thus far."

Adam scowled, and Nathan impatiently checked his watch as Sam pulled folders from the filing cabinet. Ron had sent them to find problems, to uncover reasons to close the place, which they probably had now thanks to Doc's medicine cabinet. But Sam didn't care, so long as he kept them busy until Liam arrived with Diego.

Adam exhaled sharply. "If he's not here in ten minutes—"

"Hello, gentlemen."

Sam grinned as his oldest and best friend entered the room. "Diego." They embraced. Sam was not sure Diego would be well enough to travel since his rogue encounter, not using Liam's beaming method, anyway. But he looked healthy.

"They find anything?" Diego whispered.

Sam inconspicuously shook his head. The Vessels program was still safe.

"Diego, meet Inspectors Nathan Smith and Adam Larson from the state office," Sam said. "Gentlemen, Diego Ruiz, owner of record for the shelter."

Both men looked disappointed as they shook Diego's hand.

"Forgive my delay," Diego said. "It was difficult to get a flight at such short notice."

"Flight?" Nathan asked, his sneer returning. "Don't you live here?"

"I was in Peru. Helping … family."

Diego had not lied, exactly. Sam just hoped the inspectors would not dig for more.

"Do you spend a lot of time there?" Adam asked, accusation

dripping.

Here we go, Sam thought. *Digging is why they're here.*

"My family needed more than first expected," Diego replied. "But I come back and forth as much as possible, and I've given Sam my administrative proxy. But now, I'm here to sign what you need."

"I assume you have this proxy in writing." Nathan this time.

Diego shifted slightly. Sam cleared his throat.

Nathan's sneer widened.

"And signed?" Adam added with a smirk. "It's not legal if it's not signed. But I'm sure you know this."

"We have done everything by the book," Diego told them. "We have followed every detail. Every permit is official and signed, as you can see." He pointed to the plans and folders spread across Sam's drafting table. "And, we have managed to do almost all of it through *private* funds." He paused to drive that barb home.

Adam turned red. "What about the third floor?" he asked defiantly. "The state controls building issues no matter *who* pays for them."

Sam removed his glasses and cleaned the lenses with his handkerchief to keep his hands from trembling. Their new contractor was definitely on the take. Or maybe it was Tom. Sam had caught him coming down from the third floor two days ago, sheepishly claiming he had gone up one floor too many to reach his room. Sam had not thought much about it then, but money had always been Ron's best lure, and Tom was the perfect bait. Sam wondered who had brought them together, so he could prevent it from happening again.

A fist pounded on the door, and all heads turned to a group of five or six homeless men and women standing in the hall. The police officer put a hand on his holster and instinctively stepped in to block the doorway.

"It's okay," Sam told him, putting his glasses back on. "They're guests here."

"*Guests*," Adam sniggered.

Diego seared the short inspector with a look.

A woman spoke up. "We heard they're gonna close this place, Sam. That true?" Her fearful eyes tore across each inspector.

"Is it true?" the man next to her asked, his ragged jacket patched with tape.

Take it up with Tom, Sam thought but stifled it.

"You'll be fine." Diego tried to sound reassuring. "Go on to the kitchen. I'm sure Betty has brewed fresh coffee by now."

"Who are you?" the woman asked.

Sam paled.

Both inspectors stared at Diego.

Of course, she didn't recognize him. She was new since he left four months ago. The others would not know him, either.

"They've been dealing with me," Sam told Nathan and Adam.

"Don't let 'em close it, Sam," the woman snapped, glaring at the two state men. "We ain't got no place else to go."

Nathan adjusted his silk tie. Adam studied his expensive dress shoes.

"Don't worry," Sam said. "We're working it out. Go get some coffee."

The police officer did not relax until they left.

Sam's phone buzzed. Gale again. He clicked the side button to silence it, hoping she was not in some kind of trouble.

"Let's go upstairs," Adam said, charging across Sam's dark blue carpet toward the hall. Nathan followed.

Sam leaned over to Diego. "You okay? I wasn't sure you'd be able to make it."

Diego's eyes flashed in a quick burst of golden-green.

Sam froze. "Liam?"

Liam winked and took off after the inspectors. He had evidently shape-shifted into Diego to play this role for the inspection, but *why? Was Diego okay? Had the rogue hurt him worse than they'd thought?* Sam swallowed his concern. He would find out soon enough, but for now, he just had to play along.

The group of men crossed the lobby to the elevator and pressed the button. As the elevator doors opened and the inspectors stepped inside, metal crashed from Blaze's office down the back hall.

"What's that?" Nathan stopped, holding open the door.

Sam launched a litany of silent curses. Blaze had remained invisible until now. "Nothing," he replied. "Just our tech office." *Dammit.* He had meant to say *maintenance.*

"'Tech'?" Adam asked stepping off the elevator. "What kind of tech?"

"Website admin, computer issues, internet access," Diego answered, putting a hand on Nathan's shoulder to usher him back on the elevator. "But it's more maintenance than technology."

Sam cut Diego a grateful look.

Adam's lips puckered. He resembled a mole. "I think we should go see."

Diego and Sam exchanged a brief look as the men started across the lobby. Sam held his breath and led them down the back utility hall, past the laundry room and Doc's clinic, toward Blaze's closed office door. It was the only other room that held anything connected to the vessels, and Sam had not been able to double-check before the inspectors arrived. He prayed Blaze had hidden everything.

"The tech office is right back here, gentlemen," Sam said loudly, hoping Blaze would hear them and get the hint.

Sam opened the door to find Blaze picking up a box of metal parts. "Everything okay?" he asked, entering first to look around. The metal shelving was lined with boxes and rags, cleaners, and parts. Blaze's desk was turned over, hiding his real computer underneath while staging a generic computer, phone, and rack of files in its place. Relief flooded.

"Yeah, sorry," Blaze said, turning away from the police officer. "That washing machine motor is wacked again. I dropped these looking for spare parts."

The inspectors scanned the small office.

"Cleanest desk I've ever seen for tech or maintenance," Nathan said. "Especially for an employee so young. What's your name, son?"

The officer looked up from his phone.

Blaze shifted slightly, keeping his head down and his face turned. "Name's Blaze. Blaze … Smith."

"He's just out of community college," Sam replied. "A first job. We can't pay much."

The officer returned to his phone.

"Open it," Adam stated, pointing to the locked cabinet near Blaze's desk.

"But first," Nathan said, "what's this?" He plucked Blaze's cell phone-sized GPS off a shelf in the corner.

Sam's blood drained. *The vessels GPS.* Blue, red, and green dots blinked onscreen, representing Tal, Link, and Avani.

"Put that down!" Blaze reached to grab it, but Diego's hand

on his shoulder pinned him in place.

The officer looked up again.

"Problem?" Adam gloated as he studied the device.

"It's nothing," Blaze said, eyes darting between Sam and the inspector. "It's just that—"

Sam could see the wheels turning.

"I'm working on this new game, and ..." Blaze looked down. "I'm not supposed to do that during work hours."

The boy looked appropriately shamed. *Well played*, Sam thought.

Adam and Nathan studied the small screen, the blinking dots.

"What kind of game?" Nathan touched the green dot, and a map of Miami Beach populated underneath. The blue dot brought up Pittsburgh. The red dot took him to Atlantic City. "What's it doing? What are these maps?"

Sam locked his knees to keep them from buckling.

The officer's phone rang. He stepped out into the hall.

Diego let go, and Blaze walked over, seemingly nonplussed though Sam could see the tension in his shoulders. Blaze took it from the man and explained. "It's like Pokémon GO, sort of, but collecting places you've been, fav restaurants, fun sites, stuff like that. I'm working out the bugs." He quickly stuffed the device into his pocket.

"We'll talk about this later, young man." Diego feigned reprimand.

"Yes, sir." Blaze bowed his head, sufficiently penitent. "I'll go fix that motor." He grabbed the box of parts and started to leave.

"Liang Douglas?"

Blaze jerked up.

The officer held up his phone, showing a "Missing Child"

police photo and report for Liang Douglas.

"You said his name was *Blaze*," Nathan snipped.

Sam's stomach crawled up in his throat.

"Liang is the son of attorney Howard Douglas," the officer continued, referencing the report on his screen.

"*Adopted* son," Blaze corrected, seething.

"Missing almost four months since he ran away from Mr. Douglas's home and care after being released from juvenile prison."

"Prison?" Adam stammered.

"*Care?*" Blaze hissed. "You call beating me and having me arrested, *care?*"

The officer turned to Sam and Diego. "Were either of you aware of this?"

The men exchanged a look. Blaze and his technology were the most direct connection to the vessels, and he had already compromised things by leaving the GPS tracker out, even if tucked on a back shelf. They had to lie or risk further investigation and possible discovery of the program.

"No," Sam lied, the word salting his mouth. He looked down to avoid Blaze's shock.

"You'll have to come with me then," the officer said, stepping into the room. He kept himself between Blaze and the door. "You have to stay with a parent or approved guardian until you age out or make other legal arrangements."

"He's my *step*father," Blaze yelled. "He's the reason my mother is dead. I can't go back." He whirled toward Sam. "Tell them!"

Sam swallowed hard. "I didn't know," he reiterated. The look on Blaze's face cut him in two.

"Sorry, son." The officer took Blaze by the shoulder. "You'll have to come with me."

Blaze jerked and tugged to get away. "Sam? Diego?" he pleaded.

Sam closed his eyes. Diego looked down.

"That ogre killed my mother!" he yelled. "He just wants me back for her insurance."

"You can file a complaint through Child Protective Services," the officer said. "I can help you call someone, but in the meantime—"

Blaze jerked free and tried to run, but the officer clamped both hands on his shoulders and led him toward the door. Blaze shoved the GPS device into Sam's hand as he passed.

"Thanks for NOTHIN'," he snarled as the policeman led him away.

Sam started after him, but Diego gripped his shoulder like a vise. Liam. Sam had momentarily forgotten the Spirit Guard was in there.

Sam relaxed. Diego loosened his grip.

"We'll need to see your employee records," Adam said with renewed glee. "And conduct a complete audit of your payroll and books."

"But first," Nathan said triumphantly, "let's go see that third floor."

Outside the shelter, Malina hid in the doorway of an abandoned electronics store across the street. Gang tags marked the brick walls, and metal gates shuttered its door and windows. She watched a policeman escort Blaze to his patrol car and carefully seat him in the back. The cop slid behind the wheel, called something in on his radio, and drove away.

Malina had met Blaze briefly the night before, but he seemed cool. Cute. The youngest one here by, like, a lot, so she could at least identify with him. He was not wearing handcuffs, so what had he done wrong?

Her phone rang, and she rolled her eyes before answering. "What is it, Mom?"

"Hi, Malina. How's school?" Gale was using her fake upbeat voice. Things must not have gone well with Uncle Gov.

"Fine," Malina lied. "I only have a few minutes until my next class."

"I'm going to be here longer than expected," Gale told her. "Take the bus. Get a pizza. I'll be back tonight."

"When?" Malina asked, picking black polish off a jagged fingernail. She needed to know how to plan her day of freedom. And, though she hated to admit it, she was also a little worried. After all, what would happen to her, especially here, if something happened to her mom?

Several homeless people paced and smoked outside the shelter entry. Another handful of them hunkered in front of the soup kitchen doorway, the one Malina had escaped through last night before that weird Liam guy caught up with her.

She shuddered. Homeless people gave her the creeps. They were dirty, they smelled gross, and they seemed perfectly happy letting someone else do their work. No wonder her uncle wanted to close this place.

"Malina? Hello?"

Gale's voice snapped her back. "Yeah. Um, so what time will you get back?"

Her mother sighed across the miles. "I don't know. As long as it takes for him to listen."

"Maybe he's right, you know," Malina said, knowing this would send her mother off.

"About what?"

"About closing the shelter. People would have to go back to their families, get jobs." She waited, knowing what would come next.

"That is cruel, Malina. Heartless and cruel."

Malina mouthed along—

"Just try walking in their shoes for one day and see if you say the same thing."

"Gotta go to class," Malina told her. "See you tonight."

"Text me when you …"

Malina hung up to avoid the police siren a few blocks over. Her mom would think the school was under lockdown, or Malina was skipping out on her first day. Either could have brought Gale running back.

She stowed her phone and wondered about the inspection. She had arrived early enough to see the two men go in with that cop. She hoped they'd find something wrong and shut it down. Then Sam would have to do something else, and she and her mom could go home and convince her father to move back. They could be a family again. It was her mom's fault he left in the first place. She must not have loved him enough, so he found that other woman. Going back would let Gale apologize and make things right.

Two more police cars showed up. The sirens were off, but their lights strobed. The homeless people stirred, waiting.

Sam walked out with Doc and some other old guy, all three

looking pretty sad. The inspectors seemed happy, though, and Malina learned why when the cops began pushing the homeless people back, saying, "The shelter is closed until further notice," and "You'll have to find someplace else to stay." The homeless people yelled for Sam, but all he said was, "I'm sorry. We'll get this worked out," and, "The kitchen will stay open for meals."

The cops put padlocks and chains on the front door while Sam pleaded with the inspectors. "The people need this," he told them. "The governor just wants to build stores and apartments." The inspectors replied with "government regulations, required fines," and "storing narcotics without a license." The short one said, "You're lucky not to be in jail for harboring a minor." *Is that what happened to Blaze?*

Malina was grateful to see this whole thing over. Otherwise, Sam and her mom would have had time to reconnect, she would have been forced to "get to know" her grandfather, and Gale would have bought a home, found a job, and stayed in this disgusting city.

A voice cut her thoughts and Malina turned to see Doc two stores down. She paced around talking softly on her phone. Malina snuck closer.

"Yes, love, a long time indeed." Doc held the phone tightly to her ear. "Listen, I'm sorry to cut this short, but I need a favor. Do you still have that warehouse downtown? The one you were trying to rent?"

After a long pause, Eva frowned. "I see." She paused. "All right then. I have to go and ... what's that? It is? Brilliant!" She smiled and twisted an auburn curl around her finger. "You are a godsend, love. Do you think we could use it for a bit?"

Was she ... *flirting?* Malina soured. *Gross.*

"The governor's men found out about the meds and the Oneg you sent, not to mention some wiring issues, and they're closing us down until we can fix the problems and pay their ridiculous fines. Which could take months. They simply don't care how desperately these people rely on our care. Anyway, we still need a place to work, and that sounds spot on."

Work? Malina thought. Were they going to stuff the homeless people in some kind of temporary warehouse to look after them? She bet the inspectors would *really* like to know about that.

CHAPTER TWELVE

TAL

Downtown Pittsburgh was quiet this time of night, after rush hour and before the dinner crowd. Eli led them around a corner, and Tal stopped short outside a local bar. She remembered arresting a drunken man here one time—for flashing women as they passed. The man had been docile, but he was devastated over his wife's affair and needed attention. Hurt and loss were all too often the twin roots of wrongful, reckless, and even criminal behavior.

Eli walked Tal up the block toward *The Big Easy*, a jazz club she had visited many times. The owner hailed from New Orleans, and he had made the club famous for its red beans and rice, jambalaya, and Dixieland jazz on Monday nights. Tal's husband at the time, Owen, had discovered the place soon after it opened, and he went almost every Monday night until he died. He loved hearing the music of his hometown. Tal did, too, particularly while savoring the spicy bite of their famous bloody mary.

Eli lead Tal inside where smells of gumbo, Andouille sausage and crawfish étouffée swirled with the sounds of live jazz coming from the corner stage up front. A quartet played Charlie "Bird" Parker's "Yardbird Suite." Thanks to Owen, Tal recognized the tune. The saxophonist took off on a solo that would have made Bird proud.

Why are we here? Tal asked, certain it was not to rekindle her memories.

Eli walked her to the back, to the bar that ran its length. She sat down on one of the few open stools at one end, where she could see the stage and the front door reflected in the mirrored wall behind the bartender. Images were clear but made soft and dark by the dim lighting and the mirror's swirled, decorative backing.

Why? she asked again.

You'll see.

The bartender stopped by, and Eli ordered a soda water with a twist.

But, their bloody mary is—

Next time.

Spirits. No fun at all.

Eli ignored her.

It was not long before the front door opened, and Tal suddenly understood why they'd come. And why she would need a clear head.

Tucker walked through the crowd and directly to the bar. He sat on the opposite end, where Tal could watch his muted reflection. He did not see her, but neither was he looking.

Tucker nervously removed his hat and coat and nodded to the bartender who brought his usual—a gin and tonic with an extra twist of lemon. Though often made with lime, Tucker preferred his with lemon and lots of it. The bartender obviously knew this. And knew him.

Eli amplified Tal's hearing to divine Tucker's voice from the music and drone of conversation.

"I'm in for Saturday," Tucker told the bartender.

The bartender looked around as he wiped the counter, then leaned in. "You're already in over your head, man," he said softly. "Wait a few races, then—"

"I gotta good feeling about *Harvester*," Tucker replied, anxiously hissing his words. "They say he's got a shot at the Triple Crown."

"A *long* shot," the bartender retorted. "See how he does first. Then you'll know."

Tucker's eyes narrowed. "I need this money, Jim. Put me down for twenty g's on *Harvester*." Tucker drained his glass and stuck it out for a refill.

The bartender reluctantly took the glass. "Got it with ya?"

"I will," Tucker replied sharply.

The bartender refilled his drink and topped it off with a smaller lemon twist. His expression darkened. "You've said that before."

"Paid 'em half yesterday," Tucker replied with an arrogant grin. "I'm good for the rest." He took a big pull on his drink and wiped his mouth with his sleeve.

"Hope so," the bartender said. "You'll be dead otherwise."

Tal nearly spewed her soda water. This explained a lot. But how deep in debt was he?

"Tallulah Davis? Is that you?"

Tal turned, stunned, to find a waitress standing next to her.

"It's me, Cindy Riconni. We went to high school together."

Tal caught a movement in the mirror. Tucker glared at her over his drink. *Dammit.*

"Yeah, Cindy. Wow. Been a long time." Tal tried to be polite while keeping a wary eye.

"Sorry to hear about your partner last spring," the waitress said. "Read about it in the paper. Really sad. You'ns want something to eat? Gumbo tonight. Chef special."

Her Pittsburgh accent made Tal miss home. "Um, no thanks. Not tonight."

"Okay. Well, good to see you'ns."

Cindy walked off, passing Tucker from behind. He glared daggers at Tal's reflection before downing the rest of his drink.

He stood up. Her adrenaline gushed. Thanks to Eli, she heard every squeak of his rubber-soled sneakers as they crossed the wood floor.

Tucker stopped next to her and leaned down. "I don't know what you're up to or why you've come back," he hissed. "But you better stay away, or I'll send Internal Affairs so far up your ass they'll come out your nose."

Tal's fingers curled.

Eli opened them and forced her to breathe. In, out. In, out. The bartender snuck looks at Tucker through the mirror while he mixed drinks.

Tal stood, squaring her five feet-two inch frame to Tucker's chest. She looked up to meet his gaze. "I know about Benz," she said.

His eyes widened.

"And about your little gambling problem."

He stepped back.

"And about how you arranged the gunmen that killed Jake."

His heart pounded like a timpani.

"Get help, Tucker. Turn yourself in. Or it'll be *your* ass that IA swabs clean."

His lips thinned into a straight line over his teeth. "Telling them will be the last thing you ever do." He spun on his heel and stormed out, barely missing Cindy and her tray full of drinks.

Tal sat down and sipped her sparkling water. It tasted flat. Tucker had a way of sucking the life out of everything.

Which is why he needs help, the spirit said.

Tal gripped her glass, running her finger through the condensation. *Right. So what now? Do we follow him? Take him to Benz and sing Kum-ba-ya?*

The front door opened, and Tal felt the answer arrive.

CASPIAN

Jake's spirit lit up, and Tal grinned from the bar. As Caspian started over, his hand brushed against the coin in his pocket. He mindlessly toyed with it, and tingles flew up his arm. He became acutely aware of the female customers watching him. One cute waitress turned his way and smiled invitingly. Her nametag read, Cindy.

Give it to her. The raspy voice was back.

The pull was stronger this time, forceful and driven by even stronger lust. The coin's heat drew Caspian's fingers around it, then lifted his hand from his pocket as he turned toward her.

Cindy blushed. Other women watched with envy. Tal's puzzled expression flickered in his periphery.

Jake tried to stuff Caspian's hand back into his pocket.

"May I help you'ns?" Cindy asked.

Caspian reached out in her direction. The coin began to glow.

That's it, the raspy voice urged.

"That for me?" Cindy asked, lifting her hand. "What is it?"

No. Jake's spirit yanked his hand back.

Give it to her. The raspy voice pushed his hand out again.

No!

YES. Now.

More jerks and yanks. More people watched. Cindy looked worried, and Tal stood up.

Caspian's fingers prepared to drop the coin into Cindy's palm when Jake jerked his hand even harder, and the coin flew toward the bar.

The raspy voice and intense desire ended immediately. Caspian blinked. "I, I'm sorry," he stammered. "I thought you were someone else."

Cindy frowned as he hurried toward the bar.

Stop listening to that voice, Jake commanded.

I can't help it, Caspian said. *Who is it? What does it want? And why me?*

"Tallon," Jake said, pulling Tal into a hug.

She hugged him back, not quite as hard as before, and extended her hand with the coin inside. "Lose something?"

"I, um, I thought I knew her," Caspian said, sheepish.

Jake curled his fingers around it. *Back pocket this time.*

Caspian did as instructed and dropped the coin into his left hip pocket, one he rarely touched.

Jake kissed Tal's hand and pulled her close. Heat bloomed between them.

"You just missed Tucker," Tal said.

"We saw him leave," Jake replied. The band played a ballad, and he scooped Tal into Caspian's arms. "We visited Katherine. Didn't tell her everything, just that he's in trouble."

"What did she say?" Tal held him close.

Jake shook his head. "Even after all Tucker has put her through, she's willing to help. For better or worse, right?"

"Marriage is not meant to be a sentence, Jake."

The saxophone blew long, sultry notes. Some women sighed at Caspian. Others shot Tal full of hateful glances. Cindy brushed past enviously on her way to the kitchen.

"Katherine is a better woman than me," Tal said.

Jake leaned down, so Caspian's lips grazed her ear. "And you are the only woman for me."

Tal lifted her head from his chest to look up. Jake brushed her lips with Caspian's. They were soft and sweet.

Caspian suddenly wondered about the spirit Tal carried. What did he feel about all this? By his silence, Caspian guessed he was allowing room for these two to connect.

"Tucker saw me, Jake," Tal said after another lingering kiss.

"And?"

"I told him that I knew about Benz, his debts, the gunmen he arranged. I told him to get help, to turn himself in, or IA would find out."

Jake tightened briefly around Caspian's gut. "What did he say?"

"He left."

Jake stopped dancing. He shimmered in Caspian's eyes and reverted to the safer thought-speak. *He can't see you again, Tal, not until Saturday night. We can't risk him hurting you or blowing this bust.*

I don't think that'll be an issue.

Why not?

He's scared, Tal replied. *Bartender's a bookie, and Tucker came here to place a bet, a big one: twenty g's. The guy tried to talk him out of it, but Tucker wouldn't listen. He'll need this bust to pay that bill. Otherwise, loan sharks will kill him.*

We'll make sure that doesn't happen. Jake's lips caressed her forehead, her cheek, her mouth. Tal's lips parted, and his kiss consumed her.

Visions explode in Caspian like fireworks: Kissing the dark-haired woman. Her lips and neck. Her body. An opulent bed. A tangle of sheets. The diamond on her finger. Cries of pleasure. Screams of pain. Fire licking. The snap of a red cape. A wounded bull. Horns goring flesh. A crowd screams. The old man screams. He plucks something shiny and round from the dirt. Caspian recognizes it.

"Hey!" A fist to his chest snapped him back. Tal looked up with concern. "What happened? Are you okay?"

It was a coin! he said. *The old man was holding a coin. That's what he was trying to give me.*

What old man? Where?

Caspian had finally held the vision long enough to see it. But why did the old man have a coin? Was it his or Caspian's? And who was the woman? His arms drooped. Would he ever learn the truth about his past?

In time, Jake assured.

Sorry, Caspian told Tal. *These visions, they just … pop up.*

It's okay.

Caspian could only imagine how crazy this was for her, even as an experienced vessel.

You should come back with us, she told him. *To our program. After the bust. Jake can catch the ship home, and Liam, our Spirit Guard, will know how to help.*

Caspian nodded. He was willing to try anything at this point.

Jake curled his finger under Tal's chin and lifted her face. *See you soon, Tallon.* He brushed her lips with one last kiss and turned Caspian for the door.

CHAPTER THIRTEEN

SAM

The sun sank in long streaks of red and orange outside the empty warehouse in Reno's downtown. Inside, Sam stood in those same shafts of light by the front transom windows, taking in the raw, open space. The concrete floor ran under an industrial ceiling with exposed pipes. Two half-finished stud walls defined the start of a future kitchen, and an antique wooden bar leaned against the wall in one corner, half-covered with a dusty tarp. Pipes had been plumbed for both but was more dream than reality at this point, the bare PVC sticking out of the wall alongside a handful of electrical outlets missing their protective plates.

Two sawhorses nestled in another corner, along with some large scraps of wood. Sam could turn that into a makeshift desk and use the nearby outlets for his computer and lights. Doc would not have a clinic, but hopefully, they wouldn't need one. And there would not be much IT for Blaze once he returned, but the computer and his GPS would be enough to run the program with all three vessels still out in the field.

Sam had at least persuaded the inspectors to keep the shelter's kitchen open. That paperwork, much to their dismay, was in perfect order. At least their homeless guests would not go hungry, and, on exceptionally cold nights, Victoria and the kitchen staff knew to keep the kitchen "open" with bottomless urns of coffee and some blankets to wrap around cold shoulders.

Voices wafted down from the second-floor loft, or the framed start of one, as Eva and her doctor friend, Ross, descended the open plywood stairs void of spindles or rails. Ross looked to be Eva's age, maybe a little older, a handsome man with brown hair and a short, well-groomed moustache and beard. He was taller than her by at least eight inches, with a lean frame and strong arms. Even so, Eva seemed bigger.

Ross took her hand to guide her down, supporting her until they reached the bottom. He was hesitant to let go, Sam noticed, but she pulled away. Dust bunnies kicked up under their feet. Some settled on their clothes.

"Well?" Ross asked, brushing a few from her sleeve. "What do you think?"

"It's perfect, love," she replied, leading him toward Sam. "And I think it's a dream you and your friend should finish." She grinned coyly. "As soon as we are done with it."

He laughed and stepped closer. She inched toward Sam.

"The power's working?" Sam asked, suddenly feeling like the third wheel Eva had deliberately invited.

"Power, water, one working bathroom. No heat, but you shouldn't need it much during the day."

Eva must not have told him they'd be living here. "Thank you," Sam replied. "I'm not sure how long we'll need it. Just depends on how long it takes to pay the governor's fines."

"His *ridiculous* fines," Eva added. "Thank goodness Sam here is a wiz at fundraising."

"Well, no rush from me," Ross replied. "Here are the keys.

Two of them open locks on the front door, and the third opens a padlock in the back. It's a pretty safe neighborhood. Most of the buildings are empty, and the neighbors we do have keep to themselves."

"It's perfect," Eva said again. She leaned up to kiss his cheek. Polite. Friendly.

Ross reddened slightly, and Sam could tell he wished he and Eva were alone.

"I thought you might like to go get a bite," Ross said. "I know this—"

"Another time, love. I'm afraid we have work to do tonight." She looped an arm through Sam's. "Shall we get to it?"

Ross wilted. "Right. Okay, then. I better get back to the hospital. Just let me know if you need anything else."

Sam shook his hand. "We can't thank you enough."

"Watch out for her," Ross said with a wry smile. "She can be klutzy. Not a good thing in a construction space."

Eva bopped his arm playfully and walked him to the door. They hugged once more, and he left. She closed the door and fell back against it. "Bloody hell."

"I thought you liked him," Sam said. "You told me he was your closest friend."

"He *is*," she replied. "And that's the problem. I can't afford to get emotionally involved with anyone right now, and having him around is like offering expensive Scotch to a recovering alcoholic."

Sam smiled. "Better take him in small sips."

"That's not funny," she said, sticking her hands to her hips in mock condemnation.

"Don't chug him all at once." Sam chuckled.

"That is incredibly cheesy," she said, followed by a snort that sent them both into a fit of laughter.

The catharsis soon ended, and Sam rubbed his hurting cheeks. "We are fools."

Eva dried her eyes. "The worst."

A blast of energy crackled, and Liam and Blaze appeared.

"That was sick!" Blaze exclaimed. "I want to go everywhere like that."

"It's a good thing the windows are boarded," Eva snapped, pointing to the large panes of glass in front under the transoms. "That's not exactly how we want to meet the neighbors."

"We had to leave quickly," Liam said. "His stepfather was breaking into his room."

"I'm sorry we let them take you," Sam told Blaze, remembering how Liam's *Diego* fingers had gripped his shoulder at that moment. "I hope you can forgive us, but the risk was too great."

"Yeah, well, just don't do it again," Blaze retorted, hurt resurfacing briefly before he shoved it aside. "Howard's gonna fry his circuit board over this, though. Now he knows I'm around, he'll have every cop in the city working to sniff me out."

"You should be safe here," Sam told him, handing back his GPS tracker. "Just stay inside and out of sight."

Blaze tapped the blinking dots. "At least nothing's changed in vessel-ville." He looked around the rough space. "Seriously?"

"For a while," Sam replied. "Until I can pay the fine and fix that third-floor wiring."

"Which will be never," Doc snipped. "If Governor Ron has his way."

"Wait. We have to *live* here?" Blaze's voice cracked slightly.

"Never say never," Liam told Doc. "Let's have a look outside."

Malina watched the warehouse from across the street. She had taken a cab from the shelter to follow Sam and Eva over here, then hid behind some bushes while Eva's doctor friend showed them around inside. That doctor was pretty hot, too, for an old guy, but he'd barely left in his awesome black Mercedes when a weird green light flashed inside the building. Malina couldn't see what caused it because of the covered door and windows, but since nothing else had happened, she wrote it off as weird wiring and checked her phone.

She was supposed to be back at the hotel by now. Malina fingered the meager cash she had left from what Gale had given her to buy lunch and dinner. It was mostly gone, thanks to the cab fare she'd spent getting to the shelter early this morning and then coming here, but it had been worth it. She didn't completely understand why the inspectors had kicked them out or why they needed this dump of a new space, but knowledge was power, and secrets were gold. Malina wanted as many of them as possible to lord over Sam and to force Gale's hand into leaving this place and going back home to their life, her friends, and her father.

The warehouse door pushed open, and Sam exited with Eva. Seconds later, they were joined by Liam.

How'd he get here? Malina thought. The place was locked up tight when the hot doctor opened it. And she'd been watching it since.

Wait. Did that crazy light have something to do with it? *Idiot,* Malina chastised herself. *He probably just came in through the back.*

Sam, Eva, and Liam walked around the two-story brick building. A rusted fire escape hugged one wall. Malina could climb that later, after it got dark, and peek in the second-story windows.

The warehouse sat two buildings away from the nearest intersection, between a closed pottery store and a metal warehouse with a commercial photography sign out front. The photography place had no windows, but two cars sat in the small parking lot, and a camera was mounted above the entry. That place was open, at least.

Sam and Liam noticed it, too, before the group disappeared back inside. A few seconds later, another green bolt of light, and things went quiet. Malina eyed the fire escape and wondered if she could get a closer look now without being seen. Then her cell rang. Gale.

Right on time, Malina thought and pushed the side button so it would go to voicemail. She waited until the message banner popped up, lowered the volume, and pressed the button to play it back.

"Malina, it's Mom." Gale's voice sounded sharper and more worried than it had earlier. "Where are you? Did you make it back to the hotel? Is everything okay? Do you like the new school? I hope you're making friends. And turn on your phone finder! Listen, I'll be home later than I thought. Get pizza, and wings if you want, you should have enough cash. I'll call when I'm driving back. Love you."

Malina stowed her phone and sunk deeper into the bushes. She had hours until Gale drove back, so she zipped her jacket and pulled the hoodie low over her hair, nose ring, and row of loops and studs lining her right ear. To any who might see her, she was just another homeless kid, another bullshit *victim* of Reno's streets.

CHAPTER FOURTEEN

GALE

Gale sat inside her car parked unobtrusively outside the Nevada governor's mansion. She was furious with Malina, but even more worried. Not only did her daughter not answer her phone, she had turned off the finder app and ignored every text Gale had sent telling her to turn it back on. At least Gale had made her store Sam's phone number and the school bus route into her phone. She also had made arrangements with the hotel staff to look out for Malina in case she forgot or lost her key.

When she'd called the front desk earlier, the clerk said they had not seen her arrive from school. Then again, they'd had a shift change, the employee told her, so she probably came in when no one was paying attention. Gale still worried.

She looked across at Ron's sprawling, gated governor's home. The place had been quiet since the gardener left an hour ago after weeding and pruning the hedge of roses. Sam had texted her about the inspection, how horribly wrong it had gone, and how they were being forced to close until further notice due to exposed wiring and the discovery of Eva's medicines. The fines were so steep, with inflated demands set so high, Sam was not sure he could ever reopen.

Gale had hoped to speak with Ron one more time, to beg even harder on Sam's behalf, but her brother had left the office too quickly. He'd probably seen her waiting. So, she had followed him here, parking along this adjacent dead-end street, watching his driver deposit him behind the spacious mansion before leaving, no doubt, to get the already pristine car detailed for Ron's next outing. Her brother had always been a stickler for first impressions, a vain and selfish trait her ex-husband shared as well. She hated it in both of them.

And she hated being here. If only Malina could understand that. While happy to reconnect with Sam after all these years, she did not want to be divorced, or to start her life over at age thirty-seven with a new job, in a new city, with a father she barely knew and a brother who despised her. She missed Detroit. It's where she went to college, met Vince, and became pregnant before graduation. Though the pregnancy was unplanned, she and Vince married and created a happy life together. Or so she'd thought. Now, she felt sixty, and Vince acted sixteen. Their life together was a memory, a closed chapter she'd never open again, and the only good thing to come out of it was Malina.

Metal slammed, and Gale jumped, fingers clutching the wheel. She glanced over in time to see Ron get into his Porsche at the back of the mansion. He must have put something in the trunk first.

She'd been waiting for the right moment to, to—what? Talk her way past security? Ring the doorbell until Ron came out? It didn't matter now. Following him may provide her only other chance to get him alone and talk sense into him. But where was he going this close to dark? And why would a man who lived for expensive suits go out in jeans and a ball cap?

Gale waited until Ron opened the back gate, ten or so yards away, and pulled onto the quiet street ahead of her. His windows were too tinted for her to see in. She started her engine, keeping the lights off, and waited for him to reach the stop sign and turn left onto the main road before shifting into gear.

She turned left at the stop sign, and sped up until she could make out Ron's taillights ahead. He shifted over to a left turn lane and sped through the yellow light. She hurried through it, too, staying just far enough behind to make the light as it turned red.

Ron zigzagged in and out of the Carson City traffic on his way out of town.

Where is he going? Gale wondered. *And in such a hurry?* Then again, maybe he was frustrated and just out for a drive. Maybe he needed to blow off steam and feel the road. He had liked fast cars since his first used Corvette and had never owned anything slower or less expensive since.

Gale hung back as the roads narrowed and the traffic thinned. Fewer streetlights and thicker darkness marked the shift to rural land. This was definitely not Ron's kind of place, but he seemed to know this two-lane highway pretty well.

A thought sickened. What if he were doing something or meeting someone he didn't want anyone else to know about? She wouldn't put it past him. He was not above paying people off, making deals, or delivering on dangerous promises if it would help him win. At least the hush money he'd paid her over the last eighteen or so years would put Malina through college. Something bright would come of his darkness.

Ron turned down another street, and Gale followed, staying well behind, through a neighborhood of fancy ranch- and cabin-style homes. Each home sat on several acres of land, and most featured fenced-in pastures of grazing cows and horses, their silhouettes outlined by moonlight.

Ron tapped his brakes, and the taillights winked. Gale feared he may have spotted her and was redirecting his course or stopping to catch her. She deliberately slowed and pulled into one of the driveways, then turned off her lights. She waited a few seconds before backing up and tailing him again, careful to stay well behind and keep her car dark.

Ron braked and slowed before turning into what looked like a thicket of trees. Gale followed, stunned to enter a small park with a playground at one end and a ball field at the other. The entry was thick with trees. Even more of them shaded benches near the swings, seesaw, and climbing bars.

Ron had parked by another car farther up, near one of these benches. Gale quickly pulled over, killed the engine, and opened her window to listen. Crickets chirped in the cold silence. A light breeze scented the air with pine.

A figure stepped out of the other car. A young, beautiful, very pregnant black woman waddled to the rear of her car and grinned.

Ron stepped out and grabbed what looked like a picnic basket and some kind of bottle or thermos from his trunk. He greeted the woman with a long hug and a lingering kiss. He rubbed her belly, and a rock sank in Gale. The baby had to be his.

Just like Vincent. The thought seared. What was it with men not being satisfied at home? Why did they feel this driving need to roam outside their marriage and spawn even more children than those they had vowed, in front of a priest or justice, usually with family and friends present, to love and protect?

Gale gripped the wheel so hard it hurt. She let go and rubbed her fingers.

Ron helped the woman to a bench. They sat in darkness and shared a romantic dinner from the basket. At one point, Ron opened the thermos and poured some kind of steaming liquid into the cap. His mistress drained the cup, and Ron refilled it and kissed down her neck as she drank another. Gale could hear their voices and soft laughter, but she was too far away to make out their words. They sounded happy, though. Loving. She wondered how Ron knew this woman, how long they had been together, and why they met at this park. Did the woman live nearby? Did Ron's wife have any idea she existed? Did she care?

Ron checked his watch, and Gale realized two hours had passed. It was almost nine, and she was stiff from the open window and cold night air. Never imagining she'd be anywhere this late, she'd only brought a thin jacket.

Oh, God. Malina.

She checked her phone. Malina had not called or texted, and her location app was still off. *Dammit.* Gale started to text her when Ron stood up. He capped the thermos and packed the picnic basket, then helped the young woman to her feet. Ron walked her to her car. They hugged one last time before he kissed her belly and buckled her in. He waited until she drove off, out the far entrance, before doing the same.

A horrible thought reared up. If Ron had exited the way he entered, he would have driven right past her. God knows what he would have done to her or to Malina as a result. She hadn't thought of that when she pulled in. Ron didn't take such pains to keep things this private without good reason, and he would not withhold punishment to anyone who found out, including family.

The young woman turned right from the park, and Ron waited a moment before turning left to wind back around the way he had come. Gale started the engine and the heater but kept her lights off until she reached that same entrance.

To her left, Ron's taillights sped off quickly and disappeared over a hill. To her right, the woman's taillights slowly shrunk to small dots before they began to weave. Gale thought she was seeing things, but the weaving grew more erratic, and tires squealed across the road until the car slammed into a tree with a gut-wrenching metal crunch.

Everything in Gale told her to flee, to turn left and put as much distance as she could between her and whatever this was. But she was a nurse, a school nurse with limited training, but a nurse, nonetheless. She spun the wheel to the right and stepped on the gas to see if there was anything she could do.

Moonlight cast an eerie pallor over the scene and sparkled off a sea of shattered glass, most of it from what had been the windshield. The car headlights remained on but wrapped inward around the tree that separated them. Gale reached in through the broken driver's window to feel the young woman's neck for a pulse. There was none. She wore a seatbelt, but the car was an older model that had no airbags. The engine was shoved backward against the front seat and pinned her legs. The steering wheel crushed her chest and belly, and blood pooled beneath her on the seat. Gale sunk to the asphalt remembering Ron's thermos. *What had he done?*

She started to call 911, unwilling to leave this poor young woman out here for someone else to happen upon. But as she started to dial, she stopped. If Ron was behind this, and he found out she was the one to call it in, he would see to it that she met a similar end. No doubt he would be screening emergency calls or scanning news stories to make sure this *accident* was just that. Even if they did a blood alcohol test on the woman or some other kind of screening, Gale was certain his concoction would not be found.

Gale shone her phone's flashlight into the wreckage. The woman's purse lay upside down in the back seat, its contents tossed about, including her cell phone. Gale pulled down her shirtsleeve to grip the handle and open the back door. She fetched the woman's phone, struggling to clutch it through the fabric, and dialed.

"911. What is your emergency?" the operator asked.

Knowing they would trace the call, Gale placed the phone on the woman's lap and ran.

CHAPTER FIFTEEN

LINK

Link watched as Kevin and Marie stepped inside the cemetery gate. They leaned against each other, nervously holding hands and searching until they spotted him waving them over. They soon joined him and Teddy's spirit at what appeared to be an overgrown patch of grass between two weathered markers with names and dates too faded to read.

"Well?" Kevin asked, looking around. "Who are we here to see?"

His short red hair turned copper in the sun.

"Look down," Teddy replied. "Recognize it?"

"Recognize what?" Kevin squirmed. "There's nothing here but some old stones and people we hardly know." He pointed to a distant area where Ted's mother was buried. "That's our section."

Teddy knelt and brushed aside weeds and grass to reveal a plain, flush marker:

James Dawson
April 10, 1967 - Sept. 14, 1988

Kevin's cheeks burned.

"Who is that?" Marie asked.

Kevin glowered.

"Kevin?" Marie touched his shoulder. He jerked away. She looked at Link. "What's going on?"

Link's stomach corkscrewed, but Teddy remained unfazed. "Would you like to tell her, or shall I?"

"It's ancient history," Kevin snapped. "Damn fool deserved what he got."

"Who did?" Marie asked. "Who is James Dawson? What's going on?"

Kevin glared holes into Link. "On one hand, you bring back my son and allow me a shot at salvation."

"Redemption," Teddy corrected.

"*Whatever*," Kevin hissed. "On the other hand, you're a wanted fugitive who killed a five-year-old boy in Reno during a gang war." Kevin jammed a finger against Link's chest. "That's about as low as it gets."

"I didn't do it," Link said, feeling the anger surge. Teddy extinguished it. "A car drove by and started firing. Trevor wandered out, and I ran to save him, but a bullet hit me, went into him, and—he died in my arms. That's how the cops found me."

"Right," Kevin snarled through clenched teeth.

Link wanted to punch him. Teddy eased him back.

"But I swear to God," Kevin continued. "You open this door to James, and I'm turning you in. Reward's over a hundred thousand now," he said. "Know what that could do for Marie and me? Pay off our debts. We could take that vacation we always wanted and—"

"You walked away from him once," Teddy interrupted. "Do it again, and you will *never* heal. No amount of money will fix that."

Hosting the spirit allowed Link to feel the deep wound of Kevin's shame, the guilt infecting it, and the scar of self-loathing it left behind. Teddy was prying it back open, knowing his father would not be able to do so on his own.

"Who is James Dawson?" Marie asked again with growing concern. "And what in God's name is all this about?"

Kevin's hands shook. His blue eyes blazed. "I got nothing more to say on the matter. Now let's go visit your mom or I swear I'll call the cops. Let me make my peace with her about what I did to you, and this convict you're *using* can disappear without me telling a soul or collecting a dime of that reward." He turned to storm off.

"I looked like him, didn't I?"

Kevin stopped.

"And you left him, too."

Kevin spun around and grabbed his phone. "You asked for this."

He started to call 911 when Teddy shot out Link's hand to stop him, accidentally squeezing hard enough to make Kevin yelp. Teddy pulled back slightly.

"Kevin?" Marie's voice trembled.

"He wouldn't listen," Kevin retorted. "I tried to help him, to *fix* him, but—"

"There's nothing to fix, Dad. Being straight is not a choice for you, right? You were born that way and just—are." Teddy released his grip, and Kevin yanked his hand back. "It's the same with being gay. We don't *choose* it. We just *are.* Uncle Jamie tried to fit in, but he couldn't be something he wasn't, not for you, not for your father, not for anyone. And it cost him his life."

"How do you *know* this?" Kevin asked. "I barely even knew your mom when James died, and I never told her what happened."

"There are no secrets on the other side," Teddy said.

Kevin swatted back angry tears.

"Kevin, please!" Marie said. "What is this all about?"

Kevin looked down, lips tight, so Teddy explained. "Uncle Jamie was Kevin's younger brother. He had to leave home when the family found out he was gay."

Kevin looked up. "Don't."

"He was eighteen, fresh out of high school," Teddy continued. "No idea where to go or what to do with his life."

"Stop," Kevin warned.

"He met a friend for dinner, and they went to a bar for drinks. Some guys started poking fun at them, teasing, picking a fight. It wasn't long before things got physical."

"It wasn't like that," Kevin said, his shoulders crawling up to his ears.

"The friend ran off to call for help, but Uncle Jamie stood his ground. He defended himself and his truth."

"He was a homo in a bar full of hunters!" Kevin yelled, his face turning as red as his hair. "What the hell did he *expect*?"

Marie stared at Kevin like he'd punched her.

Kevin leveled his eyes at Link. "I tried to warn him. If you're gonna be like *that*, at least carry a gun. Learn how to defend yourself. I offered to teach him, to get him a permit. He didn't listen."

"He hated guns," Teddy said. "So did I."

"And you'd both be alive right now if you had one!"

"Maybe, maybe not. But more people almost certainly would be dead."

"I've heard enough." Kevin started off again.

"You watched him die."

Marie gasped. He froze.

"You were a young cop, one of two called to the bar that night. James was already beaten to a pulp and stabbed when you arrived. You could have acted faster, called the ambulance sooner, but you didn't. You hated that James was gay, an embarrassment to you and the family, so you let him die."

Cold, windy fingers shook the trees. Link shuddered.

Kevin whipped around and stormed back. "If you're gonna *choose* a life that pisses people off, then learn how to protect yourself. Carry a gun. Have it ready. Let it speak when words can't."

Teddy clamped one hand around Kevin's arm and quickly lifted the coin from Link's pocket with the other. "Hold on," he told Marie.

She grabbed their joined hands as energy crackled around them.

Kevin's eyes went wild with fright. "What the hell are you doing?" He struggled to break free. "What's happening?"

Link braced himself as the invisible energy swallowed them into a cloud he'd never seen before. The cemetery changed and morphed until it became the mirage of a nightclub with lights strobing, people dancing, and a DJ playing Latin music. A horde of people grooved on the dance floor while others drank and ate around tables or at the bar.

It took a moment for Link to notice that most of the couples were same-sex, though a few heterosexual couples shared the dance floor.

Kevin's eyebrows narrowed in disgust as one male couple

kissed.

The spirit directed their attention to a young man across the room at the bar. Link recognized Teddy immediately from the pictures. He was broad-shouldered and strikingly handsome with short, sandy blond hair, a strong jaw, and hazel eyes that glinted at the young man with him. He was shorter than Teddy, though not by much, and thinner through the shoulders and chest. They talked, laughed, kissed—a couple in love.

Kevin looked away.

The shooter walked in.

He was young, not yet thirty, with a short, muscular frame and black hair. He wore jeans and a button-up shirt under a long, trench-style coat. A baseball cap hung low over his eyes.

"Hey!" Kevin said, but no one heard. "Hey! That's *him*!" He reached for a non-existent holster at his waist.

The music pounded. Disco balls twinkled diamonds of light around the room as the bartender poured cocktails. Teddy kissed his partner again.

The shooter flung back his coat and spun a semi-automatic machine gun into his hands.

Kevin screamed, and Marie cried out, but their voices were as invisible as their bodies. They and Link watched, helpless, as a staccato of bullets sliced the air and bodies dropped. People screamed, panic erupted, and blood stained the floor.

The bartender fell over. The DJ, too. Some patrons made it out the front, while others ran out through the kitchen in the back or hid in the bathrooms.

Link felt sick. Marie's hands covered her mouth. Kevin turned ghostly white.

Sirens drew closer, and Link noticed the number of dying and dead hands still clutching cell phones. Many began to ring or vibrate as loved ones tried to call.

The shooter scanned the carnage. A few eyes quickly closed, victims, playing dead in hopes he would not find them or finish them off. Sirens wailed outside as an army of police surrounded the club. A few officers entered the front.

The gunman fired at them and ran toward the kitchen. Kevin lunged to stop him, but his efforts were in vain.

The shooter threw open the kitchen door where more police waited, guns drawn. They yelled for him to put down the weapon, but he spotted the gas line that fueled the two kitchen stoves. Above them, grease-smeared signs warned Flammable and No Smoking.

The police barely had time to react before the gunmen fired on the stoves and exploded the kitchen and the back half of the club. The blast alone killed five officers, fifteen of the injured patrons lying outside, twenty-two patrons hiding in the adjacent bathrooms, and the shooter. Seventy-six people died in all, including those who'd been shot first.

Link smiled slightly at the shooter's death. Kevin and Marie did, too.

Teddy did not. He didn't say anything or prod Link with reprimands, but his compassion flowed equally to everyone there, including the gunman. "Every soul is sacred," he said, "even those buried in darkness."

Link knew Teddy was right, but he was also certain he could never fully embrace that concept. Not while human, anyway. Revenge, especially for such evil, felt too good. It's why Tricia Martin would continue to hate him until he proved his truth.

The spirit led them back into what remained of the club, to a pile of bodies near the bar.

Teddy lay face up on top of his partner, his arms thrown back like protective wings. His dead eyes were open, and he bled from multiple bullet wounds.

"You … saved him," Kevin whispered.

"It's been two years," Teddy said. "One bullet grazed his spine, but Mike is able to run again, and he just got accepted into Med School. He wants to be a surgeon."

Teddy let go of Kevin's arm and the music faded, the lights disappeared, and the bloody nightclub walls wavered into the sunny cemetery once more. Kevin dropped to his knees by his brother's grave. "What have I done?" His voice cracked. "What have I done? What have I done? What have I done?" His voice trailed off, and his broad back shook with sobs.

Teddy knelt next to him. He wrapped Link's arms around his father and waited for the purge to subside.

Kevin's breath eventually came back, raspy but controlled.

Teddy waited until his father looked up. "James forgives you, Dad. And so do I." He paused. "But nothing changes until you forgive yourself."

Link's tattoo ignited. His senses exploded as Teddy held his father close. They remained that way for what seemed like forever until the spirit let go.

"Love is love is love," Teddy said. "It is the deepest power and the greatest gift we humans have. And yet we abuse it, deny it, suffocate it.

Kevin's lungs shuttered. The deep furrows softened across his forehead, and his eyes brightened.

Tricia Martin had shown a flicker of that same understanding the night Link saw her last, when he had snuck over to plead his innocence before becoming a vessel. She dialed 911, but he'd had just enough time to gasp out his side of the story before sirens closed in, and he'd had to escape.

The men stood. Kevin dried his cheeks. "I looked into your case."

Link tensed, ready to run.

"Not like that," Kevin said, lifting his hands in a sign of surrender.

You're okay, Teddy told him. *I sense no harm.*

Link eased slightly.

"I still have access to the database to check files," Kevin continued. "The bullet that hit you and Trevor never turned up. That's how they pinned this on you so fast. No proof to support your story of being shot at the same time."

"There was a hole in my shirt," Link said. "From where the bullet went through my shoulder and into Trevor."

"I saw that," Kevin replied, "but the report says you must have been shot earlier. Your gun fired the same kind of bullets. Trevor died in your arms. They think you killed him. Even accidentally, it's still homicide."

"If that were true, why would I still be holding him?" Link argued. "I'd have dropped him and run."

Kevin cleared his throat, the cop in him coming out. "Your clothing and Trevor's should still be in evidence. Go back to the crime scene and find that bullet. Show the trajectory. Prove that it went through you and into the boy." He paused. "They may never learn who fired it, but it will prove you didn't."

Link sank. "It's been three years. If they couldn't find it then—"

"Check any tree trunks that would have been in front of you.

Dig into the dirt and grass you were close to. Look into any toy bins, bags, wooden house walls, car panels, anything a bullet could sink into."

"Wouldn't the investigators have done that?"

Kevin studied his nails. "Not necessarily. Not when someone … kills a kid."

Link flashed to the officers yanking him around that night, twisting the cuffs on as tightly as they could, shoving him into the back of their car with almost no concern for his bullet wound. They'd pegged him as guilty, no trial needed.

An ember of hope flickered before another thought snuffed it out. "What if they did find that bullet and … *lost* it?"

Kevin rubbed his beard. "I've known that to happen, unfortunately, especially with a crime like this. But it's more likely they just stopped looking. So they could honestly tell the court and your defense attorney that they didn't find anything."

Hope simmered again, but Link had no idea how to achieve this. Tricia would call the cops the minute he stepped on her property, so he'd have to ask Sam, Doc, and the others to search, instead. That could take days, weeks, or even months. When would they have time? And how would they convince Tricia to allow it?

"And if we find it?" Link asked.

"That bullet will reopen your case," Kevin said. "They'll look at the evidence again with fresh eyes and newer tests. If they can prove what you say, charges will be dropped."

Marie beamed and held Kevin's hand.

"You mean," Link could barely say it. "I could go free?"

Kevin nodded.

Link fought the urge to cry. "Thank you," he said as a familiar wind kicked up. This nightmare might actually end after all.

CHAPTER SIXTEEN

AVANI

"I'm not here to make some old codger feel young again," Ginger said as she and Samantha approached the strip club's bar. The bright neon and artificial palms reflected the club's Miami home.

Avani tried not to eavesdrop as she waited for Hal to mix her order of drinks. Ginger, the newest and youngest dancer, was a fiery redhead who shared her opinions with anyone who would listen.

"I told Jeffie, I work too hard to keep my body like this," she said. "The least he can do is give me the lap dances with men who *try* to do the same." She turned to Hal. "Wine spritzer."

"Ice water. Thanks," Samantha said, nudging some loose strands of long blond hair behind her shoulders. Her teeth ground against a piece of gum.

According to Hal, Samantha had recently quit smoking, and the gum was a new, less desirable replacement.

"You *told* Jeffie this?" Samantha challenged, her skin glistening with body sparkles.

Ginger huffed and sipped her drink.

At twenty-eight, Samantha was the oldest of the group and had been here the longest. But she had the saddest eyes Avani had ever seen. They only lit up when she danced, smiling and moving for the customers like they were the most important people in the world. That earned her the most tips and allowed her the most select and high-paying lap dances, both of which made her valuable in Jeffrey's club. No wonder she was his favorite.

Samantha tilted her head back to drink, and Avani caught a glimpse of a long, narrow scar hidden perfectly in the curve of her jaw. Some surgeon did a masterful job of stitching her up, but something, or someone, had done an equally skillful job of slicing her open in a place few would see.

Avani absently touched the scar on her own neck, where Sonny had poked a small hole with the tip of his knife during the attack. She could still feel the cold steel splitting open that delicate skin. Avani had feared knives since witnessing her father's stabbing when she was six, and Sonny had used that fear to control her. At least the scar was barely visible now, thanks to the poultice of herbs she had harvested and applied after Doc stitched her up.

Samantha's scar, on the other hand, reflected the work of someone who knew what he or she was doing—someone who, perhaps, wanted to keep her in line. *Jeffrey?*

Amber tingled, but Avani couldn't tell if it was agreement or rebuke.

"What's that from?" Ginger asked, brazenly pointing to the scar and, no doubt, trying to change the course of conversation.

Samantha stopped chewing and leaned in. "You can tell *Jeffie* whatever you want," she said with an unnerving calm. "But it's what *he* wants that seals your fate around here." She spit her gum the trash, adjusted her bikini strap, and strode off toward the backstage door.

Hal fired a look of caution at Avani and turned to make another drink.

So Jeffrey gave her that scar?

Amber didn't reply.

But why? Who does he think he is?

Amber swelled with kindness, but this time it angered Avani. *No*, she snapped, her first time to ever confront a spirit. *You can't love the monster* and *his victim in equal measure.* Even though she had seen many human monsters redeemed through spirit journeys. *It's not fair.*

Love is not about fairness, Amber replied. *Every soul is sacred.*

Not Jeffrey's. I doubt even God could love that guy after what he's become.

With no warning, Amber exploded inside Avani like a firework, sucking away all the negativity and throwing open Avani's soul to let her see the people around her without judgment, labels, or emotions. The waitresses and customers, the bouncer and Hal, Jeffrey in the back, and Samantha now on stage all turned into pillars of light without skin color, gender, or age. Avani could feel them more than see them, and each held varying degrees of dark spots and shadows that dimmed their brightness in different ways. She could sense their elements, too—earth, air, fire, water—by the respective green, yellow, red, and blue variations in their light. The first spirit Avani ever hosted had introduced her to this when she'd allowed Avani to witness Aaron's yellow air element light fade to darkness when he died.

Hal and Samantha were the brightest lights in this club by far. Jeffrey's light, on the other hand, flickered like a small ember buried in shadow.

That is the part we seek, Amber said.

Another blast and the sensation subsided as quickly as it had begun. The window closed, but Avani had a much better understanding of the spirit's urgency. *Why didn't you come sooner?* she asked.

He was not ready to listen.

What makes you think he is now?

The spirit vibrated happily. *A new door has opened.* She turned to Hal. "Is Jeffrey alone?"

"For now," he replied. "Until his business meeting at eight."

Avani checked her watch. Seven thirty.

"Can someone else take these?" She pointed to the full tray of drinks.

Hal nodded.

"Thanks." She turned toward the back, but Hal stopped her.

"He's bad tonight," Hal said, pulling out a special bottle of scotch and pouring two fingers into a glass. "Whatever you're up to, this'll help."

Hal was the shiniest piece of coal in this mine, for sure.

Avani found Jeffrey in his office, just off the dining room where he entertained his business associates and at an angle where he could see the stage.

He was watching Samantha dance as Avani approached. His eyes were softer, kinder ... *loving?*

"Brought you something," Avani said, placing the drink on his desk.

His eyes hardened again. "Not now." He snorted some white powder off his fingernail before closing a vial of it and tucking it back in his pocket. "It's been a long day and—"

"I came for you, Jeffrey Danielson," Amber said, her voice

echoing deep and husky in Avani's. He jerked back, but she grabbed his cheeks and turned him to face her. He struggled, helpless in her iron grip. "I'm here for that part of you that is dying and needs to live." Her eyes bathed his face in green.

"What the hell?" He pulled and tugged at her hands. They didn't budge.

"I was a dancer years ago," Amber continued. "My stage name was Candy."

"T-That's ridiculous," he said. "You're t-too young."

"I got pregnant with a beautiful child who changed everything." She leaned in. "That can be true for you and Samantha if you'll let it."

Jeffrey's jaw unhinged.

Avani stumbled against his chair. That explained the water, the chewing gum, and the extra bright light around Samantha's body during the vision. "*A new door has opened.*"

"She knows the rules," Jeffrey snapped, trying to regain control. He was more scared than angry. "You get knocked up in my club, even by me, you get rid of it. If not, you pay the price."

Samantha's scar.

Avani's lip curled but Amber twisted it into a smile. "You don't want that," she told Jeffrey. "Not with Samantha. You love her."

Jeffrey lunged from his chair and pried loose from Amber's grip. "Get the hell out of here!"

She stepped closer. "I didn't have to make that choice, not with Hal. He was a much more compassionate owner." She forced Jeffrey against the back wall. He tried to pull away, but she held tight.

"I got to love my little boy and watch him grow for four

beautiful years until someone hooked me on crack. Hal and Elaine tried to stop me, but I wouldn't listen. The drug was too strong." She paused. "Giving up my son was the hardest thing in the world to do. But it was best for him."

"Good for you." He tried to get away.

Amber blocked him. "The Danielsons gave him everything I could not." She waited for the name to sink in.

"The Danielsons …" he stammered. "The ones who adopted *me?*"

Amber smiled.

"No way. It can't be. Get away from me," he yelled. "GO."

She stepped closer. "They never told you about your real mom, about who I was or what I'd done. Maybe they were too embarrassed. Maybe they wanted to protect you." She lifted his chin. "But I know you remember some of it. Those fun and loving young women who helped me look after you backstage, who played dress-up with you in feather boas and fancy robes, who painted your face like a funny clown."

"Get out," he whispered.

"Forgive me," Amber continued. "For giving up on us, on myself. For giving you away instead of being strong enough to keep you."

He jerked her finger from his chin. "Get out."

"I never stopped loving you, Jeffrey. Not even after I died."

Maybe it was hatred, or perhaps hurt and fear, but Jeffrey grabbed Avani's wrist with unexpected strength and dragged her from the office. He hauled her past the empty table set for his business dinner and up the short hallway. She feared he was throwing her out, but Amber seemed to know better. He stopped short of the main room and pointed to the stage.

"You want me to believe you're *all that* inside, sweetheart?" Jeffrey hissed. "Then prove it." He pointed to the stage. "Any dancer knows how to shake it, but every good dancer has a signature move, something unique. With Ginger—it's this sexy ab roll against the floor. Samantha holds her body parallel to the pole before wrapping around. What was yours—*Candy*?"

The room swam as Avani teetered. She couldn't dance. Not even a little. She had tried at homecoming and prom but had always ended up with two left feet stepping on whatever partner had asked.

Amber pulsed happily. *We're getting through!* She boldly tossed Avani's hair. "How would you know Candy's move if you saw it?"

Jeffrey smiled, undaunted. "Hal!" He motioned the man over with one hand while pinning Avani with the other.

Hal joined them, a bar towel slung over one shoulder. He tried to hide his concern. "You need something, boss?"

"You remember a dancer named Candy at the old club?" Jeffrey asked.

Hal startled. "Haven't heard that name in years."

"Do you remember her move?"

Hal thought for a moment. "I think so. Why?"

Jeffrey faced Avani with a malicious smile. "Okay. Let's see it."

Hal looked confused, and Avani's heart almost stopped. Amber buttressed her insides like scaffolding, winked at Hal, and disappeared through the backstage door with rock star confidence. Avani felt numb. She couldn't breathe.

Relax and follow my lead, Amber told her. *We got this.*

The spirit strode past Ginger and a few other bewildered dancers toward the stage. She stepped Avani through the curtains and out to the center pole. Samantha's mouth dropped open as

Avani twirled around it like a seasoned pro.

The crowd erupted with catcalls and whistles.

Amber zeroed in on Jeffrey, his angry brow and smug smile. Hal stood next to him with his head down and shoulders drooped.

Ginger glared from the wings. Samantha stood next to her and watched, forlorn as if Avani had been thrown into the next ring of Jeffrey's hell.

The lights flashed, and a pop tune began, one from the late eighties that Avani barely recognized. The air conditioning chilled her bare midriff. The thin straps of her sequined bikini top cut into her back and shoulders, and the Spirit Guard coin brushed against her breast inside one of the cups. The tight, teal boy shorts hugged her hips, accentuating every move. She was grateful for the dark brown stockings that hid her tattoo.

Amber twisted Avani's hips in a figure eight, then bent her knees and circled her head around, flinging her hair in a circle.

Avani got dizzy. Amber fixed it. The audience cheered.

Hal looked down. Jeffrey poked him to watch.

Then a man entered and walked toward a table. Short blonde hair. Wide shoulders. Slim waist.

Sonny.

Oh, God. Avani stumbled, and quickly righted herself. *What is he doing here? What if he sees me?*

Jeffrey noticed her falter. Amber once more tapped the hormonal spigots of dopamine, serotonin, and endorphins to flood Avani with calm. *You'll be fine. Stay with me. Focus only on me, and this moment.*

Sonny barely sat down before a waitress appeared to take his order. He was as handsome as ever, and the waitress flirted unabashedly. He squirmed uncomfortably and tapped a booted foot.

How did he know I was here? Avani asked as Amber twisted her around the pole. Then she remembered the customer from two nights ago, the one who kept staring at her as if he knew her. Tommy Ciccone. His name had popped in her head soon after he'd left. They'd all gone to school together. He was a friend of Sonny's from the football team.

Get ready, Amber warned.

Oh, God.

Amber grabbed the pole with both hands and swung Avani's strong, shapely legs above her head, so her torso touched the pole. Upside down, she wrapped one leg around the pole as an anchor, then slowly, sensually opened her other leg to the side, like a petal unfurling from its stem. She moved to the music, arching her back, releasing both arms, and snaking them in erotic patterns around her torso, the pole, and her outstretched leg.

The crowd went wild. Hal's mouth hung open. Jeffrey stared, impressed.

Avani felt an odd sense of achievement as her muscles and limbs moved in ways she had never imagined possible. A small part of her had dreamed of performing in a Cirque du Soleil style show, an acrobat flying, twisting, and turning, seemingly weightless and with impossible strength and grace, along dangling strips of cloth or inside a narrow hoop or ring.

Her eyes accidentally caught Sonny's. She looked away, but he jumped to his feet. His beer hit the floor.

Oh no.

Hold on. Amber shut down Avani's panic, taking full control as she weaved Avani's arms seductively back around the pole to hold on. She brought her legs back together and, with incredible control, rolled in a slow forward somersault down the pole and back to her feet. She barely wobbled on her high heels.

The room thundered with applause.

Hal looked like he had seen a ghost. Jeffrey shifted nervously.

Sonny gaped. "Avani?" He made for the stage, knocking into tables and customers. Food and drinks spilled everywhere.

The burly bouncer rushed over.

"*Avani*," Sonny yelled. "It's—"

The bouncer tackled him from behind, pinning his arms to his sides. Strong as he was, Sonny was no match for this man's dense, bodybuilding strength—the main reason Hal had hired him.

Sonny continued yelling Avani's name as he struggled to break free. A couple of tough-looking male customers helped the bouncer drag Sonny to the door and yelled for him to "Get lost," "Dream on," and accept that "She's not just dancin' for you, asshole."

Amber hurried backstage.

Samantha grabbed her arm. "Thought you never did this before." Her face was drawn tight.

"I haven't."

"Well, you have now." Sadness washed over. "Welcome to the club."

Amber touched Avani's hand to Samantha's belly. "You want this baby?" she whispered.

Samantha jerked back. "How did you—?"

"Meet me at your apartment. Noon tomorrow."

"Why? What do you want? You don't even know where—"

"Be there," she said, then hurried past Ginger, who flipped her off before retaking the stage.

Avani stopped at the same door she'd entered, the one leading back out to the hall. She could hear Sonny's voice as they threw him out. He wouldn't go easily, Avani knew that. He would never come to a place like this on his own, which meant he had come to see her, and to talk. She sighed.

Amber took control and turned on the charm. Sonny would have to wait.

Hal glanced up as Avani approached the bar. He looked at her perplexed and slightly fearful but also with curiosity and respect. He gestured toward the back room.

Avani found Jeffrey in his office, at his desk, trembling and clutching his empty scotch glass. She leaned in the doorway. "Well?"

Jeffrey didn't speak. He refused to look up.

Amber stepped around his desk and stood over his chair. "Now, you listen to me, son."

He froze.

"You make things right with Samantha. Honor her life and the life of your child. Save your soul from the rot that kills it."

He wheeled back and stood up. "Whatever the hell you are, get out of my club. NOW."

Amber ignored him, a mother warrior fighting to save her child. Her eyes sparked bright enough to blind him. "Meet me at Samantha's at noon tomorrow. If you don't, I'll make a scene that will scare every customer out of here, run every one of these girls to the nearest convent and close your club for good. Are we clear?"

He glared.

"Never mind the field day cops will have learning about Elaine's secret set of books. For *all* your clubs."

His brow knitted into one fierce line over scared but steely eyes. Avani braced for resistance, but he nodded—a small, almost imperceptible bob of the head.

"Good." Amber strode from the room. She led Avani up the hall to the main room, then across to the bouncer. "He still here?" she asked.

The bouncer nodded. "You know him?"

Avani looked toward the opening. "Old friend."

"Doesn't act like it."

"Long story." She sucked in a breath.

"I can go with you," he offered.

"I'll be okay."

She exhaled and stepped out into the sticky, tropical night. Purple neon bathed her skin as she walked toward Sonny in the overflow parking lot across the street. He stopped pacing when he saw her. The bouncer watched, perched on his stool and ready to help.

Avani stood opposite Sonny on the other side of his car. She softened at the bloody cut on his lip, the growing shadow of a bruise on his cheek, the penitent look in his eye.

"Tommy called me about seeing you here. I never meant to hurt you, Avani. I never meant for you to end up like … this, in a place like this. I never stopped loving you. You have to believe me. I can't—"

"Shh." She stepped closer. "This isn't your fault, Sonny. I'm not here because of you or that night." Jasmine sweetened the air, and Prism Lake flashed in her mind: the ship, the bonfire, Captain Hugh, Chief Black, the pearly spirits of those who had made mistakes and returned to set things right. Truthfully, she admired Sonny for trying to do that while still human.

"Then, why are you here?" he asked. "This isn't like you. Especially that *dance*."

She recalled those times in the barn when she'd stepped all over Sonny's teenage toes as he tried to prepare her for homecoming or prom with one of the high school boys. That must have really hurt, too, given his feelings for her. "I can't tell you," she said, "but I am safe, and you are not involved in any way."

"But … that dance."

"Part of the training," she explained. It wasn't a lie, but he didn't need more. Bass lines thumped from the club. The breeze brushed a strand of hair against her cheek. She turned slightly so it would blow behind her. "Go home, Sonny."

"No. I … I came all this way to see you. To talk. Let's have dinner or breakfast. When are you off? I can meet you somewhere."

"Go home," she said again. "I will find you."

"When?"

"Soon. I promise."

He started to say more but stopped himself. In that moment, Avani saw the kind young boy she had grown up with, the best friend who had stood by her through nine long, awkward, and yet beautiful adolescent years.

Part of her wanted to hold him, to reassure him and encourage the good she saw inside. But she couldn't. Not yet. The memories were still too fresh of his knife at her throat, his body slamming hers against the brick, his gin-curtained breath on her face.

Amber eased her with the comforting smells of pine and cedar trees and with Avani's favorite sound of horse hooves crunching on gravel.

Avani softened. "Goodbye, Sonny," she said, then started back toward the club.

"Avani?"

She stopped.

"I haven't touched a drink or hurt so much as a fly since that night. I love you. You don't have to love me back, that's okay. But please, you have to forgive me."

Amber bathed Avani with encouragement.

Avani met Sonny's eyes for the first time. "See you soon." She crossed the street with new conviction and disappeared inside Jeffrey's club for the last time.

CHAPTER SEVENTEEN

TAL

Tal stood in the alley behind Benz's Pittsburgh pawnshop once more, seeing the memory of Tucker sneaking in four months ago to get paid for Jake's death. Her face burned. The back door suddenly opened and Tal jumped behind a cluster of shrubs. Anger shifted to curiosity when a young man exited, pulling a hoodie over his face. He was short and white with a shaved head and a teardrop tattoo near his right eye. Tal had seen many such tattoos on those she'd put behind bars, especially on gang members who had lost loved ones to street violence. It's often why they'd joined the gang.

The young man looked around nervously before darting across the side street, careful to dodge puddles of streetlight.

Tal ran to the back door and stuck her foot in the opening before it closed. She scanned the dark hall inside, the bright light coming from the store area up front. Benz's form moved around up there, but she didn't hear voices. He must be alone.

She closed the door in silence and started toward him, passing a few darkened rooms along the way. Benz's office sat off to the right, the door cracked, dim light glowing from a desk lamp. A tall filing cabinet filled one corner. A partially open blind shuttered the room's one window, and metal bars covered the glass outside.

The door across the hall from his office was also cracked open, and the light from his lamp reflected off two walls inside that room, both lined with metal shelves. Tal peeked in, and her eyes adjusted enough to make out TV sets, computers, laptops, monitors, and other large electronics that filled those shelves. A few open boxes overflowed with cords and cables. The hinges creaked slightly as she slipped inside the room for a better look. Video games and controllers were stuffed into more boxes, and another set of shelves held cameras, cell phones, tablets, and chargers.

In Tal's experience as a cop, pawnshops were sad places that served only three groups of people: those who owned them, thieves and/or desperate owners who made quick cash from selling to them, and customers who bought those goods at a reduced price, just as she had in Reno when she bought the knife that nearly took her life.

Eli turned her around to face the door. Three large wooden crates sat stacked against the wall behind it. No wonder she hadn't seen them when she entered.

The two bottom crates appeared sealed, but the lid on the top crate was open and slightly ajar. She lifted it to reveal a neatly stacked pile of semi-automatic weapons. *AR-15s?* She picked one up and held it to the light coming in from the hall. *Serial number's been ground off.* She put it back and held up another. Same thing. *Completely illegal.*

That kid who left does it for him. He's part of the crew.

Eli pointed to something atop one of the shelves, and Tal brought down an angle grinder. The tool was still warm, with a round, abrasive wheel secured in place at one end, an electric cord dangling from the other.

It was one of my first jobs, too. Eli guided her hand to put it back and led her to a stack of smaller wooden crates. He made her open one filled with twenty- and twenty-five round bullet magazines, a pile of bump stocks underneath.

So, who's throwing the party? Tal asked.

No idea, Eli replied. *He sells to middlemen who resell to multiple buyers. They let him keep one or two for his own use. Like at the drug busts.*

Like you used on Jake?

Yes. Eli made her close the lid, then led Tal from the room and up the hall to the front store. Lights sparkled off glass display shelves full of porcelain statues and figurines, high-end pottery, and framed art. Other shelves held designer handbags, musical instruments, DVD players, electronics, cameras, video games, and more.

An array of cell phones, jewelry, guns, and knives filled two glass cases mounted to the floor. Tal felt again the lightweight knife she'd bought in Reno, the memory of its sharp steel blade against her wrist.

"Shit!" Benz screamed as he stood up from behind a case.

Tal jumped, too.

"What the hell are you doing here?"

"We came to talk," Eli told him.

"We already talked. I ain't supposed to see you again 'til tomorrow night." Benz unlocked the front door and opened it for Tal to leave.

"I saw one of your crew," Eli said, ignoring the gesture. "Young white kid. Hoodie. Snuck out the back."

Benz sighed and shut the door.

"Cut him loose, Benz," Eli said. "Give him a chance to fly right."

And there it was—another additional purpose. Spirits never came with just one.

Benz opened the register drawer to check the cash.

"Let this place go, too."

Benz jerked up.

Tal did, too. This spirit was asking a lot.

Benz shoved the cash back into the drawer and slammed it shut. "Look," he said, stepping out from behind the counter. "I agreed to stop the whole drug bust thing with that cop. Asshole's messed up, anyway. But I didn't say nothin' about the rest of my business. What I do to earn a living is up to me."

"Not when it hurts others," Eli stated.

He showed no judgment, nor did he back down.

Benz reached around another counter, and Tal felt certain he had a pistol stashed there for just such occasions. He didn't bring it out, but he didn't let go, either.

"This place, the drugs and guns you sell, it's all part of the darkness, Benz. You can't come clean until you walk away, leave it all behind."

"Yeah, right," Benz sneered. "That'll get me, what, fifteen to twenty if I'm lucky?"

Eli stepped closer. "Start over."

"Doing *what*?" Benz spat. "This is all I know! It's all you knew, too, Eli, until ..." he indicated Tal. "This."

Tal crossed to the case of knives. She spied a Klaw almost identical to the one she had used in Reno. "You're just the seller, right? Doing the public a service by making expensive things affordable."

"Right," Benz said, his gold tooth twinkling.

Tal pulled back her sleeves to expose both wrists and the white scars slicing her brown skin. "I lost everything the night Jake died." Her eyes drilled into his. "A pawnshop was my last stop, too."

Benz looked down. His arm relaxed from where the gun must be hidden.

"That owner just made another sale, too, right? Just stuffed another bill inside his drawer. He may have suspected what I was up to, given the state I was in and how I must have looked, but he didn't care. Why should he, right? It's just business."

She paused. "If I'd had to work harder to get that knife, to find a place that would not sell it to me so easily, to find a person who would not just let me walk out without any question or concern, then I may not have done this."

"You survived," Benz said, scrambling for some kind of reply.

"I was lucky."

A car backfired outside. He jumped and caught himself. "So what happened?" he asked, trying to sound brave. "How'd you get hooked up with Eli and all this ghost shit?"

"Spirits."

"Whatever."

Eli stepped Tal closer. "Don't change the subject, Benz. You're not just selling someone else's stuff. You're profiting from loss and heartache you'll never see." He leaned in. "Walk from this darkness. Turn yourself in at the bust. Start over."

Benz stumbled back. "I'm not doing time again. No way. I'll help you with that cop, then I'm out."

"You're better than that," Eli told him. "Better than all of this."

"Get out," Benz snapped.

"Not until you promise to leave this."

"I'm not going anywhere. Leave me alone."

"You don't want this. You never did."

A car turned into the alley and parked in Benz's back lot. The engine shut off. Two car doors opened and closed.

Benz went rigid. "I did what I had to," he yelled. "Now GO."

Gun dealers, Eli said.

In Tal's experience, gun dealers were among the most ruthless, violent, and uncaring criminals. *We should go*, she replied. *He's too scared to listen now, anyway.*

Eli rooted her and put a hand on Benz's shoulder. "Tell them no."

Benz's mouth fell open. "You shittin' me, man? They don't hear that word. You know that."

Three distinct knocks came from the back. Benz froze. "GO," he hissed, jabbing a finger toward the front door. "Get out while you can." He disappeared down the back hall.

Tal's head swam. *If they see me*, she said. *If they recognize me or think I can ID them—*

They won't.

Eli had cut his young teeth on places like this, with people like Benz and these buyers. He knew the deals they brokered, the lives they cast aside. He knew *exactly* what they were getting into, and he was here to stop it. That scared Tal more than anything. *What if they kill me before I can grab the coin? You'll be trapped.*

It's what Aaron had tried to do by crashing that plane with Eric's rogue spirit inside. He had no idea of Eric's strength, however, or that his spirit would try to use Aaron's shattered body to escape. Thank God Aaron had called Sam, Blaze's chip had tracked where he was, Liam had notified the Spirit Guard, and they had returned Eric to the other side. Eli may not fare as well if Tal died, especially if no one knew about it.

We'll be fine. Eli eddied like a warm current, then ducked Tal back and out of sight.

She could just see Benz open the door. Two male figures stepped inside, their bodies silhouetted in the dim light from Benz's office.

Their harsh voices sounded young, probably in their late twenties or early thirties. And they wore suits. Tal recognized the squeaking hinges when Benz opened the door to the room with the guns.

Eli started down the hall.

What are you doing? She hissed, clutching a counter.

He freed her hands and kept walking.

They will kill us.

Trust me.

To do what?

He guided her toward the voices. Tal recognized the sound of wooden crates being opened, of metal guns, clips, and stocks being checked.

"All here. Plus an extra box of ammo on the house," Benz said.

"Serial numbers?" one man asked.

"All erased." Benz's voice cracked slightly. He cleared his throat. "Ain't my first time, you know."

"First with us," the second man said.

Eli inched Tal closer as the wooden lids were hammered back into place.

"Come on," the second man continued. "Give us a hand."

Tal hid inside the nearest open door as the two men carried one of the heavy crates from the room. They opened the back door, and she could just make out their features in the streetlight. Both were white, tall, and thickly muscled. One was bald.

They didn't see her, but Benz did as he exited the room carrying two boxes of ammo and bump stocks. He almost dropped them.

"Careful with that, asswipe," the bald man scolded.

Benz shook his head as Eli walked toward them, putting Tal's body in silhouette against the front room light.

"What the fuck?" the bald one yelled. Both men lowered the crates to grab their guns. "You said we were alone."

"Doesn't matter," the other replied, leveling his weapon at Tal. "She's seen us. She can—" He paused. Recognition soured his face. "Wait. I know her. That bitch is a *cop*." He turned on Benz. "You settin' us up?"

"No! I'm not. I didn't know she was—"

The bald man stuck his gun in Benz's face. "Gainz told us you were good."

"I am," Benz replied, shaking. "I didn't know, I can't—"

"You need to go," Eli told the men, his voice bold in Tal's. "Leave the guns, leave the business. Choose something that helps others."

Both men started to laugh when bolts of green light shot from Tal's eyes. The men scrambled for the door, but a strong wind met them from outside and forced them back in. They tripped over the crates.

"What the hell is going on, Benz?" the bald one asked. "Who is this bitch?"

Eli stepped Tal closer. "Leave this darkness," he told them.

The bald man aimed, hand shaking. "Get back."

Beams of green light momentarily blinded him. A gust of wind knocked the gun from his hand. Both men ran for the door a second time, but another gale pushed them back in. They landed in a heap near Benz. The wind stopped, and a tall figure with broad shoulders blocked the rear exit. Caspian.

Tal grinned. "Jake!"

"You beckoned?"

Did we?

Eli warmed.

Tal had no idea spirits could communicate with one another outside their vessels.

"Leave the guns and go," Eli commanded. "And never return."

Terrified, the bald man reached for his fallen gun, but Jake kicked up another breeze that sent it skidding across the floor. Tal kicked it behind her and picked up the second man's gun.

Tal and Caspian lifted their hands, and their spirits fired a torrent of energy through them that tore the lids off each crate, twisted the rifles like pipe cleaners, crumpled the bump stocks, and crushed the boxes of ammo into harmless scrap.

The two dealers quaked. Benz was a puddle.

"You don't want this." Jake's voice thundered.

"Leave this and live," Eli added. "Or die in the darkness."

The men clambered for the door, but Jake blocked them. "We will know," he said, then stepped Caspian aside.

The men dashed to their car and slammed the doors. The engine roared to life, and the tires squealed as the car sped from the alley in reverse.

Caspian closed the rear door and sandwiched Benz between him and Tal.

"W-who is that?" Benz pointed a quivering finger at Caspian.

"The human is Caspian, a fellow vessel," Tal replied. "The

spirit inside him is my partner, Jake. The one Eli killed."

Benz fell to his knees. "Oh God, oh God, oh God, oh God …" he cried. "Don't hurt me. I'm sorry. Oh God, I'm sorry. Please don't hurt me."

He hunkered on the floor, arms over his head until Tal and Caspian lifted him up.

"Please," he begged, legs like noodles underneath him.

"Breathe," Jake instructed.

Benz did. Several times. "I'm sorry, man. Tucker made me do it. He said you knew everything. That you'd turn him in and shut us down."

"Wait. You mean …" Tal stammered, her mind scrambling to catch up. "You mean Jake was the target all along?"

Benz nodded feebly. "You were, too. Tucker was afraid you'd find out. But Jake already knew."

Tal looked at Jake's shimmering essence. "Why didn't you tell me? At the bar, after I saw him."

"Doesn't matter now, Tallon. We're all here for the same thing, and we do it together."

Tal was lost for words, but Eli pulsed a few times and turned her to Benz. "Did Tucker drop off the body armor?"

Benz bobbled a nod.

"Good." Eli leaned close. "You see this bust through tomorrow night, Benz, then turn yourself in and leave it all behind. The shop, the drugs, the guns, everything."

"I-It's not that easy," Benz said, shifting like a bird on razor wire. "Too many people know me. They rely on me. Th-They'll kill me."

"You're dead already," Eli told him. "Leaving this is your chance to live."

Benz looked down and nodded slightly. Tal wondered if he'd really be able to give this up or if he was just pretending to agree until this nightmare was over.

Eli threw open some kind of window in Tal, an internal brightness and vibration that sparked her tattoo and allowed her to *feel* Benz the way the spirit did. That's how she knew Benz's nod was for real. A brightness was growing. His long-buried desire to get out of this life was starting to rise against the delusions of wealth and power that had entombed it. Benz was petrified, but also hopeful for the first time. The vibration subsided. The window closed.

Tal and Caspian let go, and Benz stood on his own.

"See you tomorrow night," Eli told him before he grabbed Caspian's arm and whirled them off in a gust of emerald light.

CHAPTER EIGHTEEN

LINK

Link's cells and tissue regrouped inside Blaze's office. The ship did not return for another night, and he wanted to get a jump on asking Blaze to help him find the bullet at Tricia Martin's house.

But the room was dark, the lights were off in the hallway, and no voices carried from the clinic or lobby. He reached for the light, but something told him to wait. He let his eyes adjust and took a closer look around. Blaze's office was clean, and tidy.

Something is definitely wrong, he told Teddy, then noticed the desktop flipped over to hide Blaze's computer and hard drive. *Inspectors. Had to be.* This shelter had been in those crosshairs lately. Sam said it was the governor, but Link feared it might somehow be him.

He turned to leave the room, but light pierced the dark hall, and Link ducked. Footsteps grew louder, and a police officer walked by the door. He paused briefly to shine his light around the room, flicking it across the shelves, the files, and the desk before moving on toward the lobby.

Link crawled out from his hiding place in the corner, grateful the cop didn't turn on the overhead, or he'd have been toast. He peeked out the window blinds toward the back of the building. Another cop sat in his car outside, eyes glued to his phone.

Link tiptoed toward the hall and listened. The officer's footsteps faded until the entry door opened and closed. A lock turned. Then silence.

Where is everyone? Link asked. *Do you know? Can you tell?*

No. But I do feel a presence, Teddy replied. *That way.* He turned Link toward the distant soup kitchen. Sam must have convinced them to at least leave that open.

Link dug out his phone. *I'll text Blaze. He may already know we're here.*

He barely opened the app when a flashlight blinded him. He yelped and stumbled back, throwing up both arms to shield his eyes. The phone tumbled from his hand.

A figure snatched it from the floor. "Who are you?" a girl demanded. She sounded young. "How'd you get in here?"

"Turn that off!"

She lowered the beam, but only to his chest, careful to keep herself in silhouette.

Black spots burst across his retinas. "Who are you?" he snapped. "Where's Sam? And Blaze?"

Sight returned enough for him to make out her shadowy form. She was short, wore dark clothes, and had a hoodie pulled low over her face. A nose ring glinted.

"You first," she demanded.

Link swallowed, choosing his words. "My name is Link. I live here."

"How'd you get past the cops?"

Link thought a moment, then nodded toward the window. "I

snuck in. Cop was on his phone." It wasn't a lie.

She clicked off the light and fingered open a blind.

The cop was still on his phone. Link exhaled gratefully.

She stepped back. "Inspectors came and closed it down. They made everyone leave." She paused. "Where were you? And how did you not know that?"

"Who are you?" Link asked. "How'd you get in?"

She smirked but remained silent.

Maybe she was some homeless girl who'd found a way in, trying to steal what she could between police rounds. Link cleared his throat. "Where did they go?"

She smiled, cunning. "First, tell me how you *really* got in. I saw a green light."

Dammit.

Go, Teddy said. *We'll use the coin. Your Spirit Guard will come.*

Link hesitated, inching closer to the door. Then, he shoved past her and sprinted out.

"Hey!" she yelled, chasing after him.

Link hurried two doors down to Doc's office across the hall. He closed the door and reached for the lock but—*crap.* Doc couldn't have locks per state law. Only the cabinets could be locked. He leaned hard against it as the girl grabbed the handle from outside.

"Hey! Let me in," she said, keeping her volume down.

His eyes landed on the heavy cooler Doc used to store blood. It was open and empty, most likely from the inspection, but still heavy. He held the door with his hips and dragged the cooler over, then quickly stepped aside and shoved it into place. He leaned against it and reached into his pocket for the coin. Ten seconds was all he needed.

His fingers barely wrapped around the metal when the door pushed open. He turned enough for the flashlight to blind him again.

He yelped and fell back, flinging the coin as he covered his eyes. It bounced loudly across the concrete floor.

She must have heard it, because she barged in and pointed the light in that direction. The coin rolled to a corner and glinted in its beam.

Get it. Now. Teddy's sense of urgency made Link nervous.

He lunged, but the girl got there first and scooped it into her fist. She blinded him again with the light.

"Stop it!" he shouted, burying his head in his arms.

"What is this?" she asked. "It's weird."

Get it back.

"It's, uh … a family heirloom," he said. "I keep it for luck."

NOW.

"Give it back." He softened his voice in an attempt to win her trust. "Please." He stepped closer. "I can show you what it means."

He held out his hand, so it almost touched hers. She trembled slightly. The coin glowed in her grip. Link was stunned. She wasn't a vessel, or her tattoo would have shimmered. So who was she? And what was happening?

Help me, a voice whispered to Malina. Was that from the coin?

Was it speaking to her? This boy, Link, didn't seem to hear it.

Malina was terrified, but she also felt a surge of incredible power from the coin, like it *needed* her.

Link grabbed for it, but she blinded him with the light again and ran out to the hall.

That's it, the voice said. *Hold it a few seconds more.*

Power swelled, and with it, a rising hatred for this boy she didn't even know. She ran, but a foot tripped her, and the coin flew from her hand. It barely hit the floor when Link scooped it up and shoved it back in his pocket.

Green light shimmered in his eyes. She blinked and looked again, but it had disappeared. The feeling of power drained, too, and the coin voice went away. Her hatred softened, but indignation took its place. Link had deprived her of whatever that coin needed, and she wanted it back.

Her eyes adjusted in the dark hall, and she could make out the lean but muscular torso under Link's T-shirt and jacket. His hair was short, and he had smooth skin. No beard. Her interest piqued in spite of her anger.

He extended a hand. "Sorry. You okay?"

She took it and nodded, attraction amplifying with his touch. "How did you *really* get in?"

"You first," he said.

His voice was deeper than she expected, and his Adam's apple slid up and down his throat as he talked. Rounded collarbones formed a perfect shallow dip at the base of his neck. She held up a key.

"You stole Sam's key?" He must have recognized the Chicago keychain.

"I borrowed it."

"How'd you get that? Where is Sam?"

"Tell me about that coin," she pressed.

"Not until I know about about Sam. Did the inspectors close this place?"

She crossed her arms and leaned back. "What is it? What does it do?"

He studied her briefly and leaned in.

Heat from his body shot tingles through hers. She was torn between shining the light in his eyes and kissing his soft, open mouth. "Who *are* you?" she asked again.

He tilted her chin toward his lips. Her breath caught in anticipation. Then he raced off.

Link dashed past the lobby and down the first-floor hall toward Sam's room. Her footsteps followed.

She's more scared than you are, Teddy assured him.

Link reached for Sam's door. The man never locked it unless he was changing or asleep. Link held his breath. It opened. He darted inside.

He spun around to close it, but the girl squeezed through.

"Well?" she asked, breathing hard from the exertion. "Do you want to know where they went or not?"

Link ignored her and looked around Sam's room. His drafting table was littered with plans, and shelter paperwork and bills covered the desk. Link opened the biggest drawer. Files had been rifled through, but those for the vessels Sam had hidden in back were untouched.

"Talk to me!" she demanded. "Or I'll scream."

Link closed the drawer, unsure what to do next. Teddy stepped in.

"What's your name?" the spirit asked.

She frowned at the change in Link's voice. "What is that? Why do you sound different?"

"Who are you?" Teddy pressed, flaring green again inside Link's eyes.

"M-Malina," she said. "Sam's granddaughter."

That threw him. Link didn't know the whole story but had heard enough to know Sam was estranged from his two grown kids. He had never met his grandkids.

"How'd you really get in here?" Malina asked. "What was that green light? And why do you have that coin?"

"I just want to know where they went so I can join them."

She bristled. "Sam is with Doc and Blaze at a warehouse not far from here. I can take you, but first ..." She bravely stepped closer. "Why did your coin talk to me? A weird, whispery voice. Who is it?"

Fear coiled in Link's stomach. Teddy shot a chill up his spine. *What is it?* Link asked.

Not sure, Teddy replied, *but the connection may still be active. She cannot touch it again, no matter what.*

"What, um, did it say?" Link asked, trying to sound normal.

"Tell me what it is," she replied. "And what it's for."

Link reached in his pocket and held the coin loosely against his palm. No voice came, so he let go. He only needed ten seconds for Liam to come and take him to Sam, but he couldn't risk Malina seeing that.

"I'll tell you about the coin," he countered, "but I need my phone."

She looked surprised, like she had forgotten about it, then dug it from a back pocket and handed it over.

"Thanks. Now turn around, close your eyes and count to twenty."

"You think I'm an idiot?" She stared holes into him.

"I can't leave—you have the door blocked. I just need to do something, and you can't see what." He paused, flirtatious. "Not yet."

Her breath caught again.

He held her gaze and gently turned her around.

"One, two, three …" she began.

He checked his phone and sighed relief. Blaze must have been tracking him because he'd texted a new address. That meant Teddy could transport them, after all. Link stashed the coin back in his pocket.

"Eleven, twelve, thirteen …" Malina continued.

"Keep your eyes closed." He took several steps back, and the wind gusted. Link braced to vaporize when Malina turned around and jumped, joining her body to his as the room disappeared.

CHAPTER NINETEEN

AVANI

"He won't come," Samantha said, stirring a pot of jambalaya that filled her Miami Beach apartment with the succulent smells of shrimp, onion, celery, and cayenne.

Avani resisted her gnawing hunger pains and looked around. Samantha obviously liked to cook. The compact kitchen was well stocked with appliances and a full spice rack. A planter of fragrant herbs lifted feathery stems toward the bright kitchen window.

In the adjacent room, Avani perched on a burgundy fabric couch where she could see Samantha and the front door at the same time. The apartment was clean and comfortable. The walls were painted white and mostly bare, save one near the kitchen. It bore a large, framed New Orleans Mardi Gras poster. A collection of colorful masks surrounded it on all sides, and strings of colorful beads draped one corner.

Samantha tapped the spoon on the pot. "I don't know what you're thinking, but he doesn't care enough to—"

A knock stopped her. She turned off the burner and peered out the blind. "Oh my God," she whispered. "He came."

Amber warmed. Avani held her breath.

Samantha opened the door, and Jeffrey stormed in. He walked straight over to Avani. "Okay," he snapped. "I'm here. What the hell do you want?"

"I'd like to know, too," Samantha said, closing the door and glancing between them.

"Sit down," Amber told Jeffrey, her voice turning Avani's husky and deep.

Samantha paused at the change.

Amber patted the couch next to her, and Jeffrey hesitated but sat, careful to keep space between them.

Amber took his hand. "You were not abandoned, Jeffrey," she told him. "It was never your fault." He tried to pull away, but her grip was too strong. "I gave you up because I was reckless and weak. You needed a better mother, someone who could give you security, a real home."

Samantha gasped and dropped into a burgundy chair that matched the couch.

"But I never stopped loving you," Amber continued. "I love you still."

Jeffrey glared through angry tears. "Doesn't matter now, does it?"

"Actually—it does. In fact, love is what matters most. You have a chance to start over. To make things right with your own family."

Samantha nearly fell over.

"Shut up!" He yelled and yanked against her grip. It didn't work. "Let go."

Amber stood and pulled him to his feet. She held out her other hand to Samantha.

Samantha protectively cradled her belly.

The spirit shimmered in Avani's eyes until Samantha rose on wobbly legs.

"Look at her," Amber told her son.

He looked down, around, anywhere but at Samantha.

"*Look* at her," Amber commanded.

Jeffrey lifted his eyes from floor to sofa to wall, past Samantha's belly, and, finally, to her face.

"Her eyes," Amber instructed.

He took a breath and met Samantha's frightened gaze.

"Good."

Amber joined their hands, and a million tiny volts exploded in Avani. The tattoo burned under her jeans like a bag of jewels. Her senses magnified, so a bird outside took wing like a small jet, and the Mardi Gras poster and beads burst into a blinding array of color. The experience was more intense than any Avani had felt before. Then again, she had never helped a spirit connect two outside circuits at once like this. Three with Samantha's unborn child.

Amber's energy soon ebbed, and normalcy returned. Samantha and Jeffrey collapsed onto the couch next to each other. Neither moved. They barely blinked.

Amber kneeled by Jeffrey and took his hand.

"I am sorry for what I did, son," she told him, "and I ask your forgiveness. But don't make my mistakes. Samantha, this child, their love—that is your most valuable treasure. Some people search their whole lives and never find it. Don't throw it away."

Samantha tried not to cry.

"Is it true?" Jeffrey asked her. "You … love me?"

Samantha held her belly and slowly looked up to meet his gaze. She nodded.

"But how?" he asked. "I don't, I'm not, I'm—"

"You're different when we're alone," she said. "Not the Jeffrey you pretend to be at work. You're kind and funny, and … you care." She pointed to the scar under her jaw. "You saved me from the monster who did this."

So he didn't cause that? Avani was stunned.

Amber tingled happily. Of course, she had known. She was waiting for Avani to catch up, to drop her bias and see the good inside. Like with Sonny.

"You were happy, too, when I first told you about the baby. Before you pulled away and told me to get rid of it." Samantha paused. "I knew you didn't really feel that way." She looked down briefly. "Hal knew, too. He's the one who told me to wait."

The tiniest smile turned Jeffrey's lips. "Hal's known me my whole life. Knew her, too." He pointed at Avani, at Amber. "It was just easier to push him away and keep everyone back. To stay alone."

"And unloved," the spirit said. "The way you thought I'd felt about you."

His eyes fell to the floor.

Amber lifted his chin. "Clinging to anger, hurt, and betrayal destroys everyone involved. It's time to let that go, Jeffrey. Forgive me, forgive yourself, and start over with your family."

She placed his hand over Samantha's on her belly. Jeffrey sobbed without warning or control, and years of desolation, guilt, and hatred poured out. He fell into Samantha's arms. She stroked his hair, kissed his forehead, and held him close.

Amber reopened the same spiritual window Avani had peered through earlier at the club. Samantha and her baby glowed even brighter. And the sliver of Jeffrey's soul, once buried in mud, had tripled in size already. Redemption, rebirth, and second chances were taking place right in front of her, and they held the promise of things to come.

The vision ended, and Amber placed a hand on Jeffrey's shoulder. "I love you, son." Her words dissolved with the wind and light that swept Avani away.

A single strand of LED Christmas lights strung along one wall brightened the stable just enough for Avani to see. The spirit had swirled her back into flesh and bone outside the corral on this North California dude ranch where Avani had lived. Now, she walked down the line of stalls to greet the various horses she had raised and trained over the last nine years before she'd left. Avani stroked their long noses and necks as they stuck their heads over the stall doors to neigh hello.

Sampson pranced and snorted in the back stall. He tossed his long black mane in anticipation until Avani opened the latch and ran inside. She threw her arms around his thick Friesian neck, and he leaned in for their hug. His coat and mane matched the inky midnight black of her hair.

"I've missed you, too, boy." She rubbed the withers where his broad shoulders met his muscled neck. "How about a ride?"

He snorted. His feathery hooves danced on the hay.

She grabbed a set of reins from a nearby hook, and he lowered his head for her to put them on. She placed a thick wool blanket on his back. "That'll do for tonight."

"Want some company?"

Avani wheeled around to find Sonny standing about ten feet

away, his fair hair catching in the light. She stepped deeper into Sampson's stall. "How did you know I was here?"

"I didn't," he said, standing perfectly still. "Until now. I was sitting on the porch when I saw this flash of green light by the barn. I came to check it out and heard the horses. They only whinny like that for one person." He paused. "How did you get here?"

Avani looked down.

"Did that light have something to do with it?"

Avani toyed with Sampson's mane. She had not planned on seeing Sonny yet. She'd wanted a ride first to clear her head, but perhaps it was better to jump right in. Besides, they'd always shared a love of horses. Talking on a ride might make things easier.

Amber pulsed with affirmation.

"So, is it okay if I come along?" he asked, hesitant.

At that moment, Avani saw the boy she had grown up with, the best friend who had shown her the ropes of leading trail rides and handling guests, cleaning and feeding the horses, digging rocks out of their shoes, and mucking their stalls.

"We're going to Raptor Ridge," she said at last.

Sonny grinned and grabbed another set of reins. He opened the stall to a Mustang with brown and white patches, a pinto he had favored since its arrival as a rescue.

"Hey, Rock Star," he said. "Wanna take a ride?" The horse snorted happily, and Sonny deftly buckled the reins.

Avani felt that same excitement leading Sampson from his stall. She was anxious to ride again and to be back in this place she had loved. As she passed Sonny strapping on his horse's saddle, the spirit allowed her to feel him, his goodness, as much as see him. There was no hidden agenda or ill intent, nothing that would hurt her again. This must be the same way animals sensed good or bad in people, a kind of sixth sense where they knew instinctively, immediately, if they were safe or in danger.

Sonny followed her outside. The night glittered with stars as it had so often on their midnight rides together. Avani had named *Sampson* for his power and size, as well as for his long mane that hung halfway down his legs, a mane she was thrilled to see had not been trimmed in her absence. Rock Star had earned his name after climbing down a narrow, mud-slicked mountain trail one night after a freak rainstorm had forced them back to the stable. Sonny, though scared to death of this young horse that had just arrived, sat cool and collected in the saddle, letting go and trusting the horse's instincts from cutting his coltish hooves in the mountains of Colorado. After that, Rock Star became Sonny's favorite.

Sonny cupped his hands next to Sampson's belly. Avani hesitated before placing her left foot into his stirrup of fingers. She held onto his shoulder for balance, and the touch sent sparks through her. She quickly tossed her right leg over Sampson's wide back and let go. She sat up on the wool blanket and collected herself as Sonny climbed into Rock Star's saddle.

"Ready?" he asked.

The breeze blew Avani's long hair from her face. She smiled, nudged Sampson's ribs with one heel, and took off up the dirt path.

The horses knew the route as well as their riders, maybe better. Both animals jumped easily over fallen logs and galloped up grassy slopes and across fields until they reached a small meadow overlooking a narrow canyon below.

Raptor Ridge.

The beauty and quiet amazed Avani every time. A lake anchored the middle of the canyon. Black oak and maple trees climbed up all sides, and a herd of deer grazed on one slope.

THE COIN

Moonlight painted the whole thing silver and white.

By day, this valley was filled with eagles, ospreys, and a variety of hawks riding the vectors to hunt. But now, coyotes howled from the valley, an owl hooted from a nearby copse of trees, and Avani soaked in the smells of rich, untouched earth and clean air. She had ridden here many times at night with her mom, Lani, as well, after the dude ranch was quiet and everyone was asleep. Lani would harvest a few nearby plants. Some were for cooking, while others for medicine, and still more went to make dyes for the Navajo blankets she wove. Before she died, Lani had asked to be cremated and have her ashes sprinkled here along with those of Avani's father. Sonny had come with her the night Avani honored that request. His comfort, friendship, and support got her through.

"Sampson and I take midnight rides here sometimes," he told her, looking out over the canyon. "We camp out. Roast marshmallows. Talk about you."

That night, after they'd sprinkled the ashes, Sonny had built a fire inside an old ring of stones everyone used. He and Avani had roasted marshmallows and shared stories of Lani, her arrival with young Avani, the ranch, and their years of life together. She and Sonny had shared their first kiss that night, and his touch had ignited feelings Avani did not know she had. The intensity grew, and they both had wanted more, but Avani feared the places it might lead and the commitment and expectations it would create, so she had pulled away and ridden off. It was one of the hardest things she'd ever done, but it turned out to be for the best.

Sonny, already in love with her, fell over the edge with frustration. She avoided him to try and make things easier, but his hunger grew, and he could no longer settle for friendship. His growing frustration and sense of loss finally cracked open that night in Reno, after they had taken care of the new horse, after they had celebrated her birthday, after she had rejected him yet again.

She cut a sidelong glance at Sonny now, his chiseled features, his pensive eyes.

Avani cleared her throat and shifted on Sampson's back. "I cannot tell you what I'm doing, Sonny, where I do it, or why. But it's something good. And I'm happy."

"Working at a strip club?" He didn't try to hide the sarcasm.

"No. That was just … temporary. But it's over now, and soon I'll be off on a different job. Somewhere else."

"Why? What do you do? And does it have something to do with that weird light?"

A coyote howled from the canyon. Avani's hair played on the breeze. "I can't explain it," she told him. "You just have to know it's okay. I'm okay. I'm safe and happy."

The leather saddle creaked as he shifted. "Is there someone else?"

Leaves rustled around them. "No."

He studied the reins in his hand. "Will you ever come back? To live here, I mean?"

That was it, the thing Sonny cared about most. "No," she said as softly as she could.

The word sliced, anyway. He nodded, eyes fixed on his saddle.

It's time, the spirit told her.

Avani took a breath and blew it out. "I need to tell you something." She chewed her lip. Why were these words so hard to say?

He looked up.

Amber surged with encouragement. The tattoo heated.

Avani sat straighter. Her body felt lighter like chains had

broken free.

"I need to tell you that, um … " She squirmed slightly. "That I, um …" She steeled her nerve and met his eye. "That I forgive you."

Sonny's mouth dropped open.

"What you did to me that night was unimaginable. You lost control and forced your will on another person. That cannot happen again. Ever. To anyone. Understand?"

He nodded, slack-jawed.

Forgiveness blazed. The sensation was powerful and humbling in equal measure. "You're a good man," Avani continued. "And I know that wasn't you that night, not the *real* you. But I was devastated and betrayed, and, honestly, hating you felt *good*."

The words cut, but he did not look away.

"I was wrong."

"No Avani," he said at last. "It was me, all me. I—"

"Forgiveness is not a pass, or an excuse, or a way to let someone off the hook," she continued quickly before losing her nerve. "But anger and hate are wrong, too. They keep you from healing, and they blind you to the good still there. So …" She sat up taller. "I forgive you."

He blinked at her several times before his shoulders began to shake. Tears rolled down his cheeks.

She nudged Sampson closer and leaned over to hug him. He lifted his arms to circle her waist, and they held each other a long time before he let go and leaned back.

"I'm so sorry," he said, drying his eyes on his sleeve. "I was an idiot and a coward, and I have hated myself every second since." He toyed with the reins. "I love you."

She brushed back a piece of his hair. "I love you, too, Sonny.

You're still my closest friend."

"Will I see you again?"

"Absolutely. You have my horse." She waited for him to smile, then turned Sampson around and nudged him into a trot down the grassy slope. The night air quickened her breath, and the smells of earth, pine and fir stirred her soul. She leaned over Sampson's neck. "What do you say, boy? One more before I go?"

She squeezed his belly with her thighs, and Sampson took off, mane flying and hooves pounding. They launched on wings of air into the night.

CHAPTER TWENTY

TAL

A church? Seriously? Tal grumbled as she ducked into shadow near one brick wall. Parts of the Pittsburgh skyline loomed in the distance. The arched, wooden church doors were sealed with thick chains and a rusted lock. A large, round, stained glass window was mounted over the doorway with colorful, cracked shards missing from inside the lead frame. Twin spires anchored either side of the entry, their tapered wood frames showing through under the brick.

Benz's idea, Eli said. *Dark. Empty. Closed for decades.*

And Catholic.

Maybe that will help.

Tal doubted it. Tucker had been a devout Catholic his whole life, but it didn't stop him from having affairs or moving out on his wife and kids. It did keep him from getting divorced, however, so he could live under the pretense of marriage and let his wife stay loyal and tethered and do all the work.

The spirit chastised her with a blast of heat.

Sorry. She stifled her other vindictive thoughts. Tucker had often talked about attending this K-12th grade All Saints Catholic

Church & School as a kid. It was built in the late 1800s, and his kids had been among the last to graduate before it closed. Maybe it would be a way to reach him.

A green light flared behind the building, and Tal hurried over, hugging the dense bushes that bordered this side of the building with its two-story school, and long, outside wall of broken windows. Vines crept out from inside.

Caspian hid by a rear door leading into the school. It was covered by shadow and overgrown hedge. "Where do we meet Benz?" he whispered.

He'd barely finished asking when headlights split the darkness and a black Mercedes turned into the rear parking lot.

"I think that answers it," Tal replied. This whole night had her on edge, probably because she feared something happening to Eli. Or Caspian. She'd had a similar feeling the night Jake died.

Jake made Caspian squeeze her hand. The touch calmed her.

Benz parked near the building and turned off his lights. The purring engine went silent, and he stepped out from behind the wheel. Another young black man who looked all of eighteen got out on the other side.

The young man stopped in his tracks at Tal and Caspian, but Benz gave him a flashlight, a folding table, and two small duffel bags. He broke a pane of glass to unlock the rear door, and sent him inside.

Tal recognized the kid from the party that night, one of Benz's mules. She glared.

"Don't worry," he said. "I'm cuttin' him loose. Got him a job in Ohio and some money. He's taking his mom and sisters and startin' over."

Tal had her doubts, but Eli warmed and patted Benz's

shoulder. It must be true.

Benz plucked two Kevlar police vests and black facemasks from the trunk.

Caspian took his, but Tal hesitated, thinking of Jake, the holes blown into his vest by Eli's bullets.

Be here now, Eli told her. *This moment only.*

She forced a few breaths—in, out, in, out—then strapped on the vest. Caspian did the same. Both pulled the masks over their faces until only their eyes and lips showed.

"Sadly, you make that look good," she told him.

Caspian smiled.

Benz held out two semi-automatic rifles.

They didn't budge.

"Blanks," he assured. "Loaded them myself."

Tal and Caspian took them. They only had to wield them long enough to make Tucker listen.

Good luck with that, Tal thought.

We got this, Tallon, Jake replied. *You and me. Together again, yeah?*

Tal hadn't meant to share that worry, but human thoughts and concerns were open books to the spirits. They heard everything. Jake put Caspian's arm around her shoulder. She smiled. The breeze cooled her skin inside the mask.

Benz closed the car door but did not lock it. Tal wondered why until the young man returned and Benz handed him the keys.

"Don't let me catch you doing this again," Benz told him. "Not for anyone, you hear?"

The young man nodded, and Benz gave him a fleeting, paternal-like hug before ushering him behind the wheel. The boy cast a parting, anxious look at Caspian and Tal in their masks, then started the engine and drove away.

"Won't you need that?" Tal pointed to the retreating car.

Benz smiled, sad. "Not for a while. Oh. And make sure Tucker sees you and the guns before you go in." He slipped through the same rear door and disappeared inside.

So that's how it happened, Tal thought. She had seen both gunmen that night, but she'd been so shocked by their presence, so focused on following them, she hadn't paid attention to much else. Jake was as surprised about them as she was. Dave, too. Tucker was the only one who did not seem concerned. He just kept snipping at Tal through the headset. He was closest to the door. He must have seen them go in. If she had just paid more attention. If she had just—

Don't, Tallon, Jake said. *We couldn't have known.*

Tucker had immediately, and loudly, blamed Tal for going in too soon and causing Jake's death—no doubt his retaliation for her having survived. Chief Demmings had taken her gun and badge and put her on leave pending an investigation that she knew would end her career. Tucker had accomplished his goal: remove Jake, who knew about his gambling and embezzlement, and keep Tal from looking into it.

Now, he was planning the same for Dave.

Another wave of anger swelled but Eli cut it off. *Stay focused,* he told her, pumping endorphins to steady her nerves. *It ends tonight.*

Caspian rolled his shoulders and neck. Jake must have shot him full of the same encouragement.

It wasn't long before two unmarked police vehicles drove up to the church, sirens off and headlights dark. One unit parked on the street alongside the school. The other, with Tucker at the wheel, pulled into the rear parking lot near where Benz's car had been moments earlier.

Tal and Caspian edged deeper into shadow as Tucker and his partner Dave stepped out. Tucker looked around, no doubt searching for Benz's car.

All right, Tal said, ensuring her mask covered her face. *Let's get this party started.*

Easy, Tallon, Jake replied as he eased Caspian toward the rear door.

Tal relaxed, and Eli took over.

Two more cops from the other car joined them. Tucker glanced at the rear entry.

Tal hesitated just long enough for him to see her and Caspian slip inside.

They ran down a hallway of abandoned classrooms toward the distant nave. They hurried through another set of doors that had been propped open, probably by Benz, into an open, three-story sanctuary once filled with pews and an altar. Rows of marble columns stood like soldiers on either side, chipped, scarred, and tagged with gang graffiti. Broken and weathered boards squeaked underfoot, and dust swirled in shafts of colored moonlight that spilled through the tops of partially boarded stained glass windows on either side of the room.

Benz stood in front of the arched wooden entry doors. The stained-glass window hung over his head like a fragmented halo. The two duffel bags sat open on the folding table.

Benz gestured, and Tal and Caspian ducked behind the two columns on either side of him. It was the same setup Benz had used the night Jake was killed.

Footsteps echoed softly from the back hall, then the nave. Tal braced herself as all four officers stepped through the sanctuary doors, Dave in front.

"Police, freeze!" he shouted at Benz. Pigeons took wing, warbling their discontent.

Benz held up his hands. Dave started over with a pair of handcuffs.

Tucker's eyes darted around the room before landing again on Benz. Tucker nodded slightly, and Benz gestured almost imperceptibly to Tal and Caspian—the same subtle cues Tal had missed before.

She and Caspian stepped out from behind the columns, weapons leveled.

Dave spun around. The other two cops did, as well. But Tucker backed up, easing behind the others.

Tal seethed. That's what he must have done at the warehouse, too, staying well behind her and Jake as he offered them up as targets.

Tucker nodded again, but the gunmen lowered their weapons and removed their masks.

"Tal?" Dave asked, thunderstruck.

Tucker lurched back, stunned and angry. Sweat sheened on his face.

"It's over, Tucker," Tal said, her voice more confident than she felt, thanks to Eli. "Time to end this."

All eyes turned to Tucker. He inched toward the exit, hate oozing toward Tal.

"End what?" Dave asked, gun still on Benz. "What's she talking about?"

"The night Jake was killed," Tal replied. "Tucker planned the whole thing, working with Benz to make sure Jake died. I was a target, too, but Jake saved me." She stepped in Tucker's direction. "Tonight was your night, Dave. You must have found out about him, too."

"Tucker?" one of the other cops asked. "Is that—?"

"Bullshit!" Tucker snapped. "Don't listen to her. Jake was my best friend, my partner. Why would I want to hurt him?"

"Because I knew what you were doing, Tuck," Jake replied through Caspian. His voice sounded just like him, too.

Tucker's face drained with fear and he stumbled back.

Dave and the other two officers watched, too spooked to move.

"I knew about your gambling, your debts." Caspian's eyes flashed as Jake stepped closer. "It's time to leave that behind, T-Man. Come clean and walk out of this darkness for good."

Tucker's boot hit a column, and he almost fell. "Jake?" he whispered.

"Hey, partner."

Dave dropped the handcuffs. Benz didn't move.

"That's impossible." Tucker's hand trembled holding the pistol.

"Nothing's impossible on the other side," Jake replied.

"Believe it, man," Benz said, hands still raised. "That shit's for real."

"Bullshit!" Tucker yelled again. He was almost to the door. "Jake's dead, and she got him killed." He pointed at Tal.

"It's time to end this, Tucker," Tal replied, standing with her partner. "Confess and start over."

Dave gaped. The other cops did, too.

"It's a lie!" Tucker told them. "She'll say anything to save her ass." A rotted board gave way under his feet. He scrambled to free himself as Caspian edged closer.

Careful, Jake, Tal warned. *He's a dog in a corner.*

Jake stopped but never blinked or looked away. "It's time, Tuck," he said again. "And Kathy knows."

"You told her?" Rage blistered his eyes.

"She wants to help."

"Tucker?" Dave asked, still gob smacked.

The other cops swiveled their weapons between Benz and Tucker, suddenly unsure of who was most guilty.

Benz slowly reached out and handed Dave a key. "The pawnshop. You'll find all kinds of shit in there you've been looking for."

"What are you doing?" Tucker yelled.

"I'm out, man," Benz told him. "Time to stop all this and start over."

Eli beamed at him through Tal, but Tucker fired a shot over his head. Everyone ducked.

"You *can't*," Tucker snarled. "They'll kill me if I don't pay. They'll kill my family. You'll ruin *everything*."

Dave took a step. "Whatever it is, Tucker, we can help you."

Tucker aimed at Dave, fingers trembling. "Why couldn't you just stay out of it, *partner*? Why'd you have to go snooping around my locker and fucking up my life?" He steadied his hand, took aim, and fired.

Benz must have known what was coming because he shoved Dave aside, and the bullet hit him instead. Benz collapsed. Dave scrambled to his feet. Tucker sprinted off through the open sanctuary doors.

"Get an ambulance!" Dave ordered, checking Benz's pulse.

One of the officers called it in while the other cop chased after

Tucker, calling for backup on the way.

"Hang in there," Dave told Benz, newfound respect edging his voice.

Tal sensed Eli's admiration for Benz, too. And his benevolence.

Was that planned? Tal asked. *Is it why Benz gave that kid his car?*

I'm not sure, the spirit replied. *But he found his way from the darkness.*

Sirens approached. Jake touched Tal's elbow. *Come on.* They dropped the guns, metal clattering against the wood, and turned for the door.

"Tal, don't," Dave said, his hands and arms red from holding pressure to Benz's wound. "Tucker will kill you."

Tal smiled sadly. "He already did." She sprinted through the open doors with Caspian. Halfway down the dark, classroom-lined hall, the vessels joined hands, and their bodies disappeared, mid-stride, in a swirl of wind and light.

Tal and Caspian materialized inside the old mill. "You have *got* to be kidding me," Tal groaned at the familiar warehouse columns and rickety table, the leaves still fluttering from their arrival. She checked her watch. "Shit. I have to get Eli back to the ship."

This won't take long, the spirit assured.

Moments later, footsteps pounded to a stop outside the door.

Quick. Jake led them behind some busted pallets.

The metal door creaked open, and Tucker rushed in. He pulled the door closed and fell against the paint-chipped wall on one side, his breath ragged and short. He must have run nonstop from the church ten blocks away. Dust and dried leaves scattered as he slid down to the floor, knees bent, arms wrapped around them.

Tal coiled, ready to spring, but Eli held her back. *Not yet.*

She could just make out Tucker's sweating face between some of the wooden slats. His eyes darted around the room, and he listened for sounds outside. Certain he was alone, Tucker slumped against the wall.

"Goddammit," he yelled. "Goddammit to *hell.*"

His words echoed off the concrete walls and floor.

"Doesn't have to be that way," Jake replied.

Tucker lurched to his feet, gun in hand. "Who is that?" he asked, head spinning in search of the disembodied voice. "Show yourself!"

"It is what you make of it," Jake continued, a beacon of calm inside Caspian.

Tucker's gun shook as he scanned the empty space.

"Turn yourself in," Jake continued. "Save yourself. Your family."

"*Show yourself,*" Tucker demanded, his sanity hanging by a thread.

Caspian and Tal stepped out from behind the pallet, surprising Tucker so much he dropped his gun. It clattered to the floor, and he dove for it, but Caspian kicked it away.

"Who *are* you?" Tucker said, scrambling back to his feet.

"It really is me, T-man," Jake said, holding out Caspian's open, empty hands, his emerald light ablaze in Caspian's eyes. "I came back to help you out of this mess."

Tucker shook. "J-Jake's dead. S-Spirits don't just … come

back."

Jake inched closer, with Tal shadowing behind. "The other side is beyond human understanding, Tucker," he said. "And the love is endless, even when we screw up."

Tucker trembled. "It's impossible."

Jake planted Caspian by the door, blocking Tucker's exit.

Careful, Jake, Tal warned.

Panicked, Tucker glanced at his gun on the floor, desperately measuring the distance and speed needed to grab it.

Tal moved to pick it up, but Tucker dove and rolled over in a surprisingly agile somersault to snatch it up. He landed on his feet and spun around, barrel locked on Tal's chest. His eyes flitted between her and Caspian. "You think I can just tell the mob to forget about their five hundred G's because the spirit of my ex-partner showed up and told me to get clean? They'll kill me just as easily in prison as out. You know that."

"Jesus, Tucker," Tal couldn't help herself. "You owe half a million?"

"I'll never be forgiven, not 'til I'm dead. Even then, they'll bleed Kathy and the kids for the rest. There's no fixing this, Jake! Can't you see that? I have to pay them back."

"Turn yourself in, and the rest will come." Jake slowly moved Caspian between Tal and Tucker's gun.

Tucker sensed it. "Stop," he demanded. Caspian froze.

"Forgive yourself," Jake pressed, stepping toward Tucker this time.

"Jake, don't," Tal hissed as Tucker tightened his grip.

"It all starts with forgiveness," Jake said. "With love."

"Bullshit!"

"Kathy forgives you." Jake took another step. "She knows

what you're facing, and she wants to help."

Jake, stop, Tal cautioned.

"She hates me, Jake." A tear slipped out, and Tucker swiped it back. "What I did to her, the kids. She won't help."

"She will."

"She *can't,*" he screamed. "They'll kill her, too."

"Dave can protect her. And your family. Arrange a meeting so he can set up a sting. The loan sharks go to prison. You get protective custody and help for your addiction. You'll be a new man."

Tucker laughed, a soul grating sound. "I'm a dead man, Jake. No matter what." His face twisted with self-loathing as he took aim. "Damn you, Jake," he said. "Damn you to hell." He flicked his wrist and fired before racing out the door.

Red hot pain seared Tal's chest. Her legs crumbled.

"Oh, God. Tal!" Jake cried.

Caspian caught her head just before it hit the cement floor.

Warm blood spread across her shirt, its coppery scent stinging her nostrils. Jake's voice dimmed, and memories flickered. Darden giggling with his milky sweet breath. The fiery car crash that killed him and Owen. Jake's kiss by the river. Tal's father dead in the recliner. Darden eating ice cream. Jake's kiss. His dying head in her lap.

She blinked up at Caspian and the tangle of soft black curls framing his face. His hand pulled something from her pocket, then dropped it into her palm and tightened her fingers around it. His mouth moved, but she could not hear his words.

Her pain began to fade. She reached up to stroke Caspian's olive-skinned face, his short stubble of beard and soft mumbling lips. She saw Jake instead—his short blond hair and blue eyes, his joyful smile. She whispered the words she should have said the night he died. "I love you, too, Jake."

Lightning split the room, and Liam appeared. The coin. That must be what Caspian took from her pocket.

"I've got you," Liam said, scooping Tal into his arms.

His movements were fluid and deliberate, a wave of strength. She smiled limply. "Hello, Angel Man."

Liam stood and looked at Caspian. "Hold on."

The vessel grabbed his shoulder as another bolt of energy rent the air.

CHAPTER TWENTY-ONE

SAM

Sam paced the rocky shore of Prism Lake while Chief Black sat in stillness by the fire, his legs crossed, back straight, and eyes closed. The vast water spread out like a black mirror reflecting the moon and stars, while close to shore, the lapping waves blushed orange from the bonfire. A breeze plucked at feathers on the chief's headdress.

Avani sat next to Chief Black in the same meditative state. She had shared a bond with him since the first vessel journey when Aaron died and Avani's visiting spirit had let her see the same ethereal light Chief Black had seen. Both had watched it fade and disappear once Aaron crossed over to join his deceased young wife and unborn daughter.

Since then, Avani preferred to spend her last moments of each journey like this, connecting with Chief Black and the spiritual realm while waiting for the ship to arrive. Sam suspected she was also hoping to catch a glimpse of her parents somewhere out there.

Gale and Malina sat on some large tufa rocks near Blaze and Link. Both looked apprehensive if not plain scared, and Sam kicked himself for bringing them in. But he didn't have much choice after Malina beamed to their new warehouse by hijacking a ride with Link and his spirit, or after Gale arrived from Carson City with horrible news about Ron and the woman he had poisoned and killed. Gale was terrified, certain Ron would find out and kill her and Malina, too.

Perhaps it would have been kinder to erase their memories and provide a fresh start, free from any pain, heartbreak, or fear, especially given the current state of things with Gale's ex-husband and Malina's derelict dad. But Gale and Malina had both insisted on joining the program, and Sam could not say no, not even to Malina, who he *knew* was not ready. The truth was, she may never be.

A coyote howled from high up in the mountains, and Gale and Malina cowed slightly. Sam just hoped his granddaughter would prove him wrong over time. He prayed she was not as much like Ron as she seemed and that she would mature into this world of serving others as a loyal and reliable vessel.

The ship was due in an hour or so, and Tal was still missing. Sam had a horrible feeling about it, too, a rock in the pit of his stomach he could not explain. But that rock made sense when a torrent of wind and light ripped the air, and Liam appeared with Tal limp in his arms, her eyes closed.

"Oh, God. Tal!" Sam, Doc and the other vessels rushed over.

A dark-haired stranger stood next to Liam, one hand gripping the Spirit Guard's shoulder. The man's scared eyes darted around the unfamiliar faces, but they flashed green from a spirit inside. A dim light glowed from under his left pant leg. The tattoo. Sam eased slightly.

Liam lowered Tal to the rocky ground. The stranger immediately knelt next to her and placed her head in his lap. He stroked her cheek and whispered softly in her ear.

"Tal?" Sam dropped to his knees and grabbed her limp hand. "Tal!"

Link and Avani knelt by her side across from him.

"She was shot," the stranger told them, but Sam sensed the spirit talking. "Nine millimeter. Close range."

The spirit's voice was male and confident. *Who was he? How did he know so much about guns? And why was he with Tal?* Spirits seldom worked in pairs. It must be that rogue Captain Hugh had warned them about, the one that nearly killed Diego. Had Tal died by his hand? Had he fired that gun?

"He's the one who called me," Liam whispered to Sam, obviously reading his thoughts. "He knew to use her coin."

The stranger stroked Tal's face and hair, but his movements were slightly hesitant, puppet strings being guided by an invisible master. The spirit was obviously directing this but why such tenderness, respect, and—love.

"Her pulse is weak," Doc said, pressing two fingers against Tal's neck. "She's lost a lot of blood."

"She needs a hospital," Sam said. "We need to—"

"Get the spirit out," Liam interrupted. "Quickly. Before she dies."

"*Dies?*" Sam reeled. *Tal?* Ornery, fiery Tal? His greatest skeptic going in and his bravest vessel since? It couldn't be. She was fearless, no matter which spirit chose her or where the journey led. And that included each continent at least once and back in time *twice*. She'd survived the German trenches of World War I. Certainly, she'd survive this. *Right?*

One of the tribesmen provided a wool blanket. Avani and Link quickly tucked it around Tal's shivering form.

Gale and Malina stood behind Blaze, a trio of wide eyes and slack jaws.

"But we need another vessel," Doc stammered. "For the ceremony."

"There is no time," Chief Black said, joining the circle. "Her light is weak, and the ship does not come until midnight."

"We need a volunteer," Liam said.

"I'll do it," Sam replied, desperate to help.

"No," Liam told him. "Sorry."

"Take me," Doc offered.

Liam shook his head. "You two and Chief Black are too vital to the program. We need another."

"Why? What could happen?" Gale's voice surprised them.

"A spirit can transfer from one vessel to another without harm," Liam continued, "so long as the mark, the tattoo is in place. But when a spirit enters a human, even for a little while, the energy it requires weakens them. And it can reorganize cells and damage some tissue."

"Permanently?"

"It's possible."

Sam hearkened to the humans that first rogue had commandeered before finding Aaron. One had died savagely at the rogue's hand, but the other had begun to rot in less than three days from the rogue's strength, intensity, and abuse. Liam and the other Spirit Guard had saved the man, but barely. At least he wouldn't remember any of it.

"Nothing like that, Sam," Liam assured. He looked at Blaze. "Younger bodies are stronger."

Blaze stepped back. "Heart murmur. Sorry."

"I'll do it."

Sam didn't know who spoke until Malina stepped forward, excitement in her voice.

"No." Gale reached for her, but Malina pulled away.

Liam, Sam, and Chief Black exchanged the same look. "Thank you, Malina," Liam said, giving voice to their shared thought. "But not yet."

"Why not?" Her face flushed. "I'm young and healthy. I want to be a vessel. I'm *perfect*."

"You're not ready," Liam said again, this time with authority even she did not question.

"We must hurry," Chief Black warned, his hand hovering above Tal's heart.

"That leaves me," Gale said.

"Mom. *No*." Malina threw her arms around Gale, the first loving gesture Sam had witnessed.

"She's right," he agreed. "You're too new. And you have Malina. Chief Black can ask one of his—"

Tal moaned. Her breath came in gasps.

The stranger smoothed her hair and whispered. "Shh, Tallon. Just a little longer."

Who is *this Spirit?* Sam thought. *And how does he know her?* Tal had not had anyone special in her life since her partner died. Sam looked up. Realization dawned. *Could Jake be the rogue who used Diego? Is this why he came?*

"She's mottling, Sam," Doc said, pointing out the marbled patches of purple spreading across Tal's palms and across one bare foot Doc had freed from its sock and shoe. "We don't have much time."

Sam inhaled to keep from crying. He hoped this spirit was Jake. At least she would have help and support crossing over.

Gale hugged Malina and stepped closer. "Tell me what to do."

Liam assessed her quickly, then turned her back toward Tal. He stood next to her and indicated for Chief Black and Sam to stand across from them on Tal's other side.

"Complete the circle," he told the others.

Avani and Link stepped into the opening between Chief Black and Liam.

Blaze and Doc filled the gap between Sam and Gale.

Malina cut in between Gale and Doc and grabbed her mother's hand. "What if something happens to you?" she asked.

Gale kissed her daughter's forehead. "It won't."

Seeing Malina's childlike fear at that moment gave Sam hope that she was capable of caring more than she let on. He also saw the anxiety Gale tried to hide from her daughter. It was the same anxiety he was trying to hide from Gale right now. He couldn't bear the thought of losing her, especially so soon after her return.

Drums beat, the Anaho danced around the bonfire, and Chief Black began to chant. The group joined hands, encircling Tal and the stranger holding her. One of Liam's hands gripped Tal's as the stranger held her arm aloft. Liam's other hand squeezed Gale's, Tal's coin pressed in between. The metal began to glow.

TAL

Tal's heart slowed to a bare thump as they prepared to take Eli. She wished they'd hurry. His spirit was growing weaker, too.

Spirits could leave quickly when a vessel died fast, as Eric's rogue had done with his first Vessel, Sanjay, after killing him on those mountain rocks and slipping into the body of a recovery worker. But the longer a dying vessel lingered with a spirit inside, unable to escape or cross over, the weaker that spirit became, withering like a butterfly trapped in a chrysalis. Not able to live, unable to die.

Drumbeats. Voices. Chanting. Paying attention took too much energy, so Tal let them go and focused on Jake's loving touch, on her head pillowed in Caspian's lap. The rocks pressed into her legs. She wondered if dying would hurt.

The worst is over, Eli told her, his words a bare whisper.

Tal wanted to speak, to tell them to hurry. She couldn't open her mouth.

They know, Jake assured through her muffled din and fog.

Caspian stroked her cheek, her forehead, her hair. His touch was that of an experienced caregiver. Or a thoughtful lover. She remembered Jake's kiss. Their shared desire. He would have been a sensitive lover, too. She was so stupid to make them wait.

Caspian thanks you, Jake said.

Not supposed to share all *my thoughts*, she replied, and those few words deflated her. She tried to cough, but her lungs wouldn't work. She couldn't swallow, either, and saliva and mucus began to line her throat and rattle with each shallow breath.

"We're losing her," Doc said, no doubt recognizing the sound.

She thought of Darden and Jake. Both died fast. No lingering pain. She was glad for that.

Her hand suddenly heated in Liam's grip. A flow of energy, an opening for Eli.

Let me in, another voice said. Raspy. Not Jake or Eli. *I will make you the vessel you wish to be.*

Tal struggled to hear where it was coming from, but it seemed to be everywhere. And nowhere.

Hear that? Her thoughts came in jagged rasps.

Eli didn't answer. He was busy unwrapping himself from Tal's organs, peeling away from her muscles and bones and shrinking down to his original, pearl-sized form.

Liam knows, Jake told her.

You and I are meant to be, the voice said again through the chanting. It sounded cold, hard.

Tal focused every ounce of strength she had to crack open her eyelids and search for who, or what, this voice belonged to. She could just make out the blurry silhouettes of Sam, Doc, Blaze, Link, and Avani in a circle above her.

Liam stood closest, holding her hand. The woman who'd volunteered stood next to him, her back turned to receive Eli. She held Liam's other hand, and Tal's coin burned brightly between their palms. Next to the woman stood a young girl with frightened eyes. She clutched the woman's other hand and gaped at the coin.

Take it, Malina, the raspy voice instructed. The girl's eyes widened more, in excitement as much as fear.

The voice seemed to be coming *from* the coin. Or through it. A spirit. Had to be.

Quickly now, it said. *Before they finish.*

The girl caught Tal's half-open eyes staring at her and gasped.

The others saw it, too, and murmured with surprise. A few cried. Sam whispered goodbye. But Tal focused only on the girl and her obvious connection to the coin. The voice was getting to her.

Rogue? Tal asked, her thoughts growing harder to form.

Take it! The raspy voice commanded. The girl looked anxiously between Tal and the coin.

Tal's eyelids collapsed. *Jake?*

Liam knows, he said. *Get ready.*

His words barely registered before Eli's ball of spirit moved up from Tal's chest, through her neck, to her lightly parted lips.

Thank you, he said, and his voice already sounded stronger. *You have served others well.*

She saw his brightness through her closed eyelids, and it dimmed as he floated away.

Any last warmth left with him, and Tal's hands and feet turned to ice. Her muscles went soft, and her bones sank into the rocky earth like her father's body had sunk into the recliner. A sudden heart attack. He hadn't suffered pain, either. Crickets chirped. An owl cried. Jake kissed her forehead. She was ready.

Her belly softened, her pulse slowed to a whisper, and she no longer felt the need for air. It wasn't scary. Just ... odd. Liam lowered her hand, and Caspian tucked it under the blanket.

Sam, Doc, and the others cried as they touched her arms, legs, and shoulders. She felt the love in their goodbyes.

It's time to go, Tallon, Jake told her.

She nodded or meant to. *Coin?* She could barely think the word.

See you soon. Jake leaned Caspian over to kiss her one last time.

At his touch, Tal exhaled her last. The rattle silenced, and cold consumed her like a peaceful fog, spreading from her feet and hands to her arms and legs, to her torso, where it filled the stillness around her belly, her liver, her lungs. It wasn't uncomfortable, just ... tranquil. It finally reached her chest, and the thumping stopped. Her brain fired its last thought across a cold cranium sky.

A tunnel opened above with a bright, welcoming light. Laughter rang out, and Tal's four-year-old son, Darden, appeared as if expecting her. He was beautiful and healthy, and his eyes danced with joy.

Welcome home, Mommy.

Tal took his hand and stepped into the light.

CHAPTER TWENTY-TWO

CASPIAN

Tal's white luminous spirit rose from her lips, no bigger than a pomegranate seed, and bathed the air with a sense of peace before it disappeared. *So much comfort from such a tiny source,* Caspian thought. And yet, it did not stop the tears from flowing. Especially Sam's.

The lake churned, and a submarine-like ship broke the surface. The drums pounded its arrival, and native men and women danced until it settled, a phosphorescent green band outlining the smooth, rounded metal between sides and top.

Sam kissed Tal's lifeless cheek. "I'll miss you," he whispered, then stood, dried his tears, and forced himself to join the chief on shore.

Doc said her goodbyes, too, and helped Liam care for Gale, the woman who had taken Eli's spirit. Gale's daughter, Malina, hovered by her mother, awestruck at the ship, the lake, the hatch that opened, and the burst of light from inside. Caspian wondered why Liam had been so set against her accepting Eli's spirit.

Heavy footsteps clanked against metal, and Caspian smelled a floral scent he recognized but could not recall. He'd caught a whiff of something similar when Jake's spirit had entered him from Diego. He looked up to see a tall, imposing figure of a man in a long wool coat and high leather boots crossing the ship's lighted walkway.

More images cobble in his brain. Another bonfire, a different chief, the same ship and captain. The same smell and sounds. Another coin. The same wrathful voice he'd heard recently with Jake at the shopping center and the bar. *Drop it. Don't listen to him.*

It was the same voice he'd heard during the ceremony just now. *Who was behind it? Why was it here? What did it want?*

A young, dark-haired girl remained on the ground, eyes closed, kneeling at Tal's side. She appeared to be praying, or saying her final goodbyes. A few moments later, she looked up. "Are you okay?"

Caspian startled. "Me?"

"My name is Avani."

"Caspian," he said. She was beyond beautiful, a raven-haired goddess with warm, kind eyes.

"Are you okay?" she asked again.

"I think so. Why?"

He didn't realize he was rocking until she placed a hand on his shoulder. "Oh," he blushed. "Thanks."

She lifted Tal's head from his lap so he could move back, then gently lowered it to the ground, careful to dodge the small rocks. Caspian's legs tingled from the lack of circulation. Avani helped him to his feet, her touch soothing away the last shards of memories.

The captain greeted the chief over open water, halfway between ship and shore.

"That's Captain Hugh," Avani told Caspian. "Be right back."

She joined the others in receiving this man when he came ashore. Caspian could not hear their words, but they pointed to Tal, to him. The captain's eyes sparkled like sapphires.

That other lake. This same ship. The same captain with these same indigo eyes. Misty round spirits like Tal's hover by him. People stand nearby. He can't make out their faces.

A woman's cry broke the reverie, and Caspian jerked up to see Liam, the chief, and the ship's captain surrounding Gale as Eli's ball of spirit, no longer faint or weak, emerged from her mouth and drifted over to one side by itself. Gale slumped into Liam's arms, and he gently placed her in Doc's care before joining the captain and Chief Black in a three-way circle around Avani. They surrounded her from the front and sides but left her back open. Caspian wondered why until the chanting resumed.

Avani's tattoo shimmered under her pant leg, growing brighter as a spirit emerged through her back. It glowed in human-like form with a head, limbs, and torso but no distinct features. Avani barely winced, and she did not limp or faint once it was free.

That must be the vessel difference Liam had referred to, and it must be why.

Caspian didn't hurt when Jake's spirit slipped into him from Diego. The old man had called him a vessel. Jake and Tal had, too. But when? How did it end? And why did he keep hearing that voice from the coin?

The chanting stopped, Avani's tattoo dimmed, and the spirit drifted over to wait with Eli.

The process repeated for the boy—Link, Sam had called him. His visiting spirit emerged the same way and floated over to join the other two.

Liam, Sam, and Chief Black approached Caspian next.

The man with them extended his hand. "Captain Hugh Benham," he said. His eyes glistened, and his wool coat flapped on windy fingers against his high leather boots. "It's good to see you again, Miguel."

Miguel? Caspian's heart lurched and bits of memory flashed again around the girl, the bull, the red cape, and a crowd chanting what he now heard as his name. *Miguel!*

The captain stepped back, and Liam took his place. "This will help."

He placed one hand over Caspian's heart, and memories exploded. This time, however, they were focused and linear, like someone had taped the scattered film clips in order.

An angry bull paws the dirt, blood dripping from the three decorative spears stabbing its back. The bullfighter snaps his red cape. It's Caspian! Holding the fourth and final spear. Banderillas, they're called. He remembers. The fourth stab marks the third and final act of the fight. The crowd chants his name. *Miguel, Miguel, Miguel.*

The bull charges. Caspian waves his cape and plants his spear. The crowd roars. Caspian turns to bow and the bull charges. He gores Caspian and tosses him into the air. More blood hits the dirt. Cheers turn to screams.

A hospital. The beautiful young woman. Diamond on her finger. They plan to wed. Mr. & Mrs. Castillo. His gored lung is almost healed.

Caspian lies bandaged at home in Madrid. A huge room. A mansion? He can no longer fight. His mother plans the wedding. His father frowns. *How will you provide?*

I can work for you.

THE COIN

I do not hire failures.

Fire. Smoke. The house burns. Caspian's fiancée lies crumpled on the floor. Coughing, stumbling, he carries her out. She dies. The house explodes, scattering the remains of his mother and sister. His father disappears.

High mountains. His uncle's Andalusian farm. The horses are dappled white. Their long manes and tails brush the ground. Caspian trains them in a large corral. Handicapped children ride them to heal.

A ship comes, black and metal. A vast churning lake. Another bonfire. Another chief. Tribal members dance around the fire wearing llama wool. Captain Hugh emerges. Misty marbles of spirit float from the ship. The same light flowery smell.

The horses whinny, spooked. Caspian yells. His voice is raspy and deep. Not his voice. The spirit inside him. Caspian grabs his coin. Starts to count. The spirit tries to throw it, but the old man grabs Caspian's arm. His uncle! He curls Caspian's fingers around the coin. Helps him count. The spirit makes Caspian punch the old man hard. He lands in the dirt, screaming for Caspian to hold the coin. The spirit throws that in the dirt, as well.

Caspian fights to get it back. His nose starts to bleed. His head is a helmet of pain. Uncle reaches for the coin. "Take it, Miguel," he yells, extending his hand. "Call them."

But the spirit frightens the horses. They rear up and run, trampling the uncle to death.

The spirit starts to beam them away, but Caspian forces himself to stay whole. He wades into the throng of horses, taking the coin from his uncle's dead hand. He holds it. *One, two, three* ... The spirit screams and snaps Caspian's leg. *Four, five, six* ... His lungs deflate. Blood runs from his ears. *Seven, eight, nine* ... *TEN*. A blinding light. Two figures appear with golden-green eyes. Infinite strength. The spirit breaks Caspian's arm before the two figures force it out. They call it by name—Eric Bonner.

One figure reduces Eric's spirit to a small red orb, tucks it into a clear, lantern-shaped cage, and disappears. The other figure wraps his arms around Caspian. A powerful current. Comforting words. Then ungodly pain as Caspian's bones restore, his organs reshape, his scorched tissue heals. The pain ends.

Caspian begs for something. The figure speaks. Caspian nods, and the figure places both hands on Caspian's head. The world goes cold, then blank.

Liam removed his hand, and the memories faded. The lake and bonfire returned, and Caspian blinked back to the moment. "Who were those people?" he asked. What did they want?"

"They were Spirit Guard," Liam said, having shared the memories with him. "Like me. You told them you wanted out of the program, to stop being a vessel. They asked if you understood the consequences." He paused. "You said yes."

"Will the memories come back?"

"You'd have to become a vessel again."

Caspian felt hollow, disconnected, a stranger in his own body. He couldn't remember what being a vessel was like.

Jake vibrated.

The movement startled him. Caspian had almost forgotten he was in there.

"Come, Miguel." Liam started over to where Captain Hugh

and Chief Black waited.

"Please. I only know Caspian."

Liam nodded and led him to stand in the center of the same unfinished circle. Avani smiled, reassuring as the chief resumed his chant. Tribal members danced and sang to the pounding drums one last time around the fire.

Caspian's tattoo glowed, and his insides shifted as Jake's spirit unwound and pulled free. Caspian turned around to face the luminous form. *I'm sorry we couldn't save her*, he said.

I didn't come back to save her, Jake's spirit replied.

You knew this would happen?

I knew it could.

Then why come?

To save you.

An owl's cry speared the air.

The darkness that lured Benz, that fractured Tucker and killed Tal, the evil spirit you heard from that coin, they are getting worse. Humankind is tearing apart, and the program needs your help to save it. Before it's too late.

But ...

Trust your instincts. Remember who you are.

Jake drifted away to join the others, and the three large spirits burst into pillars of light before reducing back to the same marble-sized orb as Eli. All four returned to the captain.

"I am sorry for your loss," Captain Hugh told Sam and the others. "But Tal is happy and surrounded by love." He turned to Caspian. "Until next time, Miguel." He strode toward the ship, the four spirits like pearly bubbles at his side.

Doc put an arm around Sam as the ship's hatch closed, and the metal walkway disappeared behind its narrow door.

"She's with her family now," Avani said, glancing at Tal's body by the fire. "She's with Darden."

"How do we do this without her?" Link whispered, mostly to himself.

Blaze looked at his GPS. Tal's blue dot blinked from the chip in her shoulder, the only thing still alive in her. He punched some keys, deactivated the circuit, and the dot disappeared. Only Link's and Avani's remained.

Gale and Malina held each other and watched, trembling, as the ship submerged in an emerald cloud.

The roiling stopped, the water quieted, and the lake returned to normal. Sam could almost count each star reflected on its surface. Shadows moved, rocks shifted, and Sam and Doc watched two tribal women carefully shroud Tal's body in the woolen blanket. Drumbeats sounded, and Chief Black chanted and waved a small, smoking cluster of herbs around Tal's form.

Liam clapped one hand each on Link and Blaze. "Help me build her raft." Blaze pocketed his GPS, and they followed Liam into the woods.

Avani put a hand on Caspian's arm. "Thank you for helping Tal. For bringing her home."

Firelight bathed her face. Her hair smelled of lavender, and her skin of musk and earth. He wanted to say more but settled for a brief nod.

She lowered her hand. "Where's your home?"

He paused, unsure how much to reveal. "I, um, I seem to be without one at the moment."

Her look was hopeful, inviting. Breath bottled in his chest.

"I'm sure Sam would let you stay with us," she said. "At least until you figure out what to do next."

Trust your instincts, Jake's spirit had told him. *Remember who you are.* "Until next time, Miguel," the captain had said. Was he meant to be here?

His eyes traced Avani's jaw, her soft lips, her coal black eyes, and brown skin. She was more beautiful than he'd first realized. Even more so, it seemed, on the inside. Maybe she was another part of why he needed to stay.

"Would you help me talk to Sam?" he asked.

Her smile stole his heart.

Liam, Chief Black, and two of the Anaho tribesmen set Tal's body adrift on the lake. Her shrouded form floated on a thin, narrow raft of sticks and branches that Liam, Blaze, and Link had tied together. They'd covered its surface in a blanket of fall leaves.

Sam removed his glasses to wipe his tears. Doc held him close on one side while Gale hooked her arm through his on the other. Malina hung back but remained near her mom. Avani and Caspian stood nearby.

The drums beat louder and faster as one of the Anaho women nocked a flaming arrow into her bow. Chief Black chanted, and the woman let fly.

The arrow found purchase on the raft. The dry wood, leaves, and wool blanket quickly caught fire. Tal's body would soon become part of this lake she had grown to love.

"She returns to her element."

The words took Sam by surprise. He hadn't heard Liam approach. "Her element?"

"She is water," Liam explained, then pointed to the raft. "And she takes earth, air, and fire with her."

"Metal, too, if you count the arrow tip," Link added as he and Blaze joined them. Link was partial to metal, given his propensity to weld.

An owl's cry joined a chorus of crickets as the pyre blossomed into a fiery lotus on the lake. Doc wept softly against Sam's shoulder.

"Her journey is far from over," Liam said, eyes aglow with acceptance, wisdom. "You will see her again."

Sam believed this, but he had come to love Tal like a daughter, and he would miss her wit and spunk, her courage, and her leadership.

"I pity the other side, actually," Doc said, smiling in spite of her tears. "I'm not sure if they quite know all they are getting."

Sam chuckled. Others did, too. Everyone, Sam noticed, but Malina.

One final *whoosh* of flames silenced them as Tal's raft began to sink. Water spit out the fire and sent tendrils of steam into the early morning sky. The smoke soon faded and Tal slipped out of sight. The glassy surface reflected the stars once more.

Gale let go of Sam's arm. She and Malina walked over to warm themselves by the fire. Avani and Caspian strolled along the shore.

"Whatever happened to that rogue spirit?" Doc asked. "The one Captain Hugh told us about?" Her eyes darkened. "Was it Eric Bonner?"

"No," Liam said. "That rogue was Tal's police partner, Jake. He used Caspian to try and save her."

"Why go rogue, then?" Sam asked. "Why not just use a vessel?"

"It was not his time," Liam replied, though Sam had a feeling that wasn't the whole story. "So he snuck back and found a *former* vessel."

"'Former,' as in … *erased?*" Link asked.

"Can he be fixed?" Blaze eyed Caspian warily.

"Yes," Liam said. "But only if he chooses to return."

"Hmph." Blaze walked off to join Malina and Gale by the fire.

What about this stranger inspired *that* response from Blaze, Sam wondered. Maybe because Avani was spending time with him? Sam could certainly understand her attraction, but not Blaze's sudden brooding. He had never shown any kind of interest in Avani before. *Had he?* Sam could almost hear Tal playfully chastising him for being blind to the human dramas going on under his nose, unaware of personal relationships beyond those he needed to know about or engage in. He vowed to pay more attention going forward.

Caspian and Avani paused to gaze across the lake. He was tall, strong, and powerfully built, a force to serve any spirit. Sam wondered what could possibly have happened to make being erased the better option.

See them with your heart, Chief Black told Sam about discovering vessels when he first took over the program. *Listen with your soul.*

Somehow Sam knew Caspian would become a vessel again, probably with them, and he'd be a huge asset to the program. Tal would be happy about that, too, even from Elysium. But Sam also knew with complete certainty that Caspian becoming a vessel would end in tragedy, he just couldn't tell how, why, or in what way.

A voice interrupted. "Who is Eric Bonner?"

Sam was startled to find Malina next to him.

"Eric was a rogue spirit," he replied. "The first one our program encountered. He was on his third and final journey, getting his last chance at redemption when he … began killing again. Our newest vessel, Aaron, took him on to save a dying human host."

Malina teetered slightly. "What happened?"

"Aaron stopped him," Doc said. She stood next to Sam, still staring out at the lake. "He stole a prop plane and crashed it with the rogue still inside him."

The plane was recovered three days later, once the FAA traced its signal. Authorities had called Aaron's brother-in-law, Joe, to identify the body. Liam had shape-shifted into a member of the forensics team to ensure no one found evidence of the rogue, Aaron's phone, or his unusual tattoo.

Liam had shared the condition of Aaron's body with Sam and Doc alone. No one else needed to know what Eric had done to him *before* the crash.

"What happened to him?" Malina asked.

"They recovered Aaron's remains," Sam said. "His family held a memorial."

"I mean, what happened to Eric?"

Doc cut Sam a curious look.

"He was put in The Lot," Liam told her. "Where he remains."

"Can he ever … get out?"

"Why do you ask?" Sam tried to hide his concern.

She cleared her throat. "Just wondering. You know. For when I get to be a vessel."

Liam scanned her like sonar. Malina shifted uneasily.

What is he sensing? Sam wondered.

"Other rogues exist," Liam told her. He never looked away.

He didn't even blink. "Their potential to feel the pain and anger from their past can return at any moment, more so the longer they stay. That's why it takes a special person to become a vessel—someone who has known suffering and risen above it. Someone who has experienced unconditional love and the power it wields against evil."

Sam and Doc exchanged a look. *What is he getting at?*

Malina had been pushing to become a vessel ever since she'd met Link, transported with him to the program, and learned what it was all about. She wasn't ready yet, though—they all knew that. While she'd suffered the pain of her father's abandonment, she was still too raw with hurt, anger and blame to embrace any kind of compassion or love.

Malina reminded Sam of Ron in that way. Too much, in fact. Those selfish, vindictive feelings would have to be removed before she could even *think* of becoming a vessel. Sam hoped his decision to let her remain in the program and around other vessels would help her achieve that. If not, Malina would have to be erased. And Sam could only imagine what that would do to Gale and to their tenuous reconnection.

CHAPTER TWENTY-THREE

MALINA

Eva's hot doctor friend had dropped off a used ping-pong table, and it helped the vessels pass the time at their temporary warehouse home. It also made this Reno rat hole more tolerable, and it seemed to help take everyone's minds off Tal. She must have meant a lot.

Malina served the ball, slamming it hard to impress Link. He dove to return it.

Avani, Malina's doubles partner, hit it back, targeting the opposite corner near Caspian. He lunged but missed, and the ball bounced off a wall, across the floor, and under the old bar leaning against the back wall.

"Sorry," Caspian said as he retrieved it. He was too tall and muscular for Malina's taste and not edgy or daring like Link, but he was sweet. She could see why Avani liked him.

Malina served again, and Link returned it. His veins rippled under the tattoo of his angel. Her perfectly drawn face and dress covered the underside of his forearm while her wings wound up through the fine dark hair of his arm to meet on top where his muscles flexed. Malina's whole body tingled when she learned he had inked that himself. How gifted he was, and how brave to tolerate that level of pain, especially from his own hand. His soft, full lips tightened with concentration inside the trimmed, thin beard he was trying to grow. Malina wondered what it would be like to kiss those lips right now and taste their salty sweetness.

"Fourteen to ten," Link said. He tossed the ball back for her to serve again and smiled playfully at Caspian. "Let's keep it on the table this time, partner. Okay?"

Caspian feigned a pout and winked at Avani. They had become inseparable since the lake three days ago. It drove Blaze mental for some reason, and Malina was determined to find out why. She slammed another serve, and Link returned it. They battled it back and forth several times until she hit it to Caspian, where it bounced off the corner and out of his reach, just as she'd planned.

"Fifteen. That's game," she gloated, setting her paddle down. "Take a break?"

The others nodded, and everyone walked to the refrigerator for drinks. Doctor Ross had found a used one of those, too, along with a microwave, hot plate, and laundry sink. Even temporary and strung together, it beat the hotel. Actually, just being with Link beat the hotel.

She felt Link's eyes on her as she opened the refrigerator door, and the thought sent tingles rippling. *Make him work for it*, her mom's words filled her head again. *You will mean more to him that way.* Gale had offered that advice in Malina's freshman year of high school when she had started dating a sophomore. Malina didn't listen, of course, and basically attached herself to the boy, hanging on him and kissing him all the time. It wasn't long before he pressured her for more. She gave in to a degree, but when she refused sex, he walked off and never talked to her again. Malina took a different approach with the second boy who'd asked her to homecoming. Sure enough, making him wait, even for a first kiss, made him want her more. They'd dated almost two years before Gale yanked Malina out of school and moved her to Reno. Link had made that better, too.

Malina grabbed a cold bottle of water and carried it to the far back corner, behind the stairs, where Blaze had set up shop. His plywood desk faced into the room, and he sat with his back to the wall.

"Who won?" he asked, glancing at Caspian and Avani as they laughed and shared a bottled water.

"Seriously? Did you not see us blow them out?"

He scowled at his screen.

"Want to play?"

"No thanks."

She peeked over his shoulder at the screen, and he quickly clicked on a different tab. Whatever he had been looking at disappeared, replaced by the office cam he had rigged in his stepfather's home, mounted on a bookshelf behind the man's desk. It looked over Howard's shoulder as he sat at his computer. Blaze zoomed in on the screen. Howard was writing an email to the Reno Police Department asking if they had any leads on his son. "*Son*," Blaze groused. "As if. He's such an ass."

Malina felt the hurt and loss behind his anger. She and Blaze had a lot in common that way. "Cops'll be hunting you as much as Link," she said. "Smaller reward, though." She poked him playfully.

The ball pinged off the table, and she looked up to see Link's biceps tighten as he twisted and dove to volley with Avani. The game had switched to singles, and Caspian leaned back against one wall to wait. He watched Avani the same way Malina watched Link.

Blaze glared at Caspian.

"Why the daggers, dude?"

"No one knows anything about him except he got erased, got that rogue cop spirit, and helped bring Tal back. Now, suddenly, he's the goat. And he's all over Avani, but no one seems to care."

Malina sensed more. "If you like Avani so much, tell her. She can't read your mind, moron."

He stared at Caspian a little too long, scanning him quickly from head to toe.

"Ah." A grin cut her lips. "I see."

His face turned bright red. "See what? What are you talking about? You don't know anything."

She leaned close and whispered. "Your secret's safe with me, dude, but I doubt anyone here cares if you're—"

"Gale? Malina? May I see you for a minute?" Sam asked from his desk across the room.

Gale cleaned a few last dishes in the sink and started over.

"Sorry, dude," Malina whispered. "It's only gonna get worse by the looks of it." She indicated Caspian and Avani, now arm-in-arm, playing ping-pong as one person against Link. She patted Blaze's shoulder and left.

Sam's desk was a sheet of plywood over two sawhorses. It held a phone, a laptop, and some paper and pens, thanks, once again, to Eva's friend.

"I need my files from the shelter," Sam told them once Malina arrived. "And we need the extra sheets, blankets, and pillows to make beds."

"Or to hang up for privacy," Gale offered.

"Good idea," he replied. "But Liam is away, and police are watching the shelter. They won't let Doc or me in, Avani could be recognized, and Link could wind up in jail."

"Blaze can't go, either," Malina added. "Not with his stepfather on the hunt."

"Right."

Malina shot her mom a prideful smile. It felt good to be right about something.

"I hate to ask," Sam said, "but would you two mind going? Here's a list."

He handed it to Malina. She shared another prideful look.

"Will the police let us in?" Gale asked.

"No. But you can go into the soup kitchen as homeless guests, then sneak into the lobby through the back door. There's a lockbox." He called out, "Blaze? Please join us?"

Sam was firm but polite, like her mom. Malina didn't know why, exactly, but that irritated the crap out of her. She preferred cold, hard, and direct, like her dad. And her Uncle Ron.

Blaze punched a few keys and cast a sideways, dejected glance at Caspian before coming over. "What's up, boss?" he asked.

"How do they get past the new lockbox?"

"Oh. That's easy."

He wrote some numbers on the list in Malina's hand. "This code opens the box. The key inside opens the door."

"How'd you get this?" Malina asked.

"I could tell you, but then I'd have to kill you." He laughed.

Malina rolled her eyes. *Top Gun* had suddenly become his favorite movie—only thirty-two years after it came out. "Seriously," she said. "How'd you get it?"

"I used paper clips to open theirs, then replaced it with an identical one of ours. Cops go in and out the front. No one else uses it."

"Brilliant."

"I know."

She looked across at Caspian and whispered, "I should tell your boyfriend."

He froze, terrified.

"Kidding, genius." She bopped his arm.

"Take the car," Sam said, handing Gale the keys. "Park in the back and walk around to the food line. No one knows you. The police won't, either. Sit in the far back of the cafeteria by the lobby door. Wait for the homeless guests to finish and the volunteers to clean up, then sneak inside."

"How do we get out?"

Worry tugged at the corners of Gale's mouth. She'd been doing this a lot more since Malina's dad split.

"Leave through the back," Sam told her. "That door pushes open from the inside and will lock behind you. Veronica says the police have stopped parking an officer back there, so you should be free and clear." He paused. "You'll find some cloth bags in the laundry, in the cabinets overhead. Put everything in those."

One hour later, disguised in layers of ripped, stained clothes Doc had given them, Gale parked Sam's Jeep in the back of the shelter by the empty pool and deck. She and Malina got out. Their hair was mussed, and Doc had smudged their faces with dirt. They walked around the corner and turned up the side street that ran along the kitchen side of the shelter. The long, windowless brick wall was streaked with gang tags and graffiti. Last rays of sun kicked up shadows and silhouettes from homeless people making their way to the food line.

Gale pulled her worn coat tighter. Malina tugged her hoodie around her face and winced at the street smells of soured garbage and urine. Thankfully those odors were eclipsed by the aroma of garlic bread and spaghetti coming from the kitchen. Mother and daughter hurried around the corner to find a line of people already snaking down the sidewalk, past the shelter's front door.

One police car sat out front, along the curb, with a single officer inside. He was parked where he could see the soup kitchen, the line of people, and the shelter's entry. The iron gate Link had welded that led to the courtyard was securely locked.

Darkness settled in as Malina and Gale walked toward the back of the line. Most of the people looked down or straight ahead, and many of them smoked, but none paid attention to the two women who quietly slipped in behind. Thankfully, neither did the officer. Malina caught a whiff of something vanilla and sweet, like sugar cookies. Her stomach growled, and she checked her phone. Only six o'clock.

Gale leaned over. "Smells so good. And I'm starving."

Malina nodded. Her mom had become a little more relaxed since that whole spirit-body timeshare at the lake. It seemed to have made her less worried, even though the thing was only inside her for, like, fifteen or twenty minutes. Maybe these spirits were more powerful than she thought. Sam and Eva had said they were. Avani and Link had, too. But nothing could be *that* strong, right?

Malina shivered, thinking of the dark, raspy voice from Tal's coin. It was definitely the same voice that came from Link's coin when she'd held it. *But how did it get to her at the lake when she wasn't even touching it? And how did it know her name?* No one else seemed to hear it, either—not Link that day with his coin, and not

Gale, Doc, Sam, or even Avani at the lake. Only Tal's eyes had cranked open and stared at her. And Liam had watched her more closely afterward until he had to leave for some Spirit Guard thing. They must have heard it, too.

Liam gave her the creeps. He didn't say much, and those eyes—little mirrors of gold and green that could see right through you. At least he was gone until Saturday when the ship would bring more spirits. She hadn't heard the raspy voice in five days. That was a relief, but she also had not felt that crazy weird power it gave off, like she could ride lightning or control ocean waves if she held it long enough. She really missed that.

Once they reached the kitchen, it didn't take long to be served. Malina and Gale carried their trays to the far back, away from the crowd, and sat across from each other at the end of a table nearest the door leading into the shelter. A lockbox hung on its handle.

They ate slowly, lingering over their meal, their cookies, and several cups of coffee. Almost three hours later, the crowd began to thin, and the volunteers started to clean up. Gale took their trays to empty them, then feigned tripping near the coffee urn and pulled it onto the concrete floor. Metal clattered, and coffee and wet grounds went everywhere. That diversion allowed Malina time to enter the lockbox code and retrieve the key. She quickly unlocked the door, ensured the handle could turn, then returned the key to the lockbox and clicked it shut. She sat back down and was nibbling the last bite of her cookie when her mother returned.

"All good?" Gale asked innocently.

Malina nodded.

"We're closed now," one of the volunteers called out as she cleaned up the coffee. "Please finish up." She swept up the grounds, dropped towels to soak up the puddle of coffee, and carried the metal urn back into the kitchen.

Once she disappeared from view, and with no one else to see them, Malina and Gale slipped quietly through the door and into the shelter on the other side. Malina locked the door, and they waited, making sure no cop was patrolling inside.

Malina's eyes adjusted to the dark as they listened, but she didn't hear anything except the clock ticking from Veronica's desk in the lobby. The silence was eerie compared to the cafeteria full of people, the shuffling of chairs, and the clatter of utensils and trays.

It also felt weird compared to that first night when Malina and her mom had arrived in town for Sam's birthday. The place had been bustling with homeless people and with Doc and Blaze getting ready for the inspection, with Sam and Liam showing her and Gale around and taking them to dinner in the cafeteria. That seemed forever ago, and it had only been, like, a week or ten days or something.

They tiptoed toward the lobby, where streetlights outside the front two windows cast a glow on Veronica's desk, the few chairs in the waiting area, and the large nature posters on the walls. They stepped into the laundry room, and Gale soon found the cloth bags Sam had described.

She gave one to Malina and kept one for herself. "I'll go to Sam's room. You get what Blaze and Doc need. Okay?"

Malina nodded. Sam's room would be boring, anyway. There was more to see and pick through with Doc and Blaze.

"Meet me by the back door when you're done." Gale strode off across the carpeted lobby and into the dark hallway beyond.

Malina walked the opposite way, down the back hall to Doc's office. She stepped inside and turned on her phone's flashlight. It all looked the same as the last time she'd been here, the night Link had beamed in. She opened the cabinet and grabbed the Tylenol, Motrin, and other pain relievers Doc had asked for, as well as boxes of gauze, bandages, peroxide, and cotton balls.

"*No sense wasting them,*" Doc had told her. "*We have no idea when we'll be back there to use them.*"

Malina put the armful of items on Doc's desk to load them, but couldn't resist the temptation to open some drawers first and snoop around for anything on Link. Medical records, maybe, or articles about his escape. Instead, she found a bunch of boring files on homeless patients with high blood pressure, diabetes, alcoholism, drug abuse, hepatitis, and cirrhosis. All that stupid shit adults did to screw themselves up, then wonder how it happened.

Malina closed the drawers, loaded the bag, and stepped one door down the hall to Blaze's office. She ignored the technical junk and turned over his desk to reveal the laptop hidden underneath. She unscrewed that from its base, grabbed the hard drive, then turned the false desk back over with its generic computer, phone, and files on top.

She carefully placed his laptop and hard drive in the bag and hurried toward the back door. Gale was already there with her laundry bag full of files and plans, as well as a coffee pot, small grinder, and bag of beans.

"Seriously? He can't just buy a Mr. Coffee?"

"Why spend the money? Besides, this one's broken in," Gale said. She put a hand on the door and was about to open it when she stopped. "Dammit. I forgot the bedding."

"Where is it?" Malina asked.

"Sam's closet. On top. Do you mind?"

Malina did, but she strode back down the hallway to Sam's room, anyway. She was faster and would get them out sooner. This place was starting to creep her out.

She opened the door to Sam's room and walked to his closet. Blinds were cracked on his one window, and streetlight painted the walls in bars of orange. Malina tugged open the bifold closet doors and grabbed the pile of blankets and sheets from the top shelf.

Something flew out as she pulled them down, a small wooden box that bounced off the carpet and hit the dresser. The top popped open, and something metal rolled out. It clanked against a wooden panel beneath the bed and fell over.

Malina picked it up, and her hand tingled around another coin. It was identical to Link's and Tal's, and Malina barely had wondered if it would work the same when the raspy voice filtered through.

We meet again, Malina.

The metal warmed in her palm, and the familiar sensation of power started to rise.

That's it. There's nothing to stop us this time.

Malina's fingers wrapped around the coin and her mind raced with questions. What if this were one of those rogues Sam and Liam had talked about? What if it hurt her? Or worse?

I will make you the vessel you wish to be. Stronger than Tal, Link, Avani, Caspian, all of them.

Sweet Jesus. It knew everyone. Malina was terrified yet thrilled. Whoever it was, this voice promised to give her the one thing Sam and Liam would not. She would finally have the chance to prove herself, to show them she could be a great vessel.

Your dreams will come true, Malina. Hold it tight.

"But, won't Liam find out?" she asked and opened her fingers slightly. "Doesn't holding this, like, call the Spirit Guard or something?" For a fleeting second, Malina hoped it would. She desperately wanted to be a vessel, to have the same powers as Link and Avani. At the same time, Sam and Liam had both said she wasn't ready. They'd refused to let Link give her the mark. Even Blaze had told her to give it time. What if they were right? Could she even host a spirit without the tattoo?

With me, all is possible, the voice replied, reading her thoughts. *Do as I say, and you will be the strongest vessel in the world. They will see how special and deserving you really are.*

Malina stared at the coin in her palm, then gave in to the rising temptation and squeezed it tight.

Ten seconds.

Her heart slammed against her ribs as she whispered. "One, two, three …"

That's it.

Heat traveled up her arm toward her chest. "Four, five, six …"

Almost there.

"Seven, eight, nine—"

A knock. Malina jumped and dropped the coin as Gale stepped in.

"Malina, honey, is everything okay?"

Get it! the voice said, then softened. *Or I will have to find someone else.*

Malina scurried to pick it up before the glow subsided, then tucked her hands behind her. "Yes! I'm fine," she snapped. "Sorry. Just, I'll be right there."

The same worried look tugged at her mother's lips.

"I'm fine," Malina said, trying to hide the frustration in her voice. "Just … here." She handed her mom the stack of sheets and blankets. "I'll bring the pillows."

Gale took the bundle and tried to see what was in Malina's

hand.

"Go," Malina told her mom. "I'll be right there." She forced a smile. "Sorry. This place creeps me out." She turned toward the closet for the pillows and moved slowly as Gale returned to the hall. She could feel her mother's reticence yet couldn't risk her seeing the coin.

She waited until Gale disappeared down the hall, threw the pillows down, and squeezed her eyes shut. *One, two, three ...* she said silently this time.

The thin round disc came to life once more, setting her nerves on fire. *Four, five, six ...*

That's it, the voice whispered.

Seven, eight, nine ... Malina gritted her teeth as invisible flames consumed her.

Ten.

A burst of light from the coin threw open her fingers. In her palm, a tiny ball of spirit hovered above the metal disk.

Malina's eyes widened. A cry stuck in her throat. The spirit was the same size and shape as those at the lake, but the color was more red than white. Malina barely had time to think before the ball darted behind her back, burned through her sweater, and slipped into the warm dampness of her skin. She yelped and dropped the coin as the spirit twisted around her organs. It slid like thin steel across her bones and muscles before moving her arms and legs and turning her head for control. She almost threw up, but the nausea and weakness quickly gave way to the overwhelming sense of power and strength.

You are perfect, the voice said, this time from inside her head.

"W-Who are you? What happens n-now?" She trembled with fear but also exhilaration.

Shh, Speak in thought.

"Malina, honey?" her mom called from down the hall. "You okay? What's taking so long?"

"I'm fine," Malina replied loudly, trying to hide the shakiness in her voice. "Be right there."

Who are you? she asked again.

Call me Eric, the spirit replied. *Eric Bonner.*

Malina fell against the bed. The room spun. *Oh, God. What have I done?*

Eric laughed, an evil mirth.

Malina found the coin and clutched it in both hands. She wanted to call Liam to undo what she had done. Eric uncurled her fingers, made her throw the disc across the room, then vaporized her away in a blast of wind and light.

GALE

"Malina?" Gale yelled, running toward Sam's room. Strange green light had shattered the darkness, and a sudden gust had yanked open Sam's door hard enough to sink the handle into the wall. Gale rushed in. The window was closed. All of Sam's papers and architectural plans were strewn around the room, and two pillows lay tumbled on the floor. "Malina, honey?"

Something shiny caught Gale's eye at the base of the bed. She picked it up, stunned to find a coin like Tal's.

"Malina! Where are you?" Gale peered into the bathroom, sick rising in her throat. She looked out the window. *"Malina?"*

Gale's hand shook as she retrieved her phone and called

Malina's number. The voicemail picked up. She hung up and texted. Nothing. She tried again. No reply. "Oh God, Malina. Where are you?" She called up Malina's phone on the Family Locator App. "Location Permission Turned Off." Still.

Tears sprung up. "Dammit, Malina! Where are you?" Her fingers trembled as she dialed Sam's number. Thank God he picked up.

"Sam. Malina's gone!"

"What?"

"She was in your room getting pillows when there was a flash of light and some crazy gust of wind that—"

"Oh, God."

"Oh God, *what*, Sam? Where is she? What happened to my daughter?"

Seconds ticked like bombs in the silence.

"Where is she, Sam? Where is my baby? *What the hell is going on?*"

"Was there a coin?"

Gale eyed the metal in her hand. "Yes. On the floor. Why?"

Silence.

"*Sam.*"

"Hold the coin for ten seconds."

"Why? What's going on?"

"Do it! He'll come."

"Who?"

"Grip it tight, Gale. I'll count with you."

She did as instructed, and their voices called the numbers in unison.

They barely reached ten when a crackling bolt split the darkness, and Liam appeared.

Gale fell back against Sam's desk.

Liam righted her, then opened her palm. "May I?"

She gave him the coin. He closed his eyes and held the small disc between his palms. The metal brightened, but not as much as at the lake.

Liam looked up. Worry crowned his face for the first time.

Gale felt the walls squeezing in. "Where is she, Liam? Where is my little girl?"

"Sam?" Liam took the phone from her and held it to his ear. "Eric Bonner is back."

"*What?*" Sam yelled loud enough for Gale to hear. "I thought he was locked up!"

Liam remained composed, but his concern deepened. "He found the only way out."

"How?" Sam asked. "Why would the coin allow it?"

"The coins are the only open portals between our worlds. Most spirits don't know about it, and few are strong enough to even try. But Eric is ... exceptional."

"Where did he take her?" Gale could not stop shaking. Her hands and feet went numb.

Liam touched her shoulder and sent a current strong enough to quiet her nerves and restore feeling. "We don't know," he said.

"You don't *know?*" Sam asked.

"Not yet."

"Can't you find him?" Gale stammered, her pulse slamming against her ears.

"He chose a non-vessel human to prevent it," Liam replied.

"Will he h-hurt her?"

"I don't think so."

"Why not?" Sam again.

"From what the coin tells me, she *accepted* him."

"What?" Sam and Gale asked at the same time.

"I heard him at the lake when Gale and I were using Tal's coin to remove the spirit. Malina heard it, too, but I thought it ended then. Obviously, he found her again. She took him willingly, holding the coin until his spirit crossed over and entered her body. Being symbiotic makes the bond stronger. Which is why I don't think he'll hurt her, but ..." He looked at Gale. "No one can last long with Eric's level of power. We can only hope he rewards her by getting out quickly."

"Do you have any idea what he wants?" Sam asked.

"Maybe it's that woman in San Francisco," Gale mumbled. "Doc told me about her. The one who killed him to save her baby."

"Perhaps." The green rings darkened in Liam's eyes. "But whatever it is, and whatever it costs, we must ensure Eric does not succeed."

Sam's room suffocated Gale like a tomb. She could not think clearly or catch her breath. She knew with absolute certainty, as only a mother can, that Malina would have to pay the biggest price.

Sneak Peek

THE RETURN: Book 3 of the Vessels Series

CHAPTER ONE

TAL

Tal looked out over the rusted steel mill where she had died. Well, the mill where she'd been shot and started to die. Wind from the nearby Monongahela River rustled leaves in the trees. It tickled the hair on her skin, too, though the sensation was different than when she'd been alive. She could see the hairs move more than feel them.

Tal had hosted plenty of spirits when she was alive as a vessel, but she had no idea how living as a spirit would feel. She wasn't too surprised that the sensations were more internal than external. She was part of the wind that tugged at the sagging walls and broken window frames instead of simply hearing the metal clang or feeling the breeze blow past. She was inside the sun that brightened grass and weeds in the cracked sidewalks versus feeling the warmth of it on her face and skin.

Tal eyed the metal door leading into the warehouse. That last word barely formed when she relocated inside the mill's large empty warehouse where her partner, Jake, had died, and where she'd lost her last reason to live. The drug bust played across her mind like it had happened yesterday: the dealers at that rickety table, the gunmen hidden behind those beams, the group of four cops, including herself, who had burst in to make the arrest before the gunmen opened fire. Jake had saved her life that night and paid for it with his own. Who knew that seven months later, Tucker, the same dirty cop who'd arranged those hits, would shoot her in this same space. Thankfully she was with Caspian at the time, the vessel who'd hosted Jake's spirit and used her coin to call Liam who came and transported them all back to the lake. Chief Black and Liam removed the spirit she'd been hosting, and she died in Jake's arms. Well, Caspian's arms, technically, but Jake was inside. When her time finally came and the bright tunnel opened to greet her, her beloved four-year-old son, Darden, escorted her inside.

Dying had been surreal. Serene, even. She hadn't expected that after such a violent end. She and Caspian had driven Tucker into a corner that night after he'd arranged another bust that went wrong. They asked him to give up, turn himself in, acknowledge his gambling demons, and seek help. He'd shot his way out, instead, and ended Tal's life. As a human, she would have been pissed. As a spirit, she felt sorry for him and the dark choices he'd made over the years that had impacted him and his family. While she had moved on to significantly greener pastures, he was still stuck.

Tal kicked an empty can across the floor, its metallic ring echoing across the dusty concrete. Her spirit form was so new, and she still did not quite know what worked and what didn't. It was interesting how she could interact with physical things in ways she'd never seen visiting spirits do. Maybe that was because she'd only died a few weeks ago and was still adjusting. Even eternity took a minute to get used to.

A dark stain marked the floor where her blood had spilled. She walked behind some pallets to see an even bigger, more faded spot where the gunmen had riddled Jake with armor-piercing bullets, and he'd died in her arms. At least Tal and Jake had each transitioned from this life with the other one there to hold them.

She waited for anguish and rage to flare up, but neither came. In fact, she felt free of any emotions, like a stream flowing equally over silt and rocks. The spirits she'd hosted had been like that. They'd never held a grudge, rekindled the pain of their past, or tried to get even. They just—were. Not being mired by feelings was incredibly liberating and, somehow, easy. If only she could have tapped that when human.

She wondered where Jake was now that they shared the same side of forever. She'd seen him at first, the way she'd seen Darden, her husband, Owen, and her mom and dad. But love and connection were incredibly different here. Neither visual nor physical contact was required to feel close. Souls just blurred together as one big, connected mass, everyone part of everyone and everything else. Liam had been so right. Time and distance meant nothing on this side.

Tal took a breath, not that she needed it since she was pretty sure she didn't have lungs, and she thought of home. Before she exhaled, she was standing in her old backyard near the rose bushes her mom had planted. The red blossoms and flowers had never been particularly fragrant to her human nose, but now they filled the air like perfume.

The inside of the house sat empty, dusty, and as still as the day she'd left. After Jake's funeral, she'd booked her flight to Reno with plans of committing suicide to join him and Darden. She'd become a vessel instead. Then Tucker shot her, and, well, dead was dead. At least she was back on Darden's side. She'd not been good about updating her will and power of attorney and all that, and she knew this would be a mess for someone to clean up once word got out that she was gone. As much as she was sorry for that, she also didn't care. Her favorite aunt used to say, "You'll never see a casket pulling a U-Haul." It was true. Material things meant nothing once you crossed the veil.

Tal transported into the living room. This house had belonged to her parents. She'd updated furnishings, drapes, and blinds after they died, but many of their pictures were still up. Tal's strong jaw, pronounced cheekbones, and small lean frame favored those of her Irish mother, but she had her father's curly hair and compact muscles, and she burned with the fire of his Kenyan ancestors. She'd tried to be the best of them both in life, balancing her genetics on the bullshit scale of human judgment. Now, she was just herself. Her truest self.

Author's Note

Thank you for reading! And for sharing this part of my mystical *Vessels* book series that sends us into thrilling new realms of humanity and redemption.

We have all felt lost at some point. Perhaps others have hurt us, we have hurt them, or a trusted relationship blew apart and left us shattered. Perhaps we have mourned the death of a loved one wishing we had done more, said less, or held them closer. Maybe we acted on hate, sought revenge, or crushed a caring heart without making things right.

The Vessels series sheds light on restoring those relationships. If these characters can find second chances and fresh starts in life's darkest corners, then there is hope for us to do the same.

I hope you enjoyed this book. If so, please consider writing a review. Not only does it warm my heart to hear from you, but it helps other readers who may be on their own paths toward second chances.

Thank you,

Anna

THE VESSELS Series

The Vessels

The Coin

The Return

Praise for The Vessels

"This unique novel mixes social commentary, the power of love, forgiveness, and ghostly spirits. This gothic speculative tale will appeal to sf and horror fans alike." —*Booklist*

"…fast-paced, emotionally compelling, and hard to put down … a blend of murder mystery, spiritual travelogue, and thought-provoking thriller." —D. Donovan, Senior Reviewer, *Midwest Book Review*

"Imaginative debut … Readers will be drawn in by the exploration of redemption and the afterlife." —*Publishers Weekly*

"Elias has crafted a thriller like nothing I've ever read before … a high quality, unputdownable novel, I would highly recommend The Vessels to any supernatural thriller fan looking for their next captivating read." —*Readers' Favorite*

Acknowledgements

Creative efforts like this one, while forged in one mind, take a small village to bring to life. On that note, there are several in my village I'd like to recognize:

To Diane Belk – for reading the raw stuff and sharing your incredible insights and thoughts. You made the hard work fun.

To Jonas Saul – for your immense talent as author, editor, mentor, and guide. To Mary Ting – author queen. For your wisdom, counsel, and amazing support. To Italia Gandolfo – for cutting The Vessels ribbon that got me started on this journey.

To Justin Paul – for your brilliant covers and design. To Dorothy Dreyer – for making beauty and sense of the pages in between.

To Scott – my husband, best friend, and soul mate. Thank you for sharing life's journey with me, and for encouraging and supporting my never-ending dreams.

To Kayla – our brilliant gift of a daughter. Thank you for choosing us, completing us, and inspiring us each day. Keep reaching for the stars, angel. That is where you belong.

To my God - thank you for this inspiration, and for the chance to be a spark of love in the world.

To my Readers and Fellow Sojourners – love, compassion, and

forgiveness are among the most important superpowers we can possess. Yet, they are often the most elusive. My wish in writing this book is for all of us to find them in ourselves, to tap the Vessels within us and access the spiritual peace, joy, and healing these powers can provide.

About the Author

Anna Elias is a screenwriter and author. She was born in Atlanta, raised in Daytona Beach and she graduated from the University of Florida. After college, she traveled the country working on such films and TV series as *Miami Vice, Nell, Practical Magic, In the Heat of the Night, 12 Monkeys, A Time to Kill,* and *My Dog Skip*.

Anna and her husband currently live in Florida with their Puggle dog, Karma while their daughter soars off to new heights in college and beyond. Anna loves adventure, and travel, and has been to ten countries so far plus most of the US states. She also loves to consume and write movies, TV shows and books, especially those that spark her passions of social justice, diversity, and the environment. *The Coin* is the second book in her debut novel trilogy, *The Vessels*.

www.AnnaMElias.com